SPECIAL MESSAGE TO READERS

This book is published under the auspices of

THE ULVERSCROFT FOUNDATION

(registered charity No. 264873 UK)

Established in 1972 to provide funds for research, diagnosis and treatment of eye diseases. Examples of contributions made are: —

A Children's Assessment Unit at Moorfield's Hospital, London.

•

Twin operating theatres at the Western Ophthalmic Hospital, London.

•

A Chair of Ophthalmology at the Royal Australian College of Ophthalmologists.

•

The Ulverscroft Children's Eye Unit at the Great Ormond Street Hospital For Sick Children, London.

You can help further the work of the Foundation by making a donation or leaving a legacy. Every contribution, no matter how small, is received with gratitude. Please write for details to:

**THE ULVERSCROFT FOUNDATION,
The Green, Bradgate Road, Anstey,
Leicester LE7 7FU, England.
Telephone: (0116) 236 4325**

**In Australia write to:
THE ULVERSCROFT FOUNDATION,
c/o The Royal Australian and New Zealand
College of Ophthalmologists,
94-98 Chalmers Street, Surry Hills,
N.S.W. 2010, Australia**

STRAWS UPON THE SURFACE

When Councillor Amos Cotswold's friends suspect him of killing an elderly lady, he's targeted by a greedy developer, seeking to discredit him by reporting that Amos is pressurizing old folk. Amos finds that it's not only his position which is threatened, but also the villagers who depend on his protection. Then the memory of a young woman, who disappeared forty years ago, gets painfully resurrected, but things get even worse. With three attempts on his life, a run-in with organized car crime and an ambivalent relationship with the local gypsies — Amos is forced to discover what links them all . . .

A. M. STORY

STRAWS UPON THE SURFACE

Complete and Unabridged

ULVERSCROFT
Leicester

First published in Great Britain in 2008 by
Robert Hale Limited
London

First Large Print Edition
published 2009
by arrangement with
Robert Hale Limited
London

The moral right of the author has been asserted

British Library CIP Data

Story, A. M.
  Straws upon the surface.
  1. Cotswold, Amos (Fictitious character)- -Fiction.
  2. County council members- -Fiction.
  3. Detective and mystery stories. 4. Large type books.
  I. Title
  823.9′2–dc22

  ISBN 978–1–84782–938–2

Published by
F. A. Thorpe (Publishing)
Anstey, Leicestershire
Set by Words & Graphics Ltd.
Anstey, Leicestershire
Printed and bound in Great Britain by
T. J. International Ltd., Padstow, Cornwall

This book is printed on acid-free paper

For Amber, whose story began the year
this book was published.

'Errors, like straws, upon the surface flow;
He who would search for pearls must dive
  below.'

John Dryden

Acknowledgements:

I wish to thank my husband, Christopher Farmer, for running our household whilst doubling as chief research assistant; and my friend, District and County Councillor Peter Barnes, whose tales of dubious goings-on and encyclopaedic knowledge of the area provided the inspiration for Amos Cotswold.

Prologue

Forty-two years earlier

He had to be close; the moonlight was sparse and he daren't risk prolonging her suffering by making a botch of it. Blocking his mind, he brought the gun up to his shoulder, the rustle of his jacket loud in his ears as he shifted the butt a fraction, aimed . . . and squeezed the trigger. The sound ricocheted around the meadow, echoing the crack which killed her. Her blood coursed across the grass — and him. Amos's limbs shook convulsively as he took in the slaughter, his body screaming for mercy as a thousand icy daggers lanced his veins. He hadn't expected it to feel so personal — take part of himself.

Minutes earlier he'd known he was too late. The air had been chill and ominous — the sort of night when you could imagine anything happening. Not that he'd had to imagine what had lain waiting for him. Only eighteen, Amos had felt physically sick. Sick at the sight — and sick at his own failure.

She had begged him, silently but unmistakably. How could he leave her like that?

1

Steeling himself, Amos had unsheathed the shotgun from beneath the driving seat and done what he had to.

Choosing a corner of the windswept field, under the fruit trees, he took a shovel from the wagon, dug as deep a hole as he could manage and buried her. The plums would blossom soon, fitting tribute to her blameless life and savage death.

Suddenly unable to take any more, he abandoned the grave and drove back through the village in a trance, his mind still in that field — on what he'd had to do. If only he'd realized the danger earlier.

Reaching the end of the road into Weston Hathaway, Amos swung to the right. Ahead of him lay the new Moon Cottage, which Frank Squires was building on the site of the centuries-old thatched place he'd demolished. Amos had always found it creepy. Because the property straddled a ley line, or because a previous tenant had been burned as a witch? He didn't know but he shuddered all the same.

His headlights swept round and he awoke with a start. Another second and he'd have cannoned into Frank Squires's truck parked outside. A common enough obstacle during the day, he hadn't expected it there at this time of night. As he drove past a movement in

2

the lane beside the cottage caught his eye and he glimpsed Frank running full pelt towards the road, head down, close in to the hedge — hugging the shadows.

Amos shrugged. It was none of his business what the miserable man was doing on his own building site at gone midnight — probably stealing materials in order to claim off the insurance. Nothing would surprise Amos about that family.

1

Amos abandoned his Land Rover in the street with the keys in the ignition and the engine running. He'd be two minutes. He hobbled into the entrance hall of the sixties-built council offices and was waiting for the lift when the district solicitor's secretary rounded the corner. Glancing quickly over her shoulder she whispered:

'You've been reported to the government standards board.' The lift plummeted to a stop, its gates sliding open on emptiness. Amos pulled her inside and kept his finger on the 'close doors' button without selecting a floor. 'The solicitor had to do it — he had a formal request.'

Amos stared at her, mouthing, 'Who from?'

'Don't you tell on me now, Councillor Cotswold, I could lose my job for this.'

'I'll know officially soon enough.'

'Oh, all right. It was Cyril Quartermaster.'

The lift creaked ominously, like a huge metal mastiff straining at its leash. A malign mastiff. Amos released the control and the cage began to ascend.

'I've got to go now. I don't know any more, honest I don't.'

He couldn't blame her for wanting to escape. 'Thanks, sweetheart, thanks for telling me.' He let her out at the next floor.

After she'd gone Amos rode the lift in a daze. Up and down, up and down, sometimes accompanied, sometimes not. In the struggle to assimilate the implications, he lost all thought of what he'd come for, that his truck was illegally parked outside, or of how he must appear to his transitory fellow passengers. The doors swished to and fro, shoes came and went, but Amos took no notice.

To be reported to the standards board was bad at any time but in an election year it could be fatal. It was going to be his word against Quartermaster's that he hadn't caused the office of councillor to be sullied. At the very least it would harm his chances of re-election. At the worst he could be barred from ever again holding public office.

Up and down, up and down ... as the doors opened on the ground floor he registered a crowd of people waiting to get in and came back to earth with a jolt. The Land Rover! He'd no idea how long he'd been there. Amos threaded his way back outside, relieved to find his wagon exactly where he'd left it. Unlike him, it stood enviably the same as before — unburdened with charges.

Still stunned, he drove home as far as the

bottom meadow, ploughed across it and came to a squelchy halt by the river. Where he remained for what must have been hours, gazing into the middle distance through a spattered windscreen, seeing only the ruins of everything he cared about, everything he'd tried to do. What would happen to all those villagers who relied on him to protect their interests? Who now would chase the authorities to make sure Weston Hathaway wasn't forgotten? How long would it survive as a village without being swallowed up in the urban sprawl? His world was growing dark around him.

As the light faded his obligations dragged him back to the present; he still had to check the cattle. Once back at his cottage he phoned Jack Ashley, 'I don't want to say this in the bar but . . . I'm in trouble.'

'I'll be right there.' The line went dead. Jack's pub would be full of early-evening customers and he would have no idea what sort of trouble, but Amos knew his very tone must have worried his friend. Jack had seen him take on all comers, even a stray black panther once, out on the top road; but this was different. This was like fighting an unseen enemy who could ruin you. Just like that. And for what?

In minutes Jack burst through the front

door. 'I thought you'd been shot!' His irritation hid his obvious relief in finding Amos apparently unharmed.

'I have . . . as good as.'

Jack flopped into an ancient armchair to regain the breath he'd lost sprinting down the road. Still in his shirtsleeves, his favourite orange and red checks matched his now flushed complexion.

'I've been reported to the standards board.'

'Blimey! Not that one you chaired last year?' Jack sat up.

'If only! No, that's the district council one. This is the national body, the one that investigates people in public positions. They can ban me from being a councillor for life.'

'There's obviously been some mistake. You'd never do anything to harm . . . Oh no, not like the so-called vote-rigging they put you through the wringer on before?'

'Yup, that's the one — guilty unless proven otherwise.'

'What're you supposed to have done, for heaven's sake?'

'It's this Quartermaster thing, he's making out I've used my position to con people . . . like his aunt. You know what all this is about don't you?'

'The land Nellie left you?'

'No, no, that's what he wants you all to

8

think. No, this is about his planning application. To get it through he needs me thrown off the council.'

'But you can do him for this, surely?'

'What with, shirt buttons? And anyway the damage is already done — or it will be once this gets out. 'No smoke without fire' they'll say; I can hear them already.'

'Not this village! Anyway I can't believe Quartermaster knew enough to do this all by himself?'

Jack had voiced what Amos was thinking. 'Exactly, someone — or group of someones — put him up to it. Just like the last time.'

Jack perched on the edge of the seat, his hands together in front of him. 'If I didn't know better I'd think this was a wind-up. How can anyone be petty enough to indulge in shenanigans like this at our level . . . talk about spiteful, vindictive! I'd say you were being melodramatic or exaggerating, but I've seen it myself, I know what they're capable of!'

'The worst of it is, Nellie would turn in her grave,' Amos said quietly, remembering the lovely old lady who'd cared so much for her animals that it had led to this.

'Well, you know the whole village will back you.'

'Not quite the whole village, Jack, no.'

'Oh Lord, what can we do? Can we all write to the board, say they're wasting their time and the ratepayers' money?'

'See it from their point of view. Their job is to stop crooked officials misusing our money and bringing public service into disrepute. So they can't very well say, 'OK we'll decide who to investigate based on their smile . . . or on who petitions for them'.' Amos listened like an eavesdropper to his own words of reason, unconvinced.

'But this is so obviously wrong!'

'I know, but how do I prove I'm *not* doing something?'

Jack glanced at the grandfather clock in the corner and heaved himself out of the chair. 'Come and have a pint later. We'll think of something.' He clapped Amos on the back and headed for the door, almost colliding with Lindsay Martin coming in.

'I heared you wasn't well.' She tutted, looking pointedly at her neatly laid grate as Jack closed the door behind him. 'You haven't even lit your fire.' Amos was convinced the Weston bush telegraph ran on telepathy. 'You parked your Land Rover with one wheel on the pavement. My Ted says, 'Lin', he says, 'I reckon summat's up wi' Amos'.' She cocked her head sideways. 'Then we hears Mr Jack poundin' down the lane. What's up?'

Amos went over to the answering machine and wound back the tape a couple of times until he found what he wanted. 'Remember this?'

'*Now look here, Cotswold, I've had enough of this bloody council telling me what I can and can't do. That land is mine and I'll do as I like with it. I've got important friends round here, so I'm going to build those houses at Weston Hathaway and if you oppose me any more I'll make damned sure we take this seat off you in May. And that's just for starters. No one tells me what to do, least of all a jumped-up bloody shepherd!*' Quartermaster had slammed the phone down.

'It seems he's keeping his promise. Why do they always have to drag party politics into everything?' Amos took his anger out on the curtains, yanking them shut, cheered only by the inviting smell of rabbit stew simmering in the oven. He opposed Quartermaster's plan for Hunter's Farm because it would harm Weston Hathaway, change it irrevocably. But having long since abandoned the haven of party loyalties in favour of what was good for the village, he was forced to lay his political career on the line every time he stood up for what he believed in. No party safety net for him.

11

'What do any of them matter . . . this is about what's good for Weston. I've had enough of them, always up to their dirty tricks, scoring points.'

The stalwart Lindsay Martin sympathized from the kitchen. 'Since you went independent you showed 'em! *District* councillor five elections in a row and now *county* councillor!' Lindsay skewered the meat six times, emphasizing each victory. She sat back on her ample haunches.

'Quartermaster left that message the same day Mrs Grimshaw took poorly.' She lifted the steaming casserole from the oven. 'My Ted had been there doing her windows when the doctor come to see her.'

Amos still felt bad about that, he'd not called to see Nellie Grimshaw that week.

'So I'd gone over to see if she'd like me to sit with her a bit but when I arrived the ambulance was just pulling away like. Barbara at the shop said they'd taken her to Warwick.'

Amos sat down slowly, the memory of that night flooding back. After supper he'd made sure Nellie's house was secured and checked on her sheep before going to Jack's. It felt like yesterday but it must have been six weeks ago. He remembered how the centuries-old beams that spanned the back room of the Hathaway Arms had seemed like Atlas propping up the heavens — keeping the weight from descending on to Amos's shoulders. As always a log fire had been blazing in the hearth and there would have been another in the front room, though he couldn't have seen it from where he was. Using his elbows as anchors, Jack had had the paper spread out on the counter and had been frowning down at the crossword.

'Storeman who wants to build fifty big houses — thirteen letters,' Jack had offered.

'Brown with a white head in a glass — four letters, thought I'd keep it easy for you,' Amos had countered. 'And it's not a bloody cow in a bottle either!' They'd both laughed.

'I hear he's found out you opposed his planning application.' Jack pulled Amos's pint.

'So I gather, but since he never consulted me about his scheme in the first place I don't see how he can blame me.'

'Phyllis Arbuthnot will have told him you incited the parish council to oppose it. He was in here earlier looking for you . . . ill-mannered Champagne Cyril in his Gucci suit and white loafers. Had steam coming out of both nostrils. Who does he think he is, throwing his weight around? When I asked him what the matter was he said the district council had rejected his planning application

13

— seemed to think it was your fault.' Jack had added: 'All those new houses might just be good for trade.'

'You know bloody well they wouldn't. Their sort don't drink in village pubs. The ones with money will go to the Butler's Arms or the King's Head at Lower Farthing and the others will be too stretched paying the mortgage.'

'It might help the butcher's and the post office, though.'

'Yes, it might, which is why I'm not entirely against it. We need to grow, otherwise we'll die. But in a controlled fashion, not like this — drowning in exclusive properties. Exclusive is the right word for it — excluding the ordinary folk.'

Then the outside door had opened quietly and a thoughtful-looking white-haired man wrapped in a black cloak had lifted his skirts to negotiate the way down, revealing his wellingtons in the process. They'd lowered the bar-room floor at the turn of the nineteenth century to make standing upright easier — hence the steps. Amos remembered dwelling on this inconsequential fact as, fearfully, he'd watched the man advance.

'Sad news, my friends,' the reverend had said. 'Nellie Grimshaw passed away an hour ago.'

No one had said anything. Appearing beside Jack, Marion, his wife, had made sympathetic noises in the back of her throat, two regulars round the fire had shuffled their feet and grunted. 'Oh dear,' Marion had said at last. 'I'm sure it was having to leave her home after all those years — she went downhill very quickly after that. I reckon she died of a broken heart.'

Amos had been seething. Brought up in London with his parents, Quartermaster had never lived at Hunter's. Yet he'd thrown Nellie out as soon as he'd got his hands on it after his father's death. Whereas Amos felt sure Cyril's father, Nellie's brother, had intended Cyril to stay in London and Nellie to carry on where she was. Widowed young, Nellie had run the family farm for most of her life.

'There's something else,' Reverend Whittaker had added in his soft voice. 'Before Nellie died she insisted on telling me, said it was in case her nephew tried to hide her will.' They'd all lifted their heads in anticipation. Like Nellie, Amos wouldn't have put that past Cyril Quartermaster if he'd stood to gain by it.

'Her last concern on this earth was for her few remaining animals. She wanted to be sure they'd be in good hands, unlike her own fate;

so she's left them to you, Amos — along with
the grazing land on which to feed them.'

For once Amos had been too overcome to
say anything. He'd been very fond of Nellie
and she knew he'd have kept an eye on those
sheep anyway until they were sold. He
guessed she'd wanted to be absolutely certain
her nephew couldn't ill-treat them.

'Cyril's not going to be very pleased about
that. That'll fan the flames!' Jack had said
with some relish.

'I can't see him caring about a few sheep
and an acre or two of pasture. She didn't have
much land left, you know; rented the winter
grazing.'

'Yes, but leaving it to you of all people.
You'd hardly be his first choice of beneficiary.'

★ ★ ★

'Aren't you going to eat it, then?'

Amos came to. Lindsay stood arms akimbo
looking down at him. 'You'm been muttering
to yourself the whole time I've been dishing
up.'

16

2

Bless her, thought Amos. Lindsay had remembered to send his best pink jacket to the cleaners after the village Christmas party. On his way home, in helping to stop a runaway horse he'd damaged his coat . . . lucky it hadn't been a bull. Mind you, that was nonsense, bulls are colour-blind. It's the movement that attracts them.

'There's a brace of pheasant in the back shed if you'd like them,' he yelled down the stairs, ' . . . and a sack of spuds on the step.' People were always giving him presents in return for favours. Keeping the Scotch and chocolates for him and Napoleon, his pet pig, he redistributed the rest. Lindsay used the produce to feed Amos, her own family and half of Weston's old folk besides.

He paused to survey himself in the worn glass on the wall. Pity he hadn't had time to let Lindsay give him a haircut. His shirt and tie were clean and he'd remembered to shave. He'd do.

'Where do you think you be going in them shoes?' Lindsay was worse than a wife. 'Take them off this minute so's I can clean them for you. Our Ted'll take you over there and you rings him when you wants fetchin'.'

* * *

Lord Gray, Alec FitzSimmons to his friends, lived at Moreton Hall on the far side of Stratford — an imposing stone mansion at the end of a long drive. Once a year he held a luncheon party in aid of the Injured Jockeys Association. Apart from enjoying it, Amos hoped he might learn how his peers had taken Quartermaster's action — or whether they even knew.

Favouring his bad hip, Amos climbed awkwardly up the shallow flight of steps to the front door; which opened directly on to the throng already gathered in the galleried entrance hall. Alec's ancestors gazed disapprovingly from the staircase and the crystal-encrusted chandelier lurked high above like some twinkling Damoclesian threat, ready to plunge. Having sidled around to a table of drinks, Amos was helping himself when a large florid hand clapped him on the shoulder:

'Caught red-handed! Ha ha ha,' guffawed the man. 'Red-handed, get it! Oh never mind! How the devil are you old chap?'

It was Bengy Pargitter from Snitterfield.

18

Always a buffoon, or that was what he'd have everyone believe, but pleasant with it and harmless. He lent weight to the local NHS Trust and the police complaints committee and had in the past counted the county council among his appointments.

Before Amos could draw breath he and Bengy were joined by other current and past dignitaries, party grandees, council members, and local Rotarians; some fulfilling all those roles, some a selection . . . all male. Glancing beyond them, through the double doors into the salon, Amos glimpsed their respective wives plumped gratefully on feather-cushioned sofas. Their grey heads were grouped together con-spiratorially. Jewel-laden fingers cradled cut-glass gin and tonics.

'Hear you've been giving our lot a run for their money,' Bengy said, biting into a vol-au-vent whose filling oozed oleaginously down his ruddy chin.

'When doesn't he? That's the only exercise Amos gets these days,' answered another.

A farming friend appeared at his elbow. 'You coming to the show this year, Amos? I fancy my Blonde Aquitaines'll do well.'

Feeling peckish, he extricated himself from the shop talk and was edging politely towards the buffet when Lord Gray, a small, dapper man in his early seventies, broke away from a nearby group and headed for Amos.

'I was sorry to hear about Nellie Grimshaw. I knew them quite well, you know, used to shoot with her brother when he came up. Can't say I like that nephew of hers though.'

Alec took hold of Amos's elbow and drew him away from the food, distancing the pair of them from the other guests. 'In fact I wanted a word with you about him.'

'His turning Nellie out of her farm wasn't popular with folk in Weston,' Amos replied carefully — where was this going?

'I didn't know he'd done that,' Alec gasped. 'When I heard she'd moved I assumed she wanted a little cottage to herself now she was getting on a bit.' Wistfully he looked around at his huge house — as though he too might find solace in somewhere smaller.

'Why are you asking about Quartermaster?' Amos asked.

'Because he's being unpleasant about you.'

'That's one way of putting it. You know he's reported me to the standards board — for importuning old ladies.'

'What!' Alec scanned the room. 'I'd no idea. I am sorry, Amos.'

Amos explained about the application to build fifty executive houses at Hunter's and why the planning department had turned it

20

down. 'If he'd asked me I could have told him the development needs to include at least one third 'affordable housing' and be altogether smaller. But I still don't see why you're bothered, Alec. It's nice of you but I detect there's more to it.'

'We . . . ell, don't misinterpret this, Amos, but you may or may not know that he's very generous when it comes to party funds.'

'Which means what exactly?'

'People listen to him.' Alec was clearly neglecting his other guests, but he went on: 'He's persuaded Phyllis Arbuthnot to stand against you in this year's district council elections.'

So that was it. Amos considered this. Phyllis, as leader of the parish council, was well-connected in Weston Hathaway, which was more than could be said for other opposition candidates in recent years. To be fair she did her best for the village by her own lights but she toed the party line . . . to the letter. Which meant that her party, not Weston, came first. Nonetheless she'd be a formidable opponent, since many people voted along party lines these days. Quartermaster was carrying out his threat all right, and buying support.

'Anyway, thought I'd warn you,' Alec said, squeezing Amos's arm as he moved away.

Amos turned to find Cyril Quartermaster

glaring at him from across the room. He was standing on his own near the mantelpiece, his bushy eyebrows drawn tight together, fists clenched, cheeks puffed out in annoyance. No doubt displeased to see Amos here at all, let alone buttonholed by the host, what new atrocity would he cook up next?

★ ★ ★

The following Wednesday, when Amos returned from checking the ewes at five o'clock, the papers were sitting in their bundles on the pavement outside the post office. Amos took a *Gazette* and left the money on top of the pile. Ten minutes later he saw the letter.

Sir,
Since it concerns a local councillor, Councillor Cotswold, I thought your readers should know that my aunt, Mrs Nellie Grimshaw, has left him her land in her will. So when our Independent councillors complain that they cannot contest elections to the same degree as their party-funded competitors, please remember that some of them make considerable personal gains from their so-called good works.

Cyril Quartermaster

Quartermaster had been very clever, or more likely someone who'd written it for him had. Amos didn't know whether it was libellous or not. Probably not, or the *Gazette* wouldn't have printed it. The letter only implied that Amos helped people in order to gain by it, but Amos was certain that was what Quartermaster had intended. He was broadcasting Amos's windfall and making it sound like a significant acreage. As though Amos had cold-bloodedly set out to profit from his friendship with Nellie.

Amos's reputation was extremely important to him — and people would judge by what was said about him rather than what he achieved — yet he couldn't afford to sue, and Quartermaster knew it.

His phone rang at 5.30. 'What the hell's got into that man, I'll throttle him. No, I'll do better than that, I'll ban him from the pub.'

By 8.30, when he had to go out, the phone hadn't stopped ringing with people offering help and support — from Lindsay and Ted to Alec FitzSimmons and his friends — all incensed. Yet the damage had been done.

3

The four-track came hurtling around the bend towards him at a hundred miles an hour . . . on his side of the road. The driver would straighten and swerve any second. He didn't. If anything, he accelerated — maintaining his trajectory — on target for Amos in less than a breath . . .

Amos swung the wheel hard over and careered helplessly into the nearside ditch, bumping and pitching as he lost speed. The Land Rover screamed and groaned as shrubs lacerated its paintwork, bent its torso into unnatural postures and threw it sideways. The momentum carried it yards beyond the entry point before the vehicle collapsed with a whoosh of air.

Jammed up against the muddy bank, Amos fought to open the door far enough to struggle out. His first thought was for the ram in the back.

'Come on, boy, let's have a look at you.'

He tried to coax him but the animal looked beyond help. Torn from his bindings and thrown mercilessly from side to side in the accident, his spindly legs stuck out at unnatural angles and his breathing was worse than Amos's after a night at the Hathaway Arms. Thank heavens his pig hadn't been here. Mirroring the ram, the Land Rover lay on its side, half-in and half-out of the ditch, but other than a few extra dents and a new scratch or two it looked OK. It would need pulling out, though. Amos reached for his phone.

The vet arrived first. 'How many times have I told you to take more water with it, Amos?' Seeing the wretched animal his tone changed. 'Oh no, I'm sorry.'

'Didn't think I'd call you out here at your prices if I'd had my gun with me, did you? My tup's had it.'

After a gentle examination, the vet fetched his bag, filled the syringe and dispatched the ram.

Amos patted the carcass. 'Good lad he was. Must've given me nigh on four hundred lambs over the years. Never shirked. Always keen to get on with the job. He deserved a bit more fun before he died.'

The vet packed his things, rested his hand lightly on Amos's shoulder for a moment in silent sympathy, then strode back to his car. Amos stayed where he was, unable to swallow, gazing down at the dead body.

Minutes later the breakdown truck from Broad Farthing coasted to a halt ahead of the Land Rover.

'How'd you manage that, Amos?'

Amos slowly pulled himself upright. 'Bloody gypsy — came round the corner like a whirling dervish, left me no option.'

'Lucky you had a way out if you ask me. Got to count our blessings — that's what my missus always says.'

Amos glared at him, in no mood for homespun philosophy. 'Just get me out of this ditch so I can go and thank the man who did this to me.'

'You're not going up to that gypsy camp, Amos? Leave it to the police. That's their job.'

'You must be joking. They daren't even go there in twos any more.'

'All the more reason to leave well alone, I'd say.'

The breakdown man circled the vehicle. 'Doesn't look too bad. I can have you out of here in a jiffy. I'll give her a quick check over — make sure she's safe to drive.' Spotting the dead sheep in the back he added: 'On your way to the knackers, were you? They'll be shut by now, I'm afraid.'

It was dark by the time Amos turned into the gypsy encampment at Broad Farthing. Four swarthy men advanced towards him barring his way — one of whom he'd seen already today. Only his sixty years' experience kept him from grabbing the culprit and smashing his head against the truck.

'I'm Councillor Cotswold. Where's Ma?'

Even here his name carried some weight; not, he suspected, because of his title, but because he'd helped out in the past — when Broad Farthing village had wanted the district council to evict the gypsies from their own land and when twenty sheep had gone missing and the locals had accused Ma's people. Amos had known they weren't guilty that time . . . because he'd had a fair idea who was. It also helped that he was dressed like them — only worse. Here was no visiting suit.

The human barrier relaxed its stranglehold but kept pace with Amos as he crawled the Land Rover up to Ma's tent and climbed out. She emerged from the canvas lean-to attached to the side of her caravan — a handsome woman in corduroy trousers and waxed Barbour, the deeply etched lines in her face emphasizing its sculpted structure . . . and strength.

'Your yobbo here ran me off the road, killing my best ram. He owes me.' Rumour said people had disappeared for less.

Mouthing obscenities the young man took a step forward but Ma's chilling tone intervened.

'Leave Councillor Cotswold alone and go and fetch three hundred pounds. Now!' Her eyes bored into him from behind as he slunk off. She lifted the tent flap, wordlessly inviting Amos to enter.

Inside was a cosy parlour, the whole dominated by two enormous chintz covered settees with inviting cushions. Old china and copper adorned the shelves while an ancient woodburner with a hob on top filled the atmosphere with an air of comfort and security. Amos collapsed into the only armchair.

'Why didn't you ask him about it?' he queried. Ma's acceptance of the young man's guilt had been immediate.

'Because I wasn't surprised. He left here like a pricked bull after I gave him a talking to earlier today. Besides, why would I question what you say?' She allowed him a slow smile.

When Amos departed half an hour later the only remaining guard was the one Ma had posted to mind his Land Rover. Amos clambered back into the vehicle with the cash in his pocket and several cups of Ma's tea warming his insides — wondering whether, in recovering his losses, he'd gained a new enemy.

★   ★   ★

Jack's front parlour was nicely full. Alan Tregorran and his family were sitting in the window with the butcher, Harry Fields; Vernon Squires and his eldest son Bruce were propping up the bar, their stance designed to discourage company, while Sam, one of Jack's regulars, and several elderly cronies hogged the fire. Jack and Marion were standing with the vicar when Amos walked in.

'I don't know what we're going to do about poor Brenda.'

'Is she getting worse, Reverend?' asked Marion, putting the reverend's coffee down on the bar beside him.

'Well, she may not get much better.'

Brenda Smith and her husband had owned the village garage, but when he'd died suddenly, Vernon Squires, a local builder, had bought it for Bruce to run. Before retiring last year, Brenda had stayed on for a while to help with the paperwork and to take her mind off things. Just lately they said she'd shown signs of losing her memory. Amos had overheard Vernon complaining that it had reached the point where she might say anything.

'Do you think sometimes there's a case for, well you know . . . helping them go a bit quicker, Reverend?' Jack asked. Marion glared at him. 'I mean some countries do it don't they . . . and they're going to a happier place and all that.' Sam came up for a couple of refills. 'What do you think, Sam — should

29

we help people go with dignity?'

Sam wasn't so far off 'going' himself but appeared unfazed by the question.

'I remember my old mother. Lingered for years, her did, and had to be watched every minute. Fair wore my sister out. I thought of mixing a bit of rat poison with her porridge but parson afore you . . . ' he indicated Reverend Whittaker, 'old parson said it were wrong.'

'And so it is,' Reverend Whittaker said quickly.

'I don't see why . . . ' Amos joined them, but his words hung unanswered.

Reverend Whittaker muttered: 'I really must be off,' downed his coffee like a tot of whisky, in one swig, and hurried out. Amos watched him go, wondering what he'd done.

Turning to greet him, Marion said: 'I must say you seem remarkably calm about this Hunter's business, Amos, considering the standards board thing and now this horrible letter of Quartermaster's.'

'Well, I can't do anything else, can I? Got to be careful in case he persuades the board I'm carrying out a personal vendetta against him.'

'That's outrageous! It's him who's doing that to you — for no reason.'

'You and I both know that, but since I'm

up for re-election this year I have to watch out.' Feeling worse than impotent, Amos refused to even think about the standards board any more than he had to, much less talk about it. 'So, who's going to organize our campaign against Quartermaster's resubmitted planning application? What about the Hathaway Housewives?'

'It *would* be now, Amos, when we're busy with the midsummer play.'

Many of the Housewives doubled as the amateur dramatic society, particularly behind the scenes; although the stars were people like Irene Squires, Vernon's wife . . . who wore high heels and a pink suit to go shopping.

★   ★   ★

'Seen Napoleon?' Amos called, sticking his head around the back door of Harry Fields's butcher's shop.

'I saw a black rump disappearing into Brenda's about half an hour ago,' Harry yelled from inside.

Amos retraced his steps to Brenda Smith's, hoping it wasn't the reverend's rear end that Harry had noticed. He tapped on her back door, the front had been blocked up. Unacknowledged, he peered through the bottle-glass panels and spotted the unmistakable

31

mass of Napoleon, draped against the stove. He tapped again and opened the door, Brenda never locked it. 'Halloooo,' he called, not wanting to alarm her. Napoleon grunted and Brenda came slowly through from the front room. Duster in hand, she wore neat check slippers with an apron over her trousers.

'Cup of tea, Amos?'

'If it's not too much trouble, Brenda. That would be very welcome.' Keeping his head bent to avoid the beams, Amos sat down heavily at the kitchen table, massaging his painful knee.

'I hope you don't mind me feeding Napoleon but I like to see him there,' she said fondly, giving the pig a gentle kick. In other circumstances Amos would have kept his eye out for a dog for her but folks said she couldn't be relied on any more — one day — fine, but the next away with the fairies. So the best he could do was lend her Napoleon.

'I'm glad you do, Brenda, he can come any time. How could I stop him!' Amos laughed. Napoleon appreciated female company — ladies made more fuss of him.

'What's all this I see about young Cyril Quartermaster writing to the *Gazette* about you?'

'For some reason he wants to discredit me.'

'Fancy suggesting you only helped Nellie

32

for her money. Folks here know that isn't true. Heavens, you'd be a rich man if it were — and look at you.'

How normal she seemed as she went about making the tea.

'He and Vernon Squires are quite friendly, you know. Cyril went to school with Bruce — public school,' she volunteered.

'Is Vernon going to build all these houses for Cyril, then?'

'S'pect so,' Brenda was concentrating on amassing the tea things. When she'd finished she sat down at the table opposite him while the tea brewed. Lowering her voice she said: 'I know a thing or two about that lot and their dealings, from when I did their books, after my Laurie died. Up to no good they are half the time.'

'The Squires, you mean?'

'All on 'em, all the same, they are. I don't know what it is with folk these days.' Shaking her head she rested both sets of gnarled knuckles on the table and pushed herself up to pour the tea. Uncertain of Brenda's mental state, Amos didn't pursue the point.

She handed him his tea, took her own and sat down again. 'You let me know if you want me to write to the paper for you, Amos, if that would help?'

Afraid she might reveal Quartermaster's

secrets and cause trouble for herself as well as further inflame the situation, Amos leaned across and patted her hand gratefully. 'Thanks Brenda, I'll let you know.'

'Makes my blood boil, it does,' she continued. 'Thinks he can come up here weekends and spoil our village, and us who live here all the time just has to put up with it.'

'No we don't, Brenda, we're going to fight him on this. We're getting everyone to write to the planning department saying why so many houses would be bad for Weston. Now, that's something you can do.'

'Of course I will, Amos, be very glad to. I'm not ga-ga yet, you know, though I know there's plenty thinks I am. Mind you, I have days when I don't feel myself at all.' She bent forward and wrapped her lined fingers around his wrist. Looking him earnestly in the face she said: 'Amos, if I do go really doolally I want you to bump me off, quick-like. I couldn't bear everybody laughing at me or feeling sorry for me . . . or them putting me in one of those padded places.'

★ ★ ★

Moon Cottage shone in the evening light, its whitewashed walls soaking up the sun's rays, its cottage garden a riot of late-spring colour, testament to Marion's hard work. To the right lay a broad grassy lane leading to a small field beyond the back garden. Hanging over the gate with Jack, Amos was still dwelling on Brenda's request.

'Do you know what Brenda said to me today? Quite worried me, it did. She said if she had got Alzheimer's or went, you know, round the bend, would I . . . I forget her exact words but . . . would I do her in quickly.'

'My dad always used to say that. 'Jack,' he'd say, 'If I lose me marbles, just take a heavy mallet to me one dark night, won't you, son?''

'Yes, but Brenda meant it — seemed really afraid of what would happen to her otherwise.' Amos drew in a long breath, held it for ten seconds, using the extra oxygen to dispel his dark thoughts, then turned to the notice.

'They've been quick with this, then.' He and Jack had come to inspect Jack's 'change of use' notice nailed up that afternoon; the public announcement of his request to convert the paddock at the back of Moon Cottage. Amos had insisted Jack follow the correct procedure.

'What a rigmarole, though. I still can't believe I have to ask permission to turn a field into garden.'

'Well, I'm sure you won't have any trouble. It's highly unlikely you'll encounter any opposition.'

Vernon Squires's Jaguar glided to a halt at the kerb beside them, his personalized number plate — VFS 1 — proclaiming his importance. Jack always maintained it stood for *Variable Frequency Shit of the first order*, so the effect was questionable. Noted for his ability to spot a planning notice at fifty yards in fog, Squires emerged from the car's plush interior and strode over.

'Going to extend the place, nice *en suite* for guests, is it?' he asked, beginning to read.

Before Jack could answer, Squires's face changed colour. 'What's all this then?' His tone was harsh as he jabbed at the paper. 'It's time you newcomers stopped trying to alter this village. Bloody cheek, moving in here churning up our countryside!'

'That's rich, coming from you. I hear you've got the contract for all those houses Quartermaster wants to build up at Hunter's Farm,' Amos retorted without thinking. Unsure exactly why, he'd always disliked Squires intensely but generally managed to keep his feelings in check.

'That's none of your business, Cotswold, and anyway this is different.' Thrusting his livid face into Jack's he yelled: 'You think

36

again! I'll make damned sure you can't do this!' before turning on his heel, throwing himself back into his car and roaring off up the road.

4

Jack and Amos stared after him. The performance had lasted less than three minutes — Amos could almost believe he'd imagined it. Jack recovered first. 'How extraordinary. P'raps he doesn't understand you have to apply for change of use. But for you, I wouldn't have.'

'Of course he does. I know for a fact he's had to make applications several times himself in the course of his building works,' Amos replied.

'If he hadn't sounded so ominous it would be funny.'

Amos was still thinking. 'Why on earth would he care whether or not you turn your paddock into garden . . . unless he thinks it's a preliminary to building another house on it?'

'That makes even less sense. Surely he'd like that as he'd get a chance of the business. He might even see it as paving the way for other back-land developments in the village . . . which would bring him more work.'

'Unless . . . ' Amos said thoughtfully. 'You know it was his dad that built Moon Cottage, don't you?'

'If I did I'd forgotten; it must be on the deeds I guess. But why should that have any bearing on it?'

'His old man committed suicide.'

'Not here, though?' Jack's eyes bulged and his mouth turned down in distaste.

'No, no, don't worry, it was miles away.' Amos struggled to dredge an elusive fragment from his memory. He kicked himself for having exposed Squires's hypocrisy. Once Squires had realized that for himself, the man might have simmered down and dropped the issue. He wouldn't now.

★   ★   ★

Amos often wondered how people who work in offices cope with life; at least he could escape into the open air, let the wind blow the stresses away. Nature in the raw put his world back into perspective every time — showed him what was important when he dared forget.

This week a lamb had been born horribly misshapen, poor thing — it always turned his heart over. As with humans, there could have been any number of causes. He'd wanted to take it to Cyril Quartermaster and say: 'This is what I have to face, now what have you got to bleat about.' Reluctantly, he'd refrained.

His job demanded constant vigilance. Most of the land he rented was river floodplain — sheep falling in the water consituted a constant hazard. Where the land shelved gently the river provided a useful source of drinking water but where it didn't, the lambs could misjudge the steepness and topple. Or they'd spy a succulent tuft halfway down the bank and overbalance trying to reach it.

One of the benefits of the public footpath along the riverbank was that the folk who used it provided watchful eyes, alert for animals in distress. Frequently the endangered beast belonged to another farmer but the villagers weren't to know that — Amos accepted he was the easiest man to find and was always happy to help a stricken animal.

When he arrived back from his morning rounds, the message was the most recent of the fifteen on his answering machine. Having dropped Jack off at his pub only ten minutes earlier he'd gone via Lindsay's to deliver some spring cabbage. In that short interlude Jack had phoned. 'Have I left my glasses in your Land Rover, I can't find them anywhere?' Then came the muffled voice — like someone talking on a mobile in the wind which, given the message's content, was highly likely.

'Hope you can hear me, your lamb's in the

river at Long Cast Mead . . . ' the message ended abruptly, probably because the tape was full.

Long Cast Meadow, so-called because of its fishing, was three miles or so the other side of the village, and yes, he did have sheep in that field. He'd put the ewe lambs in there — last year's lambs not yet old enough to have offspring of their own — to free up the pastures closer to home for lambing.

At this time of year, with the River Avon swollen, the drop to it would be only a couple of feet. By the same token, the water would be deep. Depending on how it had fallen, the sheep might already be dead. If it had had the sense to stay close in to the bank and avoid being caught up by the current it might still be alive, but even then, clad in its winter coat, it would become waterlogged and drown very quickly. There was no time to lose.

Ordinarily he'd have called for Jack but he'd be in the middle of serving. Now Jack would have to wait for his specs — it'd give him a perfect excuse for pulling short pints.

Amos grabbed his crook, threw it in the Land Rover, and set off much faster than usual, keeping a weather-eye open *en route* for any likely helper he could press-gang; the one day he needed them there was no one about.

Stopping to open and shut two sets of gates slowed him down and as soon as he entered the field the rest of the sheep came running towards his Land Rover, a sound they associated with food, which delayed him even more. To save time he drove straight across the four-acre field, noticing the churned up grass; another vehicle had recently done the same thing.

As he approached the bank he couldn't see anything in the river, nor any sign of his helpful informant. Had the lamb already been swept away? Clutching his crook Amos climbed down from the truck and searched along the edge. He walked over the little bridge which linked the field to a tiny offshore island popular with courting couples, to see if the lamb had swum that far.

'Baa ... baa ... baaa', the sound was weak, only just audible. He looked back to where he'd come from, trying to locate it. 'Baaa ... baaaa ... ' Then he spotted her, over to the right of the Land Rover, clinging to the base of the bank as it shelved into the river. He'd missed her the first time because she was under an overhang.

After retracing his steps back past the motor he approached carefully, talking softly all the while so as not to alarm her and send her shooting out from the bank into midstream. 'How did you get down there then? Bit wet isn't it? Were you playing hide and seek? Too old for that now, aren't you . . . ' until he was lying flat on top of the bank looking down into the terrified face of the drowning animal.

Amos had hoped he could simply lean down and heave the lamb out but she was too far below for him to get sufficient purchase on her. Hauling her up and over the overhang like that would be impossible on his own. He could see her remaining strength draining with every bleat, her legs now only feebly trying to establish a grip on the bank. He couldn't just leave her there beside her ready grave but neither would she last long enough for him to fetch more help.

The lamb slipped further in, swallowing water as her head dipped dangerously beneath the surface. The only way was to get in there with her — heave her up from behind.

Amos struggled on to his knees, whipped off his jacket in case he ended up having to swim, then sat and swung his legs over the edge. The cold liquid slurped into the top of his boots as he eased himself down; like blotting paper, his trousers conducted icy water high up his thighs in seconds.

'All right, girl, all right,' he soothed as the

sheep's terror increased with his advance.

Testing the firmness of the mud carefully, he manoeuvred round behind her, wary lest she use her remaining strength to kick out at him. Taking a deep breath, he gave her an almighty shove from the rear with both hands, simultaneously pressing down on her rump, forcing her to grip with her hoofs.

For one heart-stopping moment he feared she'd be unable to establish a hold on the overhang and would topple back on to him, or that she'd break a leg; but propelled as she had been, she scrambled on to terra firma . . . with all four legs intact and not a backward glance as she shook herself in irritation and trotted away.

Amos tottered backwards but regained his balance fast enough to prevent a complete ducking. Since his feet and legs were already sopping wet, rather than try and heave himself out he decided to wade along in the river looking for where she'd broken through. In one direction the bank was covered with thick bramble for fifty yards, so she must have fallen somewhere towards the bridge . . . yet the bank there remained stubbornly unbroken. It was a mystery.

He'd been too busy worrying about her drowning to assimilate earlier that not only had she been devoid of ear tags, but neither was she marked. So she wasn't his after all. Curious, how on earth had she got here? The neighbouring fields held no sheep this season.

He clambered through the reeds by the bridge and sloshed back across the field to count his flock — twice. Sure enough he'd one too many, he'd have to ask around. 'Someone'll be accusing me of sheep-rustling next, I wouldn't wonder,' he muttered.

On his way back along the lane he stopped to gather an armful of kindling for Mrs Pearson. She needed wood which she couldn't afford to buy and couldn't bend to collect, so Amos supplied it for her whenever he was passing.

Ever since that letter in the *Gazette*, he felt strangely guilty whenever he did a good turn for anybody. Walking up Mrs Pearson's front path with his bundle of wood, he wondered if anyone was watching.

As if reading his thoughts she opened the back door as he approached — with a twenty pence piece clutched in her arthritic old fingers, and a mischievous twinkle in her eye. 'Thought I'd best find you some money, Amos Cotswold,' she shouted. 'Else they'll think I'm paying you in kind.' She chirruped with laughter. Thank goodness his old friends had retained their sense of humour.

Back in the cottage he changed out of his

wet things and remembered to rewind the answering machine tape. Pleased he'd managed to save the sheep, yet possessed of a strange foreboding, he rang Fergus McAllister at DEFRA to check on the procedure for the unidentified addition. These days there were rules for everything . . . and people like Quartermaster ready to report him for the slightest transgression.

'What's on the tags?' Fergus asked.

'There aren't any. Ears are a bit nicked so there might have been once. Could have been a pet. Unlikely though, she wasn't keen on my company.'

'Sounds like a wise ewe to me. My guess is she lost her tags in the same incident that caused her to be so far from home — naturally or unnaturally. Maybe somebody pinched her.'

'What should I do?'

'Throw her back in?' Fergus suggested.

Would it really have been better if he'd ignored the message in the first place?

★   ★   ★

A week after Amos's extended ride in the lift, John Wilkinson, his solicitor, had received the official notification of Amos's referral to the standards board. Now Amos was forced to

46

face it — forced to defend himself and his actions.

He hauled himself up the stairs to John's office. Situated on the second floor of a converted Edwardian house it occupied most of the front elevation, with a view of neighbouring rooftops and a Stratford back street. Apart from John's desk, two chairs and a vast walnut breakfront cabinet donated by the previous occupier on account of its being too big to get back down the staircase, having originally been assembled *in situ*, the room was sparsely furnished. Piles of manila folders covered three trestle-tables pushed against the wall.

'What do you want to know, John?'

'What we need is evidence; you have to prove your innocence.' Amos was sure John's premature baldness had been due to his habit of running frustrated fingers through his hair from front to back. He still did it though the hair was long gone — the gesture now converted to a smoothing of his pate.

'Unfortunately Nellie is dead.'

John looked sideways at him and tightened his lips. 'Yes, but for a start we can show how little she left you. Leave that one to me, I can get that information from the probate office. Now, do people often give you things?'

Amos felt immediately wrong-footed. 'Do

47

we have to go through all this?'

'Why, have you got something to hide?'

John was deliberately provoking him — showing how the board would react to such an outburst — nevertheless Amos disliked it. 'You know I haven't, but this whole thing is so petty. Of course people give me things, ours is a barter economy.' Amos glared at his friend. John knew that as well as anyone; thanks to Amos's last scrape, he'd more pheasants in his deep freeze than he could ever hope to eat.

'What we have to show is that you don't do things with the express intention of gaining by it personally — in other words that you're not using your power as a councillor to indulge in bribery.'

'In a way I am.'

'What's that supposed to mean?' John groaned.

Amos didn't care, it was the truth, why should he hide it. 'I do things for people to be helpful to them and the village, but I also hope they'll vote for me. Of course I do.'

'Why do you want them to elect you as their councillor?'

'To make sure things get done. That we get Weston's roads mended and gritted, that we get Weston's share of the money allotted for the schools in this county, that Weston's dustbins are emptied properly, that our bus route stays open.'

John held up his hands, palms outwards. 'Good, good, exactly. In other words through helping people in the villages you are demonstrating the sort of person you are and the service they can expect if they elect you as their councillor. And they'd all be keen to write a letter of support for you to keep you as their representative, wouldn't they?'

'I'd like to think so, but maybe I'm deluding myself. And anyway, that would make it sound as though I'm desperate, that I've got a real problem.'

'You have.' John frowned. 'Look, there must be other people who help these old folk?'

'Yes, of course there are. The Hathaway Housewives, Lindsay Martin . . . countless others.'

'So we can demonstrate that you've been singled out for no reason.'

Amos brightened, he'd known John would come up with an answer. That was it, why pick on him? 'Ah, but the others weren't left a flock of sheep and an acre or so of floodplain, were they? It all comes back to that, you know it does. I tell you, it'll be his word against mine as to whether I wheedled those out of Nellie or not.'

John sighed. 'If you want Quartermaster to win you just carry on like this, Amos. We have to bring out your character and all the good you do, then they'll stop believing Quarter-master.'

'Well, you do that. I've got better things to do than bugger about with these people.' Losing all patience with the subject, Amos stormed out of John's office and hurled himself down the stairs, bouncing off the banisters as he went — furious with the whole affair and belatedly realizing that in his anger he'd just done his damnedest to thwart the man there to defend him.

* * *

On his way back from Stratford three police cars screamed past him. Then the dog-handler's wagon, closely followed by more police vans. They all took the turning to Weston Hathaway off the main road. Worried, Amos put his foot down. What could possibly have happened to cause this amount of police activity? He prayed they were headed beyond Weston.

As he drove into the centre of the village he saw that Mallard Lane, the narrow road leading to the butcher's and the pub, had been cordoned off. His anxiety growing, he abandoned the Land Rover on the grass verge and joined the knot of people gathered around a policeman who was guarding the entrance.

In theatrical tones, Irene Squires was demanding to be let through. 'I have an important dinner party tonight, I must get to the butcher's.'

The stalwart constable appeared unmoved. 'I'm sorry, but I can't help that, ma'am.' He was rescued at this moment by the arrival of a police four-track in which Amos recognized the local pathologist.

'What's going on?' Amos asked Sam who was on the edge of the crowd.

'Dunno, Amos. Them police cars screeching through the village was the first we knows, and this chap stopped us going up the lane.'

No one was coming down the lane either. Frustratingly, whatever had happened was beyond the bend in the road. He pulled out his mobile and punched in Jack's code.

'Ah, you're there. Are you all right?'

'Er, yes, we're all right.'

'What's going on up there — has someone died?'

No answer.

'You still there, Jack?'

'Got to go.' Jack hung up.

Odd? Amos removed the phone from his ear and examined it quizzically. Jack had sounded reluctant to talk, but he'd said they were all right so nothing dreadful had happened to him or Marion, thank goodness.

Two familiar black figures appeared, walking slowly down the middle of the road towards the makeshift barrier — the Reverend Whittaker and Napoleon. It took minutes for them to cover the fifty yards or so to the crowd but it felt agonizingly drawn out. Napoleon arrived first, pushing straight through to his master at the back. He was panting more than usual and turning little agitated circles. Then he trotted away, stopped and twisted his head round — wanting Amos to follow him past the roadblock, back up the lane. Amos suspected he knew why.

5

'My friends,' said Reverend Whittaker as he came around the barrier to join them. 'I'm afraid I have something very upsetting to tell you.' No one dared breathe. 'Our friend Brenda Smith passed away earlier today.' A gasp went up as the crowd drew breath. Like him, Amos guessed they'd all hoped whatever it was had happened to a stranger, someone visiting the pub or the butcher's.

'Oh no.'

'Good heavens.'

'Poor soul.'

'Why all the police cars?'

'The chief inspector has allowed me to break the sad news to you. Anything other than that I have to leave to him.'

Accustomed to death as he of all people must be, the reverend looked devastated as he dragged his feet up the road towards the church. Amos let him pass. Napoleon collapsed heavily under the nearest hedge, as though all the stuffing, which was considerable, had been knocked out of him. Amos assumed he must have been with Brenda when she died. He was pleased she'd had his company at the last.

Seconds later Chief Inspector Stephen Linklater strode smartly down the lane. Amos knew him — their paths had crossed from time to time. Linklater's presence boded ill.

'What's going on?'

'When can we go up Mallard Lane?'

'I've got to get to the butcher's!'

'Why won't you let us through?'

'What's happened to Brenda?'

Linklater held up his hand to speak. 'All I can tell you is that we are treating Mrs Smith's death as murder.'

The crowd was stunned. Amos had thought they might be facing the possibility of suicide — but murder?

'There's not been a murder in Weston Hathaway since young Mary Walters, and they never did find her body,' Sam muttered.

'And that was over forty years ago,' Amos mumbled in reply. He turned on his heel, collected Napoleon and the Land Rover and went home.

He dialled Jack again — no answer, just the answering machine. 'Funny, he can't have gone anywhere, he can't get out. Why won't he pick up?' Amos said aloud.

He was interrupted by a soft tap on the door followed by Lindsay's stout presence. 'They be going to come round and ask us all questions. What a thing. What a dreadful thing. I'll put the kettle on.'

Amos felt more in need of a stiff Scotch. 'Have you seen Jack, Lindsay?'

'Not since this morning, no, why? Do you think he don't know? If he be in the pub they're bound to know, ain't they?' Lindsay tutted. 'P'raps someone in his pub did it, a stranger maybe?'

Amos recalled a statistic he'd once heard, that the majority of murders are committed by someone known to the victim. He didn't voice it to Lindsay. She looked upset enough already without being told there was a murderer in their midst.

Just as the water was boiling Chief Inspector Linklater rapped on the open door and stepped into Amos's front room. He unbuttoned his jacket and leaned against the table, crossing one elegant ankle over the other. Accepting Lindsay's offer of tea he turned to Amos.

'What can you tell me about this, Councillor Cotswold?'

'Nothing at present, but if you tell me what happened, I can try and piece things together.' Amos had assisted the police many times before when they needed local knowledge. This time he'd a keen incentive, Brenda had been a dear friend. 'How was she killed?'

The chief inspector sugared his tea from the bowl Lindsay had deposited beside him, then stirred it slowly . . . saying nothing at first. The information would soon be all round the village, someone would know — the Reverend Whittaker most likely, or whoever else had found her. There was little benefit in keeping it a secret. And surely Linklater needed his help, Amos knew these people. Why else had he called here first?

'She was strangled. We obviously have no forensic report yet but there was no sign of a scarf or rope — so we're looking for someone reasonably strong, and probably someone she knew.' Lindsay gasped in the background; they'd both forgotten about her.

Amos followed Linklater's glance. 'Thanks Lindsay, I can manage now. Why don't you get off home.' He waited until the door had closed behind her. 'Why someone she knew?'

'There was no sign of a break-in.'

'There wouldn't be, she never locked her door.'

'Would you mind telling me where you were today after, say, about eleven o'clock?'

'What?' Why was Linklater asking him that? 'Eleven, eleven . . . ' Amos had to think hard, his mind still numb from the shock of what had happened to Brenda. 'Yes, that's when I dropped Jack off, came back here . . . and

56

then I went straight over to Long Cast Meadow to fish a sheep out of the river.' It seemed so long ago now, could it really have been only this morning. 'Why? What's that got to do with . . . ?' Oh, right, Linklater was probably interested in who Amos might have seen around at that time.

'When did you get back here?'

'Not until just now when I followed your police cars in. I went into Stratford to see my solicitor.'

'What time was your appointment?'

'Two o'clock.'

'So from eleven until two you were in Long Cast Meadow or Stratford.'

'Yes, that's right. So I'm sorry I can't tell you who else was in the village then.'

'Did anyone see you?'

Had he misunderstood Linklater's interest in his whereabouts? 'Look here you surely don't think — '

'I don't think anything Councillor, I simply have to ask everyone where they were and whether they can prove it. Was anyone with you?'

So why was he starting with Amos? Amos remembered how quiet the village had been earlier that day when he'd been looking for someone to help him.

'No.'

'Can you think why anyone would kill Brenda Smith?'

'Not a clue,' Amos said hopelessly. 'She was a lovely lady, well-liked. She and her husband ran the garage until he died. She was getting on a bit, that's all. Folk will be very upset. I'm sure someone will have seen whoever went into her place, they usually do here. I'll ask around for you, see what I can find out. They'll talk more easily to me than they will to you.'

'Thank you for the offer, Councillor, but until we've made our enquiries, I'll thank you not to interfere.'

Amos was stunned and must have shown it.

'You must understand we can't have our investigation hampered by amateur approaches,' Linklater explained. But by the look on his face and the questions he'd been asking, Amos had a strong feeling that that was only part of the reason his help had been so summarily rejected. Was it that Linklater actually suspected him, Amos, of murdering Brenda? How crazy could the police get?

Smarting from the snub, after Linklater had left Amos decided to find out what was up with Jack — maybe he knew why the police were acting so strangely. The road was still blocked but he could cut across the fields behind, through the old allotments and into the pub through the back gate.

As he lifted the latch into Jack's private yard he heard a muffled: 'What the hell?' from Jack who'd been on his way to change a barrel, and must have caught sight of the gate slowly opening. Everyone was bound to be nervous this evening. 'Oh, it's you.'

'Who'd you think it was, the hound of the Baskervilles? Why didn't you answer your phone?'

'Oh, I well . . . we're all a bit shaken. Anyway, what're you doing, creeping around like a burglar?'

'I wasn't creeping. I could hardly march straight up Mallard Lane, could I?' Cocooned in the Hathaway Arms at the top of the lane Jack may have been unaware the lane was still sealed off.

'I thought you'd want your glasses back,' Amos said handing them over.

Jack reacted as though he'd been stung. 'Um, er — yes I d . . . did.'

'What in heaven's name's the matter with you?' Amos asked, overwrought himself and tired of Jack's peculiar behaviour.

'Nothing, why? It's all these police, the place has been crawling with them, now they're setting up their incident room on my car park.'

'So what have you found out?'

'About Brenda's death, you mean? The pathologist, I think he was, came in here to wash his hands — don't know why he couldn't have done it there.' Jack was visibly wilting, he swallowed hard. 'Anyway, I overheard him tell one of his colleagues she wouldn't have suffered.' As an afterthought Jack added: 'Said he thought it'd been done by someone who knew what they were doing. Look, I've got to go and change a barrel over.'

'I'll come with you,' Amos offered but Jack didn't move. 'Have they asked you where you were around lunchtime?'

'Yes, and I told them I was here.' Maybe it was the way Jack phrased it, but it sounded like a lie to Amos. About to go on, Jack stopped himself. Instead he snapped: 'And where were you, then?'

'Fishing a lamb out of the river.'

'What's that supposed to mean? How am I supposed to support you when you give answers like that? If you're going to be cagey about it I won't bother asking again, I'll just make my own assumptions!'

Even allowing for today's stresses, Jack's outburst was uncalled for. Amos had come to discover why the police were being odd, only to find that Jack was too. What was going on that he hadn't understood? Brenda Smith had been murdered, here in Weston Hathaway, in cold blood. He'd have thought something so evil would have drawn them closer together, not forced them apart.

★ ★ ★

Harry Fields's butcher's shop was the only property from which Brenda Smith's house could actually be seen, diagonally across the lane. The following morning, Amos went to see him.

'Did you notice anything, Harry?'

'Well I think I saw Napoleon headed that way and I saw the reverend later, which must have been when he found her . . . but I had a shopful that day. And it was quite sunny you know; it streams in through the window so's I can't see a thing.' Why did Amos have the feeling Harry was inventing this as an excuse for not noticing Brenda's murderer enter her house? Guilt, he supposed.

Amos would miss Brenda. Yes, she'd been worried about getting older and about forgetting things and going off into a little daze; but that had been more about having insufficient to occupy her than about becoming senile.

She had loved Napoleon. As Amos came out of the butcher's he spotted him sitting by her gate — prevented by the police from going any further. Susan, Lindsay's daughter, was giving him a cuddle.

'Did you know he'd hurt himself?' she asked, looking up at Amos from her crouched position, one hand still on the animal's head. 'Look,' she pointed to a tear in his hide and he flinched when her hand went near it.

'Been trying to stick his snout in where it's not wanted, I expect.' Napoleon was wont to sustain injuries during the course of his insatiable foraging. Amos was more con-cerned about who could possibly have wanted Brenda dead. Like the police, he couldn't believe that in a village this size no one had seen anything, in broad daylight, in the centre, opposite the butcher's. It was incredible. If only old Napoleon could talk.

Linklater was waiting for him on the corner. Neither man smiled.

'Have you found anyone who saw anything unusual?' Amos asked.

'Nothing unusual, no. Not yet. We have found a lady who says she saw you going into Mrs Smith's.' Linklater was watching Amos's face intently.

'Not yesterday she didn't,' Amos replied with as much innocence as he could muster under such scrutiny.

'You were down at Long Cast Meadow, you said?'

'Yes, that's right.'

'Because there was a sheep in the river?'

'Yes, I told you.'

'Did you manage to get it out?'

'Actually, yes I did.'

'And then you went to your appointment in Stratford?'

'Yes.'

Linklater stared pointedly at Amos's clothes. 'Didn't you change first?'

'No, he's used to seeing me like this.' Amos surveyed his mud-caked ex-charity shop trousers with the missing left knee, his sweater covered in wisps of straw and his tattered jacket held together with pink bailer twine — his working clothes.

'You didn't get wet pulling the sheep out?'

Amos felt ridiculous. 'Oh God, of course I did. I came back, I did come back! I came back to change out of my wet trousers.' Why on earth had he said he hadn't come back, of all stupid things to say. Now Linklater really would be concerned about him.

'And what time was that?'

'I don't know, about one-ish I guess.' He was flustered now. How could he have been so dumb? All he could think was he'd not been paying much attention to his answers, especially last night; had been far too caught up in feeling sorry for Brenda, worrying if there was a murderer loose in the village . . . and wondering what was eating Jack.

'And did you go to Brenda Smith's?'

'I told you, not yesterday.'

Linklater pursed his lips. Amos could see him thinking that last night Amos had said he'd gone straight from Long Cast Meadow to Stratford and that had turned out not to be true. What else might the councillor be forgetting?

'Were you in the habit of visiting Mrs Smith?'

'Yes, sometimes. Who thinks they saw me yesterday?'

'You know I can't tell you that.'

'I don't see why not. If I'm to be accused I think I should know who's doing the accusing.'

'No one's accusing you of anything.'

At that point the Reverend Whittaker appeared round the corner. 'Oh, Amos, Chief Inspector. Any news?'

'Not yet, sir, no.'

'Was it you who found her, Reverend?' Amos asked gently.

'Yes Amos, yes it was. Napoleon was there you know, didn't want to leave her. The police had to help me get him out. I hear you'd been

64

in earlier.' By his tone Amos could tell the reverend meant he was pleased Amos had had the chance to speak to Brenda before she died.

Amos stared at Linklater then turned to the reverend and asked: 'What makes you say that, Reverend?'

'Oh someone said . . . oh yes, it was Mrs Squires, saw you from the butcher's.'

Linklater's lack of reaction told Amos this was the same informant. If not, Amos would now be under even more suspicion as seemingly there'd be more than one witness to his alleged visit to Brenda's.

'I didn't go in yesterday. I only wish I had.'

6

Inconveniently, his interview with the standards board was set for the same day as the district council planning meeting to which Cyril Quartermaster's latest application would be presented. Quartermaster and his cohorts had moved it up the list — Amos knew why . . . and how. However, Amos had persuaded the committee chairman into an inspection visit which would buy the campaign the extra time it needed to get everyone's support . . . and meant today he could concentrate on his interview. Despite his reaction to John Wilkinson's questions, Amos knew that in order to remain a councillor, he had to persuade the inquisitors of his innocence.

'Councillor Cotswold, I believe you understand the nature of the complaint against you. Do you understand the purpose of this interview?'

The chairman glanced at Amos, then across to John Wilkinson, who murmured assent.

'This is an unusual case, Councillor, because we've been deluged with letters on the subject — one hundred and thirty-seven at the last count, I believe. All but three are in support of you and the work you do in your constituencies.' Peeking at the sheaf she held, Amos spotted Alec FitzSimmons's crested notepaper. John said he'd written, they had copies of all the letters. 'However, we cannot ignore the three from Phyllis Arbuthnot, Vernon Squires and his wife, Irene.'

John stood. 'You should understand, ma'am, that Mrs Arbuthnot holds opposing political views to my client and may well stand against him at the next local election so it would be in her interest to have him discredited — or barred altogether. And Mr Squires has the contract to build fifty executive houses for Mr Quartermaster whose planning application has so far been refused — he believes due to my client's intervention.'

'Why do you think Mr Quartermaster believes you shouldn't hold public office, Councillor?'

'What, really?' Was this a trick, was she trying to catch him out? He turned to John for the answer. John nodded.

'Because he can't bribe me.'

The lady blinked her eyelashes rapidly — that clearly wasn't the answer she'd expected.

'I thought it might be because his aunt left

67

you some land, and he felt he should have had it — so this was a way of getting back at you? People do that all the time you know. Anyone in public office is very vulnerable, but I don't have to tell you that. Believe me . . . ' she leaned forward, 'we are aware that the unscrupulous may try to use us as a means of punishing their enemies.'

By appearing to be on his side was she trying to soften him up, lure him into betraying himself? Amos replied: 'No, ma'am. It's because he wants to build fifty new houses in our village and he thinks I'm blocking him.'

'And are you?'

'Yes, ma'am.' Amos opened his mouth to say more but John audibly shuffled his feet so Amos shut it again. John had counselled him not to offer information, only answer the questions. Instead he gave her one of his most winning smiles.

'Well, I think that's all we need,' she said, gathering her papers.

What did she think? Was that it? He had to find out. 'Can I buy you lunch, sweetheart?' John gasped but the attractive lady inter-viewer removed her glasses and patted her hair into place at the back.

'That's very kind of you, Councillor, but I'm afraid we've another meeting we have to get back for this afternoon. Another time, perhaps?' She returned the smile. Amos felt he'd given it his best shot.

As they walked out John exploded. 'For heaven's sake, Amos — now she's in no doubt about how you con those old ladies.'

'You're only jealous,' Amos retorted, hobbling swiftly out of the building, convinced it had gone well. Head held high he was nonetheless aware he'd still have to wait a month for their draft report, so it would be close to the election before he'd know the outcome. To which, even then, Quartermaster could append further comment.

★ ★ ★

Amos finally left the council offices at twenty past eleven that night, along with two fellow councillors. They crossed the road to the car park, which was tucked behind some old buildings opposite and left open for the use of councillors on meeting nights. Concentrating on their discussion, it was only as the others were peeling away that he noticed.

'Hey, where's my Land Rover?'

'Where you left it, I expect, Amos. Try the middle of the road,' came the riposte. The others laughed in the dark.

'No, seriously, it was here, against this wall,

where I always park it.'

The others climbed back out of their cars and wandered towards him, casting around. They could see the whole car park. Save for their own and two or three more cars it was empty — no Land Rovers.

By the time he'd summoned the police, waited for them to arrive and assured them with some difficulty that the vehicle had been stolen as opposed to abandoned, Amos eventually arrived home in a police car at one o' clock in the morning. His mind was racing. Wide awake, even he couldn't very well ring Jack at this hour so he paced the cottage instead. With a full glass of Scotch in his hand and Napoleon following him with his eyes, he circled the room, pondering.

It had been ten days since Brenda's murder and from what Amos could gather the police were no further forward. They hadn't been near him since the day after . . . which surely meant they didn't really suspect him, although they might suspect he'd deliberately lied about returning to the village. But neither were they confiding in him, as they had done in the past. And why had Irene Squires said she'd seen him going into Brenda's? Amos had no idea.

And now someone had stolen his Land Rover. Were these things linked? Was this more of Quartermaster's doing? Oh no! Amos stood still in the middle of the room. Were they trying to frame him? Was Quartermaster intending to plant some evidence, put something of Brenda's in the Land Rover . . . but hang on, he needn't steal the Land Rover to do that, the back was wide open anyway. P'raps he'd wanted to tuck it away, say under a seat or something, as though Amos had tried to conceal it. Why would Amos have done that when he could easily have buried it in any one of a dozen fields — or burnt it? Nothing made sense. He continued his pacing round and round, mentally and physically. Napoleon grunted, wound his head around as far as it would go, shook it, wound it back and closed his eyes.

At six Amos rang Ted and Lindsay. He needed to borrow Ted's pick-up to check on the sheep.

'Maybe someone's put a spell on you.' Lindsay suggested when she and Ted arrived.

'What on earth makes you say that?'

'I dunno. It's just that you be having a run of bad luck, like.'

Which set Amos wondering whether indeed anything at all had gone right recently. 'Not entirely I haven't, Lindsay. We got what we wanted from the planning committee last night. They're going to pay us a visit.'

'No one in their right mind would steal your Land Rover. It has to have been a stranger — everyone else knows they'd have to fumigate it first.' Jack was in buoyant mood after the minor triumph at the council meeting — as indeed Amos would have been were it not for this. 'What did the police say?'

'When they'd finished laughing you mean? I told them when your animals and your livelihood depend on your having a certain vehicle it actually isn't remotely funny. Anyway, they said the predictable — that it was gypsies.'

'Well, it could have been. They steal cars to order these days, you know, I told you not to get that fancy model.'

'Yes, it could. When I thought it was part of a bigger plot — what with Quartermaster and Brenda and everything — I dismissed that idea. But if it was just common or garden theft then, yes. It could have been.'

'You don't sound very convinced.'

'I know this sounds odd but I just don't think they'd take mine. On the other hand one of them's not very pleased with me after he had to pay for driving me into the ditch.'

'The police may not have meant our local gypsies.'

'Oh, I'm sure they did. Fact is they don't know what goes on over at the gypsy encampment because they daren't go there. For all I know my lovely Land Rover is sitting at Broad Farthing this minute.'

'I know what you're thinking. Leave it to the police, Amos.'

'Mmm, I think I might just nip over there and have a look. Don't worry, Jack, contrary to what Lindsay thinks, I live a charmed life.' It was Amos's turn to laugh. In a way he'd feel more comfortable if the gypsies had stolen his Land Rover, then he could eliminate the Quartermaster theory.

★ ★ ★

This time the welcome party waved him straight on as he turned into the camp in Ted's truck.

Ma greeted him. 'Twice in as many weeks, Amos Cotswold? To what do I owe this honour?'

'I came to see you.'

'Flattering as that is, I somehow doubt it's the real reason.'

'Can I have a look around?'

'Now why would you want to do that?'

'Because I've never been round your estate.'

73

She regarded him very steadily for a whole minute, then offered her arm. 'Let me show you our camp, Councillor. You'll have to take us as we are, we would have tidied up if we'd known you were coming,' she said with a straight face.

'I'm glad you haven't.'

They set off down a cinder track bordered on either side by caravans drawn neatly into lines, each with its own fenced off garden. Behind these were trucks and other vehicles.

'Can we see the motors, Ma?' Amos pointed in their direction.

'Like your motors don't you.'

'How long have you been here now, Ma?' he asked as they performed their tour of inspection along the ranks of trucks and pick-ups . . . and Land Rovers. It was a big camp.

'About eight years off and on, since my Jacko died. It's our land you know. His family bought it years ago fearing that one day we'd have nowhere left to go. Far-sighted, weren't they?'

'But you still move around?'

'Oh yes, now and then. But some of the younger ones need to settle for a while, raise their kids, give them a decent education. Things have changed so much. We can't teach them all they need any more — about

computers and electronics and science
. . . and the law. And there are fewer and
fewer places, even across Europe, where we
can still wander at will. So now we have to do
it the other way around. Give the kids a
grounding in every sense — an education,
other skills, and then let them put those to
use across our communities. Which means
they travel later. Problem is we're not allowed
into your villages — couldn't afford it
anyway. So the youngsters are damned before
they have a chance.'

'And are you still accused of being
'Travellers'.'

'See for yourself Amos. Does this look like
a Traveller's place? Look how clean and tidy
it is — even when we weren't expecting
visitors.'

'OK, OK, Ma, I know that. I wonder if
anyone else does? You bar outsiders so, as
with all secret societies, people think the
worst — especially the police.'

'Oh, we're supposed to let them in so they
can plant their evidence and blame us for all
the crime in the neighbourhood, are we? So
they don't have to work at finding the real
culprits.'

Quietly he said: 'There have been occasions
when it was your boys.'

'Of course. We've got our roughnecks and

our no-goods just like any other society — and we deal with them.' Ma stood still, catching her breath. She looked him directly in the eye. 'Why are you here, Amos?'

'My Land Rover was stolen from Stratford last night.'

'And you think it's here?'

'I wanted to be sure it wasn't.'

'Don't think much of us, do you.'

'That's not fair, Ma. I've supported you against all sorts of accusations. It's the police who think it was your lot.'

'How are we ever going to get out of this vicious circle?' she asked wearily, more to herself than Amos. 'We're hated regardless, so what are our hot-headed young men, like my granddaughter's husband, going to do? Behave accordingly of course. What's that old saying: *Might as well be hung for a sheep as a lamb.*'

How very apposite. 'So they thieve because they're being blamed for it anyway — think they should reap the benefits as well as the penalty. Is that it?'

'I suspect a few of them do, yes.'

'And has he got my Land Rover?'

'I don't think so, but I will find out,' she said stiffly. 'Give me a day or two. He's not here at the moment . . . but he *was* here last night.'

They strolled back to her van, having cleared some long overdue air in Amos's opinion.

'I heard about Brenda Smith,' Ma said.

'Who would kill an old lady, Ma? And why Brenda?'

'Some folks say she wanted to die.'

'She was afraid she'd got Alzheimer's.'

'Understandable then.'

'Yes, but I don't think she had.'

'Suicide maybe?'

'She didn't fall on her sword if that's what you mean. She was strangled.'

'I meant someone might have helped her.'

'What makes you say that?'

'I heard you were seen there that day.'

Amos stopped dead. 'For heaven's sake, Ma, don't you start! The police have already told me that and I've told them I wasn't there!'

'All right, all right, it's just that I know you're as soft as butter. I'll never forget the time when that badger had been run over and you spotted her milk all over the road. You spent hours locating her sett because you knew her cubs would die unless you rescued them. There aren't many men who'd realize that needed doing, let alone would bother to do it.'

Amos stopped and turned towards her.

'I've always thought you had second sight. You knew she'd asked me to kill her if she got any worse, didn't you?'

'No, but I'm not surprised. I could see myself making the same request if I were in her shoes. Don't worry, I'm not going to say anything.'

Amos took hold of her arm, turning her to face him. 'Ma, let's get one thing straight. I did not do it! I was not there, OK?' He released her roughly.

'OK. So who did?'

'How do I know?'

'You must have a clue.'

'Not really, why?'

'Well, you may not have been the only one she asked to . . . you know.'

'Who do you have in mind — Reverend Whittaker perhaps!'

'Funny you should mention him. He was in the parish in Cornwall where I once lived. His mum had Alzheimer's, you know. There were rumours.'

That explained why the reverend had been so good with Brenda. 'You're not suggesting . . . ?' Amos couldn't begin to believe the reverend would do such a thing. Not him, not a man of God. He refused to consider the idea.

7

'Bit ambitious isn't it?' commented Amos, leaning against the stainless steel worktops in Marion's spotless kitchen, drinking coffee.

'I don't see why.' Marion drew herself up to her full five feet nothing. 'I can't understand why we've never done it before, it's such an obvious one for us to do. The really clever thing is that *A Midsummer Night's Dream* provides a key role for Irene Squires without requiring her to be a beautiful young princess. Titania, Queen of the Fairies, was a mature woman.'

'And is *Mister* Squires in it this year?' Jack asked. Amos understood the emphasis on the Mister. Jack hadn't recovered from Squires's peculiar outburst over the change of use notice.

'No, said he didn't want to be, which is a pity because as usual we're short of men. Either of you fancy being an elf?'

'P'raps you should ask these policemen who've become a permanent fixture.' Amos peered out of the window unsmiling, indicating down the road with his mug. 'Have you heard how they're getting on?'

'No more than you know already,' Jack answered. He was still distinctly tight-lipped on the subject of Brenda's murder. Everyone was upset but Jack had taken it particularly hard. Maybe because it had happened within spitting distance from him, so it was all the more awful for having taken place so close.

'Anyway, are you fit now?'

Still using Ted's truck, he and Jack drove up to the barn to inspect the ewes. The wind whistled across the field where the open-fronted barn stood alone, exposed to the elements.

They'd been so busy that neither of them had heard or seen anyone arrive, but on emerging from the barn Amos saw the note tucked under his windscreen wiper. Though he usually gave some indication of visitors, Napoleon had failed to alert them, hadn't stirred from where they'd left him propped up against the front offside wheel, just where anyone leaving a note would have had to stand.

Amos unfolded the dog-eared scrap and read aloud: '*WE AINT GOT IT. LOOK IN THE GARAGE.*'

'Very cryptic,' Jack said. 'How many letters? Haven't got what?'

'I can guess who it's from. It's about my Land Rover.'

'You went to Broad Farthing, didn't you?'

'Yes, and this is my answer.'

'Do you believe them?' Jack sounded incredulous.

'Absolutely.'

'What do they mean: 'Look in the garage'?'

'Since I don't have a garage I can only assume they mean the one in the village.'

'But your Land Rover would hardly be sitting there in broad daylight without being returned to you?' Jack lapsed into silence but temptation soon overcame him. 'Well? What are they getting at?'

'I don't know but I think it's time for another trip to Broad Farthing to find out — alone.' He added that before Jack could think of accompanying him. It was the last place he'd take anyone, partly because he didn't want to be responsible for their safety and, more practically, because the gypsies would clam up in front of a stranger.

'Leave it to the police, Amos. It's their job.'

'Oh I can see the gypsies talking to them, can't you! Don't tell anyone about this, please, Jack.'

'What would I tell them anyway? Seems very odd to me.'

⋆ ⋆ ⋆

They met Amos halfway — in a small copse a mile or so on the Weston Hathaway side of

Broad Farthing. The same surly youth who'd driven him off the road was standing half on the verge and half under cover, visible only because Amos was looking for him. Amos pulled off the road and got out.

'Thought you'd be coming.'

'I'm too busy for guessing games.'

'You expect us to write it down for you?'

Amos understood why they'd left a note when they'd seen Jack in the barn with him, otherwise they'd have talked to him there.

'What do you want?'

'Ma said to tell you we ain't got it.'

'You're Ma's grandson.'

'I'm married to her granddaughter.' Perhaps that explained the surliness — a gypsy taking orders from a woman.

'Did you steal my Land Rover?'

'No'

'But you know who did?'

'Maybe.'

Amos glowered at the young man.

'Ma said you'd get the police off our backs if we help you.'

'Oh?' It was Amos's turn to be enigmatic.

'They're always blaming us.'

'Maybe with good reason.'

The gypsy glared at him. His sidekick stared at the ground during the whole exchange, perhaps he didn't speak English.

Must be here as muscle, Amos concluded but without any idea why they might think that necessary.

'They've done a lot of them you know.'

This was more like it, but he mustn't interrupt the flow.

'They nick posh motors up here — Mercs, Beemers, the odd sports job.' Still Amos held his tongue.

'They swap 'em over on Thursdays, always Thursdays. We reckon somewhere down the M5. He brings another one back for the Friday auction in the Black Country.'

'Who?' Amos had to have a name — though the clue had been in the note.

'Bruce Squires and his brother. Ma doesn't like them.' This last remark was presumably added to protect their *machismo*, explain why they were telling him all this.

'Why haven't you told anyone this before?'

'Who would've believed us — we're gippos, remember.'

'Thank you,' Amos said.

'Thank Ma,' replied the man, melting back into the trees; obviously uncomfortable with this unaccustomed civility.

Why hadn't he taken Jack's advice and left it alone? Because he was furious. He marvelled how other car-theft victims could accept their fate so philosophically. Not him, he had to act. Which was why he couldn't ignore what he'd been told. He supposed he should go straight to the police with his information but he shared the gypsies' dilemma — doubted if the police would believe him, especially when they learned his source. Nor did he have a single scrap of evidence. He couldn't accuse upright citizens of being mixed up in organized car crime just because someone had told him they were. He must have proof — substantiate the story for himself.

Today was Wednesday, the insurers had promised him a temporary vehicle tomorrow afternoon. He'd need someone to share the driving because heaven alone knew where he would end up. He rang Jack from his mobile: 'I need your help, but don't tell anyone, not even Marion. Don't worry, it can wait until after you've closed.'

Jack appeared an hour later looking as though he'd seen a ghost. 'What's all the cloak and dagger about?'

Amos told him what the gypsies had said and Jack visibly relaxed. 'What did you think I was going to say?' Amos muttered.

'The Squires boys?' Jack repeated.

'That's what they said.'

'But why?'

'Beats grafting, I s'pose. Bruce is never in the garage.'

'The younger one, Keith, is it? Went away, didn't he?'

'A few years ago — got mixed up in that tobacco racket. It never went to court because his old man paid for him to disappear until the suspicions had died down — Cornwall somewhere, I think; which would tie in with the M5 bit.'

'Their dad's not my favourite man at the moment.'

'Did I tell you, he's put in a written objection to your paddock application?' He could tell he hadn't by Jack's face. 'I'm sorry, it slipped my mind with all this carry on. I'll get you a copy — he goes on about changing the character of the village. Bloody hypocrite. I'm sure Quartermaster's put him up to this.'

'It didn't look like it that day he spotted my notice. He started off OK, then went peculiar.'

'Don't forget he's been into amateur dramatics for years.'

'What's his real problem?'

'Dashed if I know. I'm as baffled as you are, which is why I think Quartermaster must be behind it. Or maybe it's some sentimental reason to do with it being the last house his dad built . . . which I doubt. More likely his stuck-up wife's afraid your new garden will outshine hers at the Open Gardens afternoon. I've really no idea.'

'So what're you going to do about the car thing?'

'Ah, that's where I thought you might like to help,' Amos said, grinning. Jack's eyes narrowed with suspicion. 'I need proof, right?'

Jack nodded. So far, so good Amos thought. 'Well the only thing I can think of is to follow Bruce tomorrow night . . . it's Thursday.'

'Oh, we're going to play Gumshoe and Greenhorn, are we?'

'Have you got a better idea?'

'Go to the police.'

'Oh, they're going to believe my possibly slanderous accusations, are they? 'And where did you learn about this, Councillor',' he mimicked. ''Oh, the gypsies told you did they? Ha ha. You don't think they were trying to deflect the heat from themselves at all, do you? Ha ha.''

'OK, just forget it then. The insurance company will cough up, why should you care?'

'Good point . . . but strangely I do. Maybe I don't like the idea that our villages will get a reputation for harbouring thieves. Maybe I want to give the gypsies a break — stop them being automatically accused of everything.'

'Can't see why you're bothered about them.'

'So, are you game?'

'What, for following Bruce tomorrow night? Worst it can be is excrutiatingly boring — waiting for something to happen. Where does he live, anyway?'

'Outskirts of Stratford. There's a pub opposite which is handy, we can sit in the car park unnoticed.'

'But he'll know my car.'

'No, he won't. I get my loan Land Rover tomorrow afternoon, no one will recognize that.'

'OK, I must be certifiable but . . . count me in.' Then, as an afterthought, Jack added: 'We'll be tucked up in bed by ten, you see.'

★   ★   ★

The more Amos turned it over in his mind, the more he realized how simple it was for Bruce — being in the trade. He could leave his own car anywhere locally and send his men to pick it up afterwards — garage people did that all the time. If he needed an excuse he could always say he'd had one too many to drink and decided to walk home.

Bruce Squires could easily have a set of skeleton keys which would fit most cars — or even use a trailer and a hoist if necessary. No one would think twice about it if they saw him driving a strange car . . . or indeed if they'd seen him driving Amos's. He was a garage man, they'd just assume he had permission. Come at last, if caught he could pretend innocence — or stupidity — by saying he'd been sent to pick up a car and had picked the wrong one by mistake.

By seven o'clock Amos and Jack were skulking in the car park of the George and Dragon, their eyes trained on Bruce Squires's driveway. They could see his black BMW — Amos recognized the number plate — and a coupé, presumably his wife's.

'You do realize how ridiculous this is,' Jack moaned. 'Supposing, just supposing he does go out for a spot of thieving tonight — what makes you think he won't realize he's being followed?'

'Well, even if he does, what's he going to do about it?'

'I say we give it until ten o'clock, then I think we should call it a night.'

'All right,' Amos agreed reluctantly.

At eight o'clock Bruce emerged from his house, climbed into his car and turned out of his drive. Amos was shaking with excitement.

'Well, go on then or we'll lose him before we've even started,' Jack urged.

The roads were quiet as the BMW drove sedately up the Warwick Road.

'He's going north,' Jack said.

'He could be going anywhere. Let's see what happens at the Longbridge island. You keep your eyes on him while I worry about the traffic.'

'He's in the left hand lane so it's either London down the M1, Coventry . . . or west on to the M40.'

'Thanks a lot.'

'It's the M40. Come on.'

Once on the motorway Amos found it easier — staying in the inside lane, hoping to make their presence less obvious.

'Where'd you think he's going?' Jack asked.

'How do I know? Looks as though it could be straight for the M5.'

'But he hasn't stolen anything yet?'

'Shall we stop him and remind him of that? Don't ask me, just make sure you don't lose him.' Amos was relieved they hadn't had to watch Squires stealing any vehicles. He hoped the evening would continue that way — kept telling himself he was there to gather evidence, not confront people. But he couldn't have sat idly by while a crime was being committed — couldn't have squared that with his conscience, and even less with the conduct required of a councillor.

They passed the last junction of the M42

westbound, which meant Squires was definitely headed for the M5, but whether south to the west country or north to the M6 remained to be seen. Proceeding at a steady seventy-five miles per hour in the middle lane, Squires was being careful not to draw attention to himself.

'Look, it's south,' Amos yelled, as Squires pulled into the inside lane.

'Which means he hasn't seen us. He could have left that lane change right to the last minute if he'd really wanted to wrong-foot us.' Jack caught sight of Amos's withering look.

'Just keep your eyes on him, he could switch back yet,' Amos yelled.

But the BMW swept on. They settled down to a steady purr down the M5 for about an hour. Worcester, Gloucester, the turn-off for Slimbridge . . . all slid past in the night; on he went.

'I can think of things I'd rather be doing than wasting my time like this — he's probably got a bit of stuff tucked away down here, that's all,' Jack grumbled. They reached the outskirts of Bristol, carried on where the road rises up on stilts, then Squires moved across into the slow lane.

'He's going to turn off,' Jack shouted.

'Mmm.'

'The services — it's the services — Gordano — they're set off the motorway.'

'P'raps he wants a pee,' Amos suggested.

'Don't say that or I shall want one. Yes, he's turning for the services. Not the petrol area, he's heading for the main car park. Slow down, Amos, or we'll overtake him.'

'If you were coming northbound up the M5 you'd use exactly the same services, wouldn't you? I mean, it's not one of those where they're on both sides of the road is it?' Amos asked.

'No. You turn off the motorway regardless of which way you're travelling and join the ordinary road system at that roundabout we came by. It's the same at Exeter. Why?'

'Because the gypsy said something about a swap-over down the M5.'

'But what're they going to swap? They haven't stolen anything?'

'Bruce hasn't, no.'

'But if they swap, then Bruce's car'll end up in the West Country?'

'I don't understand it any more than you do; let's just watch and see what happens.'

'Would you recognize Keith if you saw him?' Jack asked.

'In context, if I got a good enough look . . . yes.'

'Look, he's parking in the back of the car

91

park, farthest away from the services building, in the dimmest light.'

'I'll park in the middle facing towards them. You get out and look in the back or something, so we don't look so conspicuous if he glances this way.'

Jack had only just alighted when a pristine white Saab swept in and drove purposefully across the car park, stopping nose in, beside the BMW. Both drivers got out. Amos was straining to see in the poor light. He could hear Jack clambering about in the Land Rover's open back, heard him fiddling with the restraining straps against the cab. The brothers wasted no time. They couldn't have exchanged more than a dozen words before they climbed into one another's cars and prepared to move off. Jack scuttled back inside the cab.

'Well, that's it then,' Jack said. 'Now we know what happens.'

'I'm glad you do because I sure as hell don't.' Amos was afraid Jack would want to go home now. 'Fancy some crab?'

8

'You're crazy. How do you know he's going west?'

'Just a hunch he's going home — he could just as easily be headed for Holyhead and the ferry to Ireland. We'll soon know depending on whether he heads for the Severn Bridge or not.'

'You really are cuckoo you know. You're going to keep following the BMW, aren't you? My guess is that car's going back to Stratford, for a good night's sleep, like we should be.'

'Then why did the drivers swap over?'

'Search me.'

The cavalcade left the car park, first the Saab, then the BMW, and way behind them, an innocuous-looking Land Rover.

'This could be tricky,' Jack said as they reached the roundabout. 'It helps that the Saab's white. Yes, he's turning back towards Stratford. Yes damn it, you're right. The BMW's going south. You win.'

Amos and Jack were able to follow comfortably. They travelled mostly in silence — afraid to lose concentration on the black car in case it suddenly turned off. But something was gnawing at Jack. 'I still don't understand why Bruce is sending his BMW down to Cornwall . . . I guess there's an innocent explanation for it, though.'

'That's why we have to keep going, have to understand what they're up to. OK, if it's innocent so be it, but somehow I don't think it is. Perhaps that's not Bruce's BMW.'

'But you said that was his licence number.'

'And it is — what safer way is there to transport a stolen vehicle than to use your own number plates. Think how easy that would be for him.'

On they went, soaring high over the Severn, inky-black in the darkness beneath them, bypassing Bridgwater, past Somerset's answer to the 'Angel of the North' — its ill-proportioned form bestriding the country-side — past its camel tucked into a hedgerow a mile further on, past Taunton and on down to Exeter. Which way now, Plymouth perhaps? No, the BMW took the A30 to Okehampton and on to Launceston. Although they hadn't stopped long at Gordano, it was getting on for midnight as they approached Bodmin Moor. In this eerie, empty landscape their presence behind the black car was much more obvious.

Being in a Land Rover helped until they picked up more traffic on the Bodmin bypass. It wasn't a motor you'd choose for a car chase, nor one that stood out in the country. Amos thought they were headed for Newquay when the BMW suddenly turned off the road from St Columb and dived down an archetypal Cornish lane with breathing room only on either side. Keeping their distance they followed him in.

Luckily nothing came the other way to hold them up, otherwise they'd never have found their quarry again in this maze of eight-feet high tunnels. Forced to retain a tantalizing 200-yard gap, they drove in constant fear that he'd bolt down a hidden opening and they'd lose him.

At last, as they rounded a sharp corner, there he was, only fifty or so yards away — crossing a main road which had materialized from nowhere. When they arrived at the junction they could see he must have taken a single cart track on the other side, like the entrance to a farm or smallholding.

Amos had already pushed his reliance on Keith Squires's blindness to its limits; he could hardly follow him down that track unnoticed. He turned left on to the main road and drove another quarter of a mile — far enough for anyone listening beside the path to assume the engine had faded into the distance. Then he pulled on to the grass verge and stopped.

'Now what?' Jack asked.

'I think we should do the rest on foot.'

'But we've no idea what we're going to find or how many people live there or anything. It could be a whole gang.'

'You're just finding excuses.'

'You're damned right I am — talk about walk defenceless into the lion's den. No one even knows where we are.'

'Who said anything about being defenceless?' Amos felt around under his seat, producing a twelve-bore shotgun.

'For God's sake, Amos!'

'Don't worry, I haven't got any ammunition for it — last lot I had went all mouldy, had to take it into the police station.' Amos chuckled in the dark. 'I just thought it might help.'

'More likely to get us killed if they think we're armed,' Jack yelled. Calming slightly, he added: 'Are you seriously thinking of going in there?'

'I certainly haven't come all this way just to exchange pleasantries with you.'

'I'm dying for a Jimmy Riddle,' Jack responded.

'Well, let's get out, then we can stroll back up there and at least get an idea of the set-up.'

'You leave that thing in the motor.' Jack

indicated the gun.

'Somebody might steal it. Tell you what, I'll keep it well hidden under my coat.'

'It's a wonder you didn't bring Napoleon too.'

'I would have, only he's another one who can't go very long without responding to the call of nature, so I couldn't risk it — not in a borrowed Land Rover.'

Amos knew this banter masked their fear. What were they getting themselves into? Yet he couldn't stop now, not when he was so close to getting proof that the gypsy's story was true. He only wanted to see what was there.

The moon lit the road and the track the BMW had taken. Conscious that Keith Squires might have driven only a few yards along, they walked on the verge to muffle the sound of their footsteps. As they turned in they met with head-high brambles on either side of a path a car's width across, which stretched into infinity. Grass grew down the centre and a stiff breeze blew in their faces, laden with salt. They walked for ten minutes — the road neither veered nor branched, just stretched inexorably ahead.

'What's that whirring?' Jack asked, cocking his head to one side. 'Sounds like a power tool.'

'What whirr — ' Amos grabbed Jack's sleeve and pulled him in to the side. The track had widened into a courtyard. He could make out the vague shape of a house over on the right along with what in the dark looked like caravans. Further bushes and sheds occupied the middle distance and next to them, on the left, stood a couple of large barns. One was undergoing some sort of renovation, the builders had left their paraphernalia scattered around. The other, the one nearest to them, had ill-fitting corrugated-iron doors with light showing beneath them and a grubby window beyond. No sign of the BMW.

Amos felt compelled to take a peek through that window. Gesticulating to Jack to stay back on the corner by the track, he tiptoed across the corner of the yard. The whirring had stopped. He looked in. Keith Squires had his back turned to the door and was busy screwing new number plates on to the BMW. Bruce's lay discarded on the floor.

With the shotgun tucked under his arm like any farmer out for a stroll, Amos pushed open the door and walked in. Keith started, staring at him open-mouthed, clutching his screwdriver ineffectually. His white, chinless, face — adorned with patchy fuzz — pre-sented a singularly unprepossessing sight.

'W . . . Wh . . . What are you doing here?' he stammered, backing away as Amos began to inspect the car. Once inside, Amos could appreciate the size of the barn, with gleaming black BMWs lining its walls — six in all, counting tonight's addition.

'Taking on the local dealership are you, Keith? I didn't realize there was such a big market for BMWs down here.' Amos struggled to assess exactly what was going on. 'Got a Land Rover or two as well, have you?' He walked further round the car. 'Oh, and what's this then? Tut tut, fancy the factory forgetting to put the serial number on, now there's a shocking omission. Wouldn't it be awful if the chassis number were missing as well.' Amos looked under the propped up bonnet where an electric filing gadget lay on the edge, presumably the source of the whirring sound.

'How did you get here? What do you want?'

'I thought you might have my Land Rover.'

'Well, I haven't.'

'Had a customer for it, did you?'

'Why should you care, insured, wasn't it.'

'Oh, so that's it. It doesn't count because you were only robbing the insurance company — is that it?'

'Lots of people do it.'

'Oh yeah. On this scale? Got a regular

container load here, haven't you.'

'What's it to you?' Keith started to walk towards Amos just as the shotgun was feeling a bit heavy under his left arm, so he shifted it slowly to his right. Keith froze.

'I just drive for Bruce, that's all,' he said in a different tone.

'Oh, and file off engine numbers and change number plates . . . and where did that nice white Saab I saw you driving come from?'

Keith sank down on his haunches beside the BMW, looking beaten. 'I don't know, I just does as I'm told. It's only the insurance companies that get hurt. Anyway, Mrs Smith never kicked up about it, like she did about other things.'

'What's that supposed to mean?'

'When she kept the books, she used to bitch if we didn't have the receipts for our expenses, like. But she never said anything about this.'

'I don't suppose your brother's little transactions went through the books, do you?'

'I dunno. I just thought she knew like and it was OK. I didn't think it was really bad.' Like a schoolboy, Keith was trying to wriggle out of having any responsibility for his shed-load of stolen BMWs. By the sound of it this sideline had been going on for years, probably since the spineless Keith had been exiled.

'What're you going to do?' Squires asked.

'Well, I'm not going to stop here gassing to you all night, that's for sure.' Amos took out his mobile phone and dialled the Stratford police number — the only one he knew.

'Constable? . . . Sorry, Sergeant. This is Councillor Cotswold. I'm fine thanks. Actually it's a bit complicated to explain now, but I've found a barn full of stolen cars in Cornwall . . . yes Cornwall . . . oh the weather's quite good, yes. This barn is off the main road from Newquay to St Columb, about halfway along I'd say, down a long track on the right, coming from St Columb, that is. Got that? Would you be so good as to ask your Cornish colleagues to hurry up. Thank you . . . oh, and Sergeant, if you see a white Saab — what do you mean, they're all white? No, not a memsahib, an SAAB. Yes, that's right, registration number UA08 XWT, it's been stolen too. You might tell your patrols that. Not at all, always pleased to help the police. Goodnight Sergeant.'

Amos knew Bruce Squires wasn't stupid enough to have taken the Saab home with him. He would have dropped it off and been given a lift back together with the set of his BMW number plates which had been in its

101

boot — returned by Keith from the previous BMW driven down to Cornwall. He'd be innocently tucked up in bed by now. Amos envied him, it must be gone half past one. Jack would want to be off.

'Goodnight, Keith, sleep tight.' Amos turned on his heel leaving the stupefied Keith sitting on the floor.

'I wonder who'll win the race?' Amos said to Jack as they walked briskly out of the yard.

'Aren't you going to wait for the police?'

'What for?'

'To see that Keith gets caught, of course.'

'I can't be bothered. Anyway, that's what I meant, want to bet me?'

They heard the barn door scrape on the yard, the sound of the BMW start up, the squeal of tyres as it was gunned into action and the flying gravel as it tore up the track — no sedate driving this time. Amos and Jack leapt into the hedge to escape being knocked down. Simultaneously they heard the wail of police sirens coming down the Newquay road.

'My guess is it'll be a dead heat at the end of the track.' They heard the squealing brakes and the skidding tyres but no further car sounds, no motor tearing away down the road. 'See, what did I say.' They kept walking. 'Let's just nip across this field here — it's bound to be quicker because it cuts off the corner.'

'Aren't you even going to stop and talk to the police?'

'Not tonight, no. I thought you'd be in a hurry to get back, I owe you that much, you've been very good coming all this way with me.'

Although too dark to see clearly, Amos could imagine the look on Jack's face by his body language. He had stopped, with his legs apart, hands on hips, jaw jutting forward.

'I haven't got a licence for the gun.'

They made good time going back. Jack drove. 'You took a huge risk going in there like that. Whatever possessed you?'

'I don't know, really. I wanted to make sure. Perhaps I just wanted to see the look of surprise on his face.'

'That gun was giving you false courage is what I think. Didn't it occur to you the builders could have been living on site, or other people?'

'Not until I was in the barn, no.'

'Well, I couldn't think of anything else, hanging around out there in the dark. I thought someone was going to jump me any minute.'

'Once I saw all those cars lined up ready to go, what worried me was whether they were coming for them tonight. That's why I wanted to get out of there fast. I should have just told the police so they could have lain in wait for the transporter and nabbed the others as well,' Amos realized. 'Not gone in there.'

'But you said it yourself before, they probably wouldn't have believed you.'

'Oh yes they would, once I was able to tell them exactly where all those stolen cars were.'

'But just think, Keith might have got away. They all might have escaped while you were busy telling the police.'

'Not if Keith hadn't known he'd been rumbled.'

'Well, what's done is done,' Jack said, ever practical.

'No, but you're right. I was wrong to go in there.' They lapsed into companionable silence, Amos kicking himself for not playing it better, for not thinking before he acted. It took the edge off his sense of elation at having so successfully proved the gypsy right. Not that he'd found his Land Rover, but he was sure the Squires had taken it — Keith had virtually admitted it. So there was some satisfaction in their night's work. But he'd made enemies needlessly. If he hadn't gone in there they need never have known who'd shopped them.

'Keith said a funny thing, though,' Amos

said aloud. 'Something about Brenda knowing what they were up to. He said it by way of
a defence — as if that made it all right.'

Jack said nothing. Amos sighed inwardly,
watching Jack clam up at the mention of
Brenda. 'I think that's a bit unlikely, don't
you?'

Still Jack said nothing. They had just
turned off the main road into Weston
Hathaway, it was 6.30, nearly light.

Four minutes later Jack drew up outside
Amos's cottage and switched off the ignition.
Instead of getting out he turned to face
Amos: 'I've been struggling with myself ever
since . . . not knowing whether to tell you this
or not, but I've got to. I can't keep it from
you any longer.'

Jack drew a sharp breath, his waver of
indecision audible. 'I saw you kill Brenda.'

9

Jack's words lay on the surface, unabsorbable. They were both very tired. They'd been up all night, driven 500 miles, apprehended a multiple car thief . . . now what was he saying?

'What?'

'I saw you kill Brenda Smith.'

'Don't be ridiculous.'

'Well no, that's not strictly true. I saw you bending over her and she was leaning back in her chair with her head at an odd angle. Somehow I knew she was dead.'

'You saw me bending over her, you say, the day she was murdered? You're sure it was that day?' Not that Amos could recollect ever having been party to a scene at Brenda's which could remotely be construed that way.

'Positive. Do you think I haven't asked myself this over and over again — but it's not something you'd forget — or muddle up.' Jack looked down at his hands as though they'd performed the act themselves. 'I didn't know what to do. I couldn't believe what I'd seen. If only I'd got there a minute or two earlier . . . p'raps . . . well . . . But as it was . . . '

Amos was wide awake now, his brain beginning to function again. 'So what were you doing at Brenda's? The police reckon she was killed around lunchtime. You'd be in your pub.'

'Yes, normally, only we'd run out of mustard so I nipped down to Harry's to get some. I thought nothing of it when I caught sight of you going up Brenda's path, but then I remembered you still had my glasses and thought you might've popped in there on your way over. So I decided to save you a trip. Believe me, I've wished so many times since that I hadn't.'

'So what happened exactly?'

'I crossed over and went up Brenda's path and round the side but just as I reached the door I peered through the glass . . . and well, I've told you what I saw.'

Amos couldn't accept that Jack thought him capable of murder. But wait a minute, he'd already forgotten that he'd come back to change that day; maybe he was having blackouts and doing things he didn't remember. Maybe he had killed . . . No! no! That was insane. But things like that did happen. Amos had heard stories where people moved in and out of different planes of existence. Maybe it had happened to him. Had he committed this atrocity whilst in a different universe? That way lay madness. There had to be a rational explanation for this and Amos had to find it, fast; had to persuade Jack he'd got it wrong.

Jack was still gazing at his hands, misery etched in his posture.

'So why didn't you stop me?'

'Because it was too late . . . and because I didn't want to know, didn't want to be a part of it. I told you, I just couldn't believe it. Then I remembered what you'd said — about her asking you to do it if she was going senile. I knew she'd been to the hospital the day before because Marion arranged for the Housewives to drive her there and back.'

'But you can't think — ?'

'And I remembered that conversation we'd all had in the bar one night.' Jack paused. 'You know, when Reverend Whittaker was there and we were talking about whether sometimes it might be kinder to help people go and you said something like you didn't see why not. And then there was tonight.' Now the floodgates had opened, all Jack's pent-up cogitations poured out. 'With the gun and everything.'

Amos was stupefied. 'So you think I killed Brenda because she wanted me to?'

'Yes.'

'Why haven't you told the police this, then?'

'Because I didn't want to be the one who betrayed you and because I understand why you did it. You did it for her.' Jack looked at Amos. 'I'm not going to say anything, Amos, I haven't even told Marion and I won't. But I had to tell you.'

Amos regarded his friend with gratitude, appreciating his loyalty.

'I didn't do it, Jack.'

'But I saw you.'

'It wasn't me.'

Jack wrung his hands. 'Look, I know you don't see it as murder. In the circumstances . . . neither do I.'

Amos fought to suppress his exasperation. 'How can I get this across to you? I'm not playing with words, or talking in euphemisms or twisting things or denying it because I can't bring myself to face what I've done. I'm telling you I was nowhere near Brenda's house that day — at all — at any time!'

If he couldn't persuade Jack of his innocence, he stood little chance with a jury. A jury! What was he thinking about? Then he realized. If it hadn't been him — Amos — whom Jack had seen . . . then Jack had let the murderer escape. He alone could have identified him. Jack didn't want that on his conscience.

'I don't understand,' Jack said, rubbing his glasses with vigour, as if cleansing his sight of the dilemma. Did he want to believe Amos yet couldn't face the consequences of his error? 'I see Lindsay's let Napoleon out for you already,' he went on, glancing up from his task.

'Where?'

'Up the road there,' Jack gesticulated with his spectacles.

'That's not Napoleon, that's Ted's fat black Labrador. Look, there's Ted just coming out of the alleyway. They've been for their morning constitutional.'

Jack replaced his glasses on his nose. 'Oh yes, I see now.'

Amos grabbed Jack's arm. 'That's it!' he cried in relief. 'That's it!'

'That's what Amos? What?'

'You didn't have your distance glasses on that day. I had them. That's why you thought it was me when it wasn't.'

'Well I . . . ' Jack stammered. He took off his glasses and angled his body to focus hard on an oak tree up the road, then replaced them and went through the same performance with them on. He repeated the process, twisting first one way then another, using various targets at different distances.

Amos watched him. 'Satisfied?'

'I want to be, Amos, you know I do.'

'And that old bottle-glass in Brenda's door is very misty and distorting.' Amos was conscious of sounding as though he was trying too hard. 'It wasn't your fault. I'd have thought the same myself.'

'All I can say is, it was someone awfully like you.'

'Well, that's a start at least.'

Whether or not Jack accepted his eyesight deficiency, Amos had been aware of it for some time — which helped him feel better. For a while there he had really begun to think he must be in thrall to the dark forces; there could have been no other explanation. But to think that Jack could for one minute have believed him capable of murder . . . And if Jack could think it so would others. The only way he could prove his innocence was to find his own double.

★   ★   ★

Linklater arrived about ten o'clock. Amos wasn't surprised.

'Chief Inspector,' he said holding the door open. Linklater ducked his head under the lintel and preceded Amos into the cottage. Spotting the computer set up in the corner of the sitting room he wandered over and peered at the screen — as he might a painting or a photograph. Whether he'd expected to find something unsavoury displayed, Amos couldn't tell. The screensaver was a picture of Napoleon.

'I expect you're tired.'

Since this came across as a statement rather than a solicitous enquiry into his health, Amos took it as rhetorical.

'Cornwall, I hear.'

So that was it. News travelled fast in the police — when they wanted it to.

'Any progress on who killed Brenda Smith?'

'I was going to ask you the same thing.' They stared at one another.

'I take it the answer's 'no' then?' Amos said.

'Yes. We have the sighting of you going in there at about the right time. Ordinarily we'd have taken your clothes, checked for DNA etc to put you at the scene of the crime . . . but since you openly admit to visiting the lady frequently — it would prove nothing.'

Is he trying to tell me I'm still number one suspect, Amos wondered, fervently thankful that Linklater remained ignorant of Jack's erroneous identification.

'Why are you telling me this, Chief Inspector?'

'Because I think you know more than you're admitting.'

'Well, if I do I'm not aware of it,' Amos said with a half-laugh.

'Actually, I haven't come about that. I've come about last night.'

Amos groaned to himself. He hadn't followed Keith Squires to help the police — but he'd had to tell them once he'd found those cars.

'Keith Squires has been telling the Cornish police you had a gun. We said he must be mistaken because we have no record of a licence for you.'

'Mmm.' With all the other accusations flying about, no one would ever believe him if he started to lie now. 'I didn't threaten him with a gun, if that's what he's saying.'

'I didn't think you had, Councillor. As I said to my colleagues down there, Squires wouldn't have been able to make the escape attempt that he did if you'd had a gun to detain him with — now would he?' Linklater held Amos's gaze.

'What'll happen to Squires? Was his brother in it too?' Amos asked.

'Denies any involvement whatsoever, I'm told — the brother, that is. Why do you ask?'

'Slippery bugger.' Amos was debating whether to confess what they'd seen Bruce do — the police might be able to charge him for being in possession of a stolen vehicle on his and Jack's evidence, but he doubted it. Best to make light of their part in this.

'Can I ask how you came to be at this place in Cornwall?'

'It's a long story, Chief Inspector, and I'm not too sure you'd believe me anyway. Does it matter?'

'Not really, no. We've recovered the cars and we've got Keith Squires. So we're obliged to you. But if you did know any more it could help us get the rest of the gang.'

'What'll happen to him?'

'Oh, he'll be out on bail by this evening. His father's seen to that.'

'I expect Vernon's taken it hard.' Amos would need to avoid him for a while, what with the contretemps over Jack's paddock and now this. They'd never got on anyway. He wasn't sure why, there'd been no overt quarrel as such, except Squires always sought to get what he wanted by force — bully-boy tactics — an approach Amos found unacceptable. No wonder Squires and Quartermaster hit it off so well, they were two of a kind. At least Keith hadn't seen Jack, so he'd be all right.

'Yes, but it was odd. He was angry with his son, which you might expect. Kept yelling at him that it was 'all he needed right now!' and yelling at us saying we'd never make it stick;

that the lad was innocent and he'd be bringing his solicitor in, do us for wrongful arrest. We get it all the time from men like him. But the minute he found out you'd been involved he suddenly climbed down off his high horse, muttered something about he was sure we'd deal with it and as good as crept away. Suddenly distanced himself from the subject.'

'What do you think?' Amos asked, puzzled.

'I think six newish BMWs in one barn counts as suspicious, but without engine and chassis numbers it'll take us a while to find their owners.' Linklater had a sense of humour after all.

The chief inspector made a move towards the door. 'Oh, by the way — we've found pig hairs and even some tiny fragments of flesh on Mrs Smith's clothing.'

'Oh, if you can't pin it on me you're going to blame Napoleon. Is that it now?' Being suspected of killing someone he'd been fond of was getting to Amos. 'You knew Napoleon was in there when she was found. He was often in there — most days in fact — ask anyone in the village. They'll all tell you that.'

'Did he just go there on his own, then?' So that was the trap. Linklater had 'gotcha' emblazoned across his face. They think if

Napoleon was there, ergo I must have taken him.

'Yes, oh yes. Again, ask anyone.' Being a townsman the chief inspector had clearly not understood. Pigs can't wander at will in Stratford, but in Weston Hathaway Napoleon could.

Catching sight of Phyllis Arbuthnot bustling past on the footpath, Amos flung open the door and called, 'Mrs Arbuthnot, could you spare a moment?'

The matronly figure halted her progression, turned and glowered at Amos, her distaste for him amply illustrated by the visible stiffening of her nose and her reluctance to approach any closer. He'd picked the perfect witness. Even if she hadn't been standing against him in the local elections, her loathing of Amos was palpable.

On seeing the chief inspector she smiled. 'Good morning, Chief Inspector Linklater, what can I do for you?'

'Mrs Arbuthnot,' Amos said in his most charming manner, 'the chief inspector was wondering if my Napoleon ever wanders around the village on his own — on the odd occasion like?'

She took the bait beautifully. Puffing out her ample bosom and summoning her best Margaret Rutherford tones she pronounced:

116

'Odd occasion! Odd occasion! All the time, Chief Inspector, revolting beast that it is. I'm sure it's against the law and I'm extremely pleased to see you people taking the matter seriously at last.'

Linklater opened his mouth to speak but Phyllis was in full spate: 'In and out of people's houses it goes — continually — poking its filthy snout into other folks' rubbish bags. Not a day goes by but that it's out here spreading disease and trampling flowers. It shouldn't be allowed and the sooner you make him keep the animal in a proper sty, the better.' With which she turned on her heel and marched off up the road.

Amos felt sure it was him she thought belonged in a sty, along with the pig, and wondered idly if he could train Napoleon to chase her whenever she walked past.

'All right, Councillor, all right,' Linklater manfully choked on his laughter until she was out of earshot.

'I think that tells you what you wanted to know, Chief Inspector.' Then a thought occurred to him; seriously Amos asked: 'Could that have been what Irene Squires saw?'

'She said she saw you going into Brenda Smith's that lunchtime.'

'Yes, but what if she assumed she saw me

117

because she saw Napoleon?'

'I'll ask her. But what I really need from you is some help. Who disliked Brenda enough to kill her?'

Amos relaxed. Could Linklater be trusting him at last. 'Not robbery, then?'

'Doesn't look like it, no other room was disturbed.'

Amos was loath to share his lookalike theory with Linklater lest it incriminate him even further — like a tale he would dream up to explain why people thought they'd seen him. Instead he asked:

'Who benefits from the will?' He cursed inwardly. That sounded as though he expected Brenda'd left him something, as Nellie had. He hadn't meant it that way at all. Linklater appeared not to have noticed. Embarrassed, Amos hurried on, 'I wondered if it was the motive, that's all. Either that, or it actually was robbery and the thief was disturbed.' Amos was thinking about Jack and whether the attacker had heard him and fled empty-handed.

'Someone local, do you think?'

'The killer you mean? I'd prefer it not to be, Chief Inspector. Wouldn't you if it were your village?'

* * *

118

At half past eleven at night, Amos strolled back down the hill to his cottage. Passing Brenda's house, he was struck by how still and empty it appeared. Whereas the other dwellings had some signs of life even at this hour — a porch light, open windows in the bedrooms, a rosy glow behind drawn curtains — hers was shrouded in darkness, the police tape flickering in the night breeze like blue and white bunting. Still mounting his Cerberuslike guard on her property, Napoleon rose to his feet at Amos's approach and fell silently into step beside him. How could he be expected to understand she wouldn't be coming back?

With Amos muttering to himself as usual, they carried on along the lane, past the old forge, and into his front garden. Where a shadowy figure detached itself from the cherry tree inside the gate and followed them up the path.

10

More sensitive to their visitor than Amos, Napoleon stopped dead. 'Get on you old fool, don't stop there.' Turning, Amos caught sight of the figure.

'What on earth?'

She must be about eighteen and, in the dim light, fleetingly reminded him of someone.

'Who are you?' he managed, shocked.

'I'm Ma's granddaughter.'

'And does Ma know you're wandering around the countryside at this time of night?' He said it sharply, still thrown.

'I've a car around the corner. I've been waiting ages.'

'You'd better come in, then.' Amos lifted the latch on his front door and ushered the girl and Napoleon inside.

She stood motionless on the doormat while he lit the lamps and filled the kettle.

'Like some tea?'

'Mmm . . . please.' She was clearly chilly. He put on a fan heater and indicated a chair beside it. She sat down gratefully, holding her hands out into the warm airstream while he busied himself in the kitchen. Once she'd thawed a little he could hear her moving around the room.

He brought the tea in two large mugs, ladled both with sugar without asking for her preference and handed her the steaming beverage.

'So, have you something to tell me?' Maybe her husband's enforced lapse into helpfulness had led to him sending her with yet more information.

Napoleon had taken a fancy to her, at least he was keeping her feet warm by lying on them. 'What happened to him?' she asked looking at the wound on his head.

'Oh, likely as not pushed through a fence or something after someone's rubbish.'

'I don't think so,' she examined the wound more closely. 'I'd say he'd been hit.'

'I suppose someone could have fetched him one if they caught him poking his nose into their things. I can think of one or two as might.' Phyllis Arbuthnot sprang readily to mind.

Her knowledge of animals didn't surprise him. He was sure the Romanies' legendary ability with horses must extend to other livestock.

'The council people came tonight, didn't they?' The unexpected subject caught Amos unawares. 'Council people? Oh! the site visit to Hunter's Farm, d'you mean?'

'Yes, all those houses they're going to build there, they came to look, didn't they?'

'Where's this leading, young lady . . . I don't even know your name?'

'Naomi.'

'Where's this leading, Naomi?' He would dearly have liked a slug of Scotch in his tea but he had better not set such a bad example.

'Are they going to build council houses?'

Amos's conversation with Ma came back to him. *The younger ones sometimes want to settle for a while, problem is they're not allowed into your villages, can't afford it anyway.*

'What do we have to do to get a council house, Mr Cotswold, — Jem and me? Thing is I want to go to college and I don't think they'll take me if they know I live in a gypsy camp.'

'What does your husband think about this . . . and your grandmother?'

'I know Jem's a bit rough but he's clever, you know — particularly with engines and cars and things and he'd do anything for me. Ma hasn't said much, I think she knows how impossible a dream it is and doesn't want to see me hurt.' Amos admired the girl's perspicacity.

'To answer your question — you have to be on a waiting list for affordable housing. Though I have to warn you, those properties are in short supply. Still, you should have a fair chance — same as everyone — and I'll do all I can to make sure that happens.'

'Will you really, Mr Cotswold?'

If he were honest, right now Amos had no idea how to fulfil his promise.

'What do you want to study?'

'I want to be a vet,' she said, smiling down at Napoleon. 'Hang on, I'll be right back.' She ran out of the cottage and came back a minute later carrying various packets and lotions. 'Can I have some warm water to dissolve this so I can bathe him with it?'

Amos fetched the bowl and watched while the girl tended Napoleon's wound. The pig didn't stir.

Amos got up. 'Thank you, young lady but now I think it's time you went home, give me a chance to see what I can do. I'll see you to your car.' He walked down the lane with her, waved her goodbye and walked slowly back indoors, wondering. He suspected Ma knew exactly where Naomi had been tonight. But why had she really come?

* * *

123

'Isn't it about time you put your signs up?' Marion chided him in the bar one evening at the beginning of May. 'If this were a national election they'd have been up weeks ago.'

'Well, that's the difference, Mrs Ashley,' Amos replied, wagging a grubby finger at her. 'This ain't a national election and most folks around here have far better things to do than worry about the district council.'

'Phyllis has had hers up for over a fortnight,' Jack said.

'Yes, all two of them,' laughed Amos. 'And one of those is in her own window.'

'She's just being discreet.'

'Has she always lived here?' Marion asked, curious. She looked over at Sam who'd lived in Weston all his life, as had his family for untold generations before him. Sam knew all about everyone.

'Only about thirty year, I'd say,' he answered. 'Her married a chap who had that big house at the end of the village . . . what's it called?'

'Hathaway Court?' Jack offered.

'Aye, that's the one. Proper stuck up they were.'

'That hasn't changed,' Amos muttered.

'He had it built but I don't know why he chose Weston — unless it were to be near Catherine.' Sam gave no one a chance to

124

enquire who Catherine was. Clearly enjoying himself now, he went on: 'We always reckoned he married Phyllis because of her posh friends, or maybe he thought she had some money. Trouble were though he were no good. Stole people's savings in some crooked scheme of his; then ran off with his secretary.'

'Doesn't sound like the sort of person Phyllis would associate with,' commented Marion, looking shocked.

'No, I daresays it don't,' agreed Sam, 'but tis true. Proper scandal it were for a week or two ... specially seeing as Catherine, his secretary, were Brenda's sister like.'

There were audible gasps around the bar. Jack had his mouth wide open.

'I didn't even know Brenda had a sister,' Marion said.

'Well, she never spoke of Catherine after that so there's no reason why you should. But I had the feeling she never heard from her again,' Alan Tregorran added in corroboration. 'I'd forgotten, but Sam's right.'

'Have you told the police about Brenda's sister and this embezzlement? It could be important.' Amos remembered part of the story now that Sam mentioned it. He'd been away when it happened, so it wasn't something he'd ever known much about

125

— and as Alan had just said, Brenda never spoke of it.

'What for?' Sam said. 'They knew thirty year ago, they've only got to look in they's records.'

'Puzzles me why Phyllis stayed after that,' Marion said. 'All I can think is she hoped he'd come back.'

'Don't know why,' Sam went on. 'House were sold to pay some of his debts and she moved to where she is today. Used her connections in Warwick, they say, to keep her. She must've had some family money salted away.'

'Phyllis has a brother. You see him here occasionally,' Alan said. 'As a matter of fact, he was here the other week.'

'So why does she think she's so above us all?' Marion asked.

'Inverted, isn't it? She looks down on me,' here Amos paused to survey himself and they all followed his gaze, ' . . . as though my appearance were important.'

'You have to admit she's always immaculately turned out,' Marion said.

'That's Amos's point,' Jack said, 'but look what lurks underneath.'

'It doesn't make her a bad person, just because her husband was a crook.'

'No, Marion, it doesn't,' Amos agreed. 'But

126

her keenness on what is only outward appearance is . . . well . . . let's just say I disagree with her approach.' They all looked him up and down and laughed.

'Surely there's a happy medium though!' Jack ducked to avoid the blow Amos aimed at him.

★　★　★

Early for his evening meeting, Amos was sauntering along the road towards County Hall, enjoying the spring light, when a beautiful old Bentley crawled along beside him — he'd always loved that strap over the bonnet they had, like a muzzle, curbing their power.

'Jump in, Amos, I've got something you might like to hear.' Amos needed no second invitation — a ride in that beauty alone was enough to entice him. Hearing the satisfying clunk as he closed the door, he could almost be envious.

'Didn't think kerb-crawling was your thing, Alec.'

'Oh, but I do it in such style don't you think?'

Amos had to laugh.

'How's the standards board enquiry going — I wrote to them, you know.'

'Yes, and I'm very grateful Alec, thank you.

They're due to issue their draft report in election week.'

'Not the best timing.'

'No, even assuming I'm cleared — mud sticks. Then both sides have a chance to correct any errors or make any points they think have been forgotten. So I won't be surprised if our friend gets up to some more of his tricks.'

'How's his planning application going?'

'We've done the site visit, I think that went well but I don't know what the outcome will be. Because of the elections it won't get back on the committee agenda for a few weeks, by which time a number of members may have changed — including me.'

'Not like you to be pessimistic, Amos.'

'Funny thing, you know — Quartermaster didn't appear at the site visit. Too arrogant I suppose, thinks it's a done deal.'

'Actually it's Quartermaster I want to tell you about. I was down in London the other day, had to pop into the Lords then over to the City to see some old chums for lunch. One of them asked if I knew Quartermaster.'

'P'raps they know he has a place up here.'

'Yes, maybe. Anyway it seems our friend Cyril may be getting in over his head.'

'In to what?'

'That I'm not too sure about, not my

subject really, but something to do with a 'spread betting' syndicate?'

'Get rich quick but highly risky you mean? Are you saying he's short of money?'

'He could be soon, I was told.'

'What do you think the effect will be on his plan for Hunter's — do you think he'll shelve it?'

'Well, I wouldn't get too excited. It'll depend on exactly how he's fixed won't it, and whether he can raise some money? It could mean he'll try all the harder to build at Hunter's because he badly needs the profit from it.'

'Or, might he be more inclined to compromise to avoid further delays?' Amos suggested.

'I don't think that word's in his vocabulary. Believe me, if I thought having another word with him would help I'd gladly pitch in — but he ignored my advice earlier in the year.' That was the first Amos had heard of Alec's intervention. 'He thinks he's got divine right. Anyway, I thought you might like to know what I'd picked up.'

'Thanks Alec, most interesting. If you hear any more . . . '

Alec smiled and nodded. He came to an accomplished halt outside County Hall and saluted. 'Your stop, sir.'

★ ★ ★

Amos had installed himself on the low wall outside the village hall with Napoleon at his feet. It was early in the morning on polling day and he could do little more now except be there smiling encouragement — show his commitment to serving the community. Amos enjoyed elections, especially if the weather was fine. He could indulge in his favourite occupation — talking to people. In the course of the day he would converse with most of the village.

The first person to arrive was Vernon Squires, who drove towards the hall, slowed to park but, and this could have been Amos's imagination, on sight of Amos accelerated away again. Amos hoped his presence would similarly deter other opposition voters.

Since he and Jack had discovered Keith Squires's shed-load of, yet to be proven, stolen cars — the Squires family had been noticeably missing. They'd failed to appear in the Hathaway Arms, neither he nor Jack had seen Bruce in the garage — not that he'd ever been there much — nor had Amos caught sight of Irene. He wanted to ask her what she'd seen on the day of Brenda's murder; it might just tell him more about his *doppelgänger*. In more normal circumstances he'd have sought her out at home but he didn't want to run into Vernon.

Strangely, Vernon appeared to reciprocate this aversion. His usual reaction would have been to come looking for Amos to blame him for Keith's arrest — but he hadn't.

Lindsay came running across the lane holding Amos's mobile phone aloft like a hand grenade with the pin pulled.

'You forgot this and it was going off. Oh — it's stopped now.'

'Thanks, Lindsay,' Amos said, glancing at the dial to identify the caller — John Wilkinson. He'd got this far, to this very day, without the standards board report being issued — which was good; many would have forgotten about it by now. Releasing the draft today would be like loosing the stopper from that metaphorical bomb — even if it did clear him. Quartermaster would soon broadcast its contents just to stir things up, remind voters of the accusation. He dialled John. 'You rang.'

'Wanted to wish you luck . . . '

'And . . . ?'

'You must have a guardian angel is all I can say. I had a call from that nice lady at the standards board . . . ' John paused.

'Go on, go on.' Amos had to know the verdict even if it was election day.

'The draft clears you completely.'

11

The following morning Amos hammered on the back door of the pub. 'Biggest turnout ever and biggest turnout of the whole district by miles!'

The door was opened by a dressing-gowned Jack. Cautiously he whispered: 'That's good . . . isn't it?'

'Seventy-eight per cent! I got seventy-eight per cent, Jack!' Amos yelled at full volume. Jack took hold of him and yanked him indoors but Amos could hardly contain himself.

'Amos, Amos,' Jack gesticulated with his hands. 'Calm down, man. It's six o'clock in the morning, you'll wake Marion. Come on through and stop making such a row.'

He led Amos into the bar where a magnum of champagne stood waiting on the counter in its bucket of ice . . . and where Marion, Ted and Lindsay, Sam and his son, Alan Tregorran and his wife and many others were already gathered.

For once Amos was tongue-tied. A loud cheer went up as they pressed forward to pat him on the back and ask about the results.

'Look out Cyril Quartermaster is all I can say,' Jack shouted.

'Let's drink to that,' Ted replied and they all raised their glasses.

Stepping out of the pub two hours later, Amos found Stephen Linklater propped against one of Jack's sturdy table-and-bench affairs in the front garden. He looked like a harbinger of doom.

'Have you come to congratulate me, Chief Inspector?' Amos beamed, bubbling with *bonhomie* and Jack's champagne.

Linklater uncrossed his arms and levered himself upright. He fell into step with Amos as they turned out of Jack's and into the lane. 'I think I mentioned that we found pig tissue on Mrs Smith's clothing?' He turned to Amos for confirmation. Amos nodded, puzzled, trying to sober up. 'Well, and we should've thought of this before, I know — there might be traces of the murderer on your pig.'

'What? Even now?'

Linklater shrugged. 'Worth a try — as long as you haven't washed him.'

'Have you ever tried washing a pig, Chief Inspector?' A hint of a grin crossed Linklater's face. 'There'll be traces of lots of people on Napoleon, folks are always petting him.'

'We know, but it's really for corroboration.

For instance, if the suspect is an outsider, who denies being in Weston Hathaway, he'll have trouble explaining how he came to be anywhere near your pig.'

Amos stood still, Linklater too. 'He had a gouge out of the back of his head. I didn't think much of it at the time, it's not that unusual; though it was a nasty one. Young Susan, Lindsay's girl, pointed it out the day after Brenda's murder. The wound has been bathed.'

'You didn't notice it the evening before?'

'Did you? I was more concerned with what had happened.' Bad choice of words again Amos realized, but surely it was natural to be upset when a friend has been murdered. Stephen Linklater might seem amiable enough at eight o'clock in the morning after several glasses but Amos was under no illusion — he was still very much a suspect. The mild approach was designed to relax him into making mistakes. 'Anyway, why are you interested in the wound? You're not thinking the murderer did it, are you?'

'Quite feasibly. Why not? Maybe Napoleon was in his way.'

'Or tried to defend Brenda?'

'Would he do that?'

'Possibly ... yes, quite possibly.' It happened to be true but it might also help establish Amos's innocence. It was unlikely that Napoleon would attack Amos, and even less likely that Amos would strike him — or need to. 'Was there any blood around?'

'No.'

'Mind you it was more of a big bruise just lifting at the edges. That's why Na . . . ' Amos stopped himself, for some reason preferring not to mention Naomi. 'That's why a friend of mine thought someone had hit him. Even then it didn't occur to me. I'm sorry, Chief Inspector, I should have thought.'

'So should we, Councillor. Can I send someone to go over him? Would you mind?'

'I don't mind but I can't speak for Napoleon. That'll depend on what they want to do to him and how many chocolates they bring.'

★　★　★

'Here, have you read this?' Jack asked, cradling his head in one hand while clutching a tomato juice with the other. He had the local paper spread out on the back bar. '*Farmers are warned to be watchful after a South Warwickshire farm was targeted by distraction burglars who let the cattle out on to nearby roads. While one of the men helped the farmer round up some of his animals, the other burgled his home.*' Jack straightened up. 'I've never heard of it happening to farmers before,' he said.

'Nor I; most of us haven't anything worth stealing.' Amos stopped. 'But why go to all that trouble?'

'To make it less likely they'd be caught of course. The longer it is since the event the less people remember who they saw . . . and when. It would take some time to catch the animals which escaped and then check all the others — just in case. You know that better than me. By which time the thieves would have been long gone and any witnesses along with them.' Jack stopped. 'Amos?' Jack was shaking him by the arm. 'Amos?'

'Mmm,' Amos was thinking hard. Bells were ringing in his mind but he couldn't quite tune into them. 'It's this distraction idea — you've hit on something.' Amos looked around to see who else was in the bar to overhear. It was still early, Sam and his son were the only ones by the fire. Lowering his voice, he said: 'Do you remember me telling you about the lamb in the river?'

'You don't think . . . ?'

'Yes, I do. The more I think about it, the more blindingly obvious it becomes. That's why I could never find out whose sheep it was — I thought that was odd at the time.' Amos reduced his words to a whisper, 'You saw me, you reckoned. Only someone else made quite sure I would not be in the village while they stole my identity. They even chose lunchtime so I couldn't send you instead; even knew I'd have to come back and change — slightly later but nevertheless showing my face in the village around that time. And I daresay I was watched going out to the river, so they knew exactly when to strike.'

'Hang on, though, isn't this just a teeny bit far-fetched! All sorts of things could've gone wrong with that plan.' Amos raised a 'such as' eyebrow. 'For starters you might not have picked up the message.'

'So they send me another one.'

'There might've been someone at Brenda's when they arrived.'

'Possible. So they'd either have to wait or else abort for that day. Who knows how many tries they had?'

'You don't think it was burglary or an accident then?'

'Do you?' Amos felt even now that Jack still suspected him, albeit for a worthy motive.

'And what about the lamb? It could've already drowned or been towed away by the current by the time you arrived. Or someone else might've already fished it out?'

'With all those, I still had to go right down

137

to the riverbank to find out, didn't I?'

'Yes, but you wouldn't have got wet so you might not have appeared back in the village.'

'I don't think that mattered too much; I think it was a happy accident, so to speak, for the murderer — makes me look guilty even to myself, when I know I'm not.'

'But someone might've seen you by the river — given you an alibi?'

'Yes, possible — but unlikely at that time on a weekday. It wasn't in the school holidays, or the fishing season. It's not a popular time for walking dogs and too early in the year for most pleasure craft. It was worth a punt. And that's why it was the sheep, not the cows. Everyone would've seen me rounding up cattle. I was much less likely to be spotted rescuing a sheep out of the river — but I'd be bound to respond just as quickly.'

Jack ran both hands through his hair, sucking in air through his teeth as he did so. Amos went on: 'Don't you see? That's why I couldn't find out where the lamb had fallen in, there was no obviously broken bank. She'd been thrown in. And that's why there were fresh tyre tracks going right across that field.'

'You're serious about this, aren't you? Did you recognize the voice?'

'It was on the answering machine — sounded as though he was in a wind tunnel, which wouldn't be surprising if he was down by the river. I thought nothing of it.'

'But you must've noticed something. The voice was male, you say?'

'I think so — it was very muffled.'

'What did he say?'

'How on earth do I know now? Something about one of my sheep being in the river and which field. You see, that's what I mean — it was the field that's farthest from here. Ah yes, I remember, it was cut off. I assumed it was the end of the tape.'

'I was just going to say, you've probably still got it?'

'No. I'm sure I rewound the tape.'

'It might still be worth rescuing, especially if you turned it over instead. Or if you haven't reached the end again maybe you won't have overwritten it yet.'

'Oh I'm afraid I must have, there've been no messages for a while — with the election and everything I haven't had time to change it.' Jack sighed with exasperation. 'All right, all right. I'll do it tonight. Do you have a spare I can borrow?' Pre-empting that request, Jack was already rummaging in a drawer beneath the bar. He produced a small Perspex oblong and held it aloft triumphantly.

Amos downed the remains of his drink, pocketed the spare tape and went home — accompanied by an inexplicable sense of foreboding, like he felt when he'd drunk too much gin. He put it down to over-excitement and not enough sleep.

The answering machine winked at him knowingly. It knew the tape had gone. Amos tried to remember who had been in his house lately? No surely not . . . what could Naomi want with the tape? She was the last person he'd suspect of involvement with Brenda's murder.

He rang Jack. 'It's gone.'

'Well I'll be . . . Are you sure you hadn't already taken it out yourself?'

'No, I'm not sure, but I don't recollect doing it. So that's that, anyway.'

'You haven't got it kicking around in a drawer somewhere? Where would you have put it?' Amos heard Jack shout over his shoulder: 'With you in a tick, Sam.' Then, 'Where would you have put it if you had taken it out to replace it?'

'In the bin.'

'Really?'

'Really. Why not? I've never needed to keep evidence of my telephone messages before.'

* * *

140

A few days after the election John Wilkinson insisted on coming over.

'Can't we do it over the phone — whatever it is?'

'No. I'll be there at three, if that's OK?' And three it was when he arrived at Amos's cottage. Amos ushered him in and offered the seat by the fireplace but John chose the wooden chair next to the table, and perched uncomfortably on the edge of it, balancing his briefcase upright on his knees. Amos remained standing. 'There's no easy way to say this, Amos. Brenda Smith has left you a fair amount of money. She called me after that letter in the *Gazette*, said she wanted to change her will and didn't want her previous solicitor to know. So after I'd had a word with her doctor, to make sure she knew what she was doing, I wrote a new will for her — as it turned out, only days before she died. In which she left express instructions that I should break the news to you personally. You'll see why in a minute.'

Amos was stunned — and horrified. 'Oh no! Oh no,' was all he could say. 'Why on earth has she done that?' He clutched the mantelpiece to steady himself before collapsing into his armchair.

'It seems, because Nellie did. Brenda too wanted to express her gratitude for all the

141

help you had given her.'

Amos could feel the colour drain from his face. 'Now they really will believe I killed her,' he moaned, hiding his face behind grimy hands.

'Nonsense. It's not a fortune, not worth killing someone over.' He looked again at Amos. 'Here, I'll fetch you a glass of water.' John put the briefcase down and went into the kitchen. Amos could hear him looking for the glass, heard the tap running. His own legs wouldn't move.

After he'd sipped the water he said levelly: 'I don't want it John, what can I do?'

John resumed his seat. 'After what happened over Nellie's legacy, Brenda realized you might feel that way. So she provided an alternative in the wording of her will.'

'Why didn't you flaming well say so?'

'Because I had to have your reaction before I was allowed to. Presumably because otherwise you might've felt duty bound to take the latter course even if you'd not wanted to. Are you sure you don't want the money? Why don't you think about it? No one thinks ill of you over Nellie's legacy — you can see that yourself from the election results. Quite the reverse in fact.'

How would John understand. If Jack could believe Amos had killed Brenda — albeit at her own request — then so would others; especially when they learned she'd paid him for his trouble.

Amos leapt to unsteady feet. 'Here, I'll write it down for you.' Grabbing the latest council minutes he scribbled on the back: 'I hereby relinquish any right I may have to anything Brenda Smith has given me,' and signed it.

'I'll keep it for a few days,' John said, putting the paper in his pocket. 'The sum is fifty per cent of her house, by the way.'

Amos remained impassive. Then recalling his conversation with Linklater he asked in a detached voice: 'What happens to the rest?'

'Her house is to become a part-owned, thus affordable, house for someone on a low income. And if you don't accept fifty per cent of the money, then that goes to fund a second such house here in Weston. Her personal belongings and investments, after a few legacies to local people, will be shared amongst her husband's nephews and nieces.'

'No mention of her sister?'

'No . . . why? Is there a sister?'

'Just wondered. Does anyone else have to know about the first option?' Amos asked.

'The will becomes a matter of public record, I'm afraid. But if someone makes an issue of it we can go public on your decision

143

which will instantly defuse any slur. Otherwise it need never be mentioned.'

'And the police?'

'They know already.'

And there he'd been, burbling on to
Linklater about the beneficiary being the
likely culprit. Had Linklater thought that a
bluff, that Amos had been feigning ignorance?
No wonder the police suspected him.

12

Now more than ever Amos had to find Brenda's killer. What with the Land Rover theft, the election, the standards board fiasco and still the lambing — he'd lacked the time to brood over her death. Lately he'd allowed events to run him, he admitted that. He must take hold of things, find out what was really going on.

Why would someone want to lure him out of the village that day? Was it just in case he called in on Brenda at the wrong moment? But that could have applied to lots of people — Lindsay, Susan, Marion, the reverend, and others. Had they too been lured away by some invisible pied piper? No. So there must have been another motive for calling Amos to Long Cast. Could it seriously have been done to deliberately deprive him of an alibi?

Put that together with Jack's having seen someone very like Amos, albeit through bottle glass and without his glasses, and the conclusion was obvious. The killer wanted people to think it was Amos. No, he was being paranoid. Why should this thing centre round him at all . . . just because Napoleon had been there and Jack thought he'd seen someone like Amos at Brenda's? There were plenty of other dishevelled sixty-year-olds about.

But Jack wasn't the only one who said they'd seen him, was he? Mrs Squires had said so too. So it seemed likely that someone similar to himself had been at Brenda's house at the time she'd died. Hang on — he was always around this village, in and out of people's homes. He smiled, maybe that's how Napoleon had learned his bad habits. So Irene Squires could have been mistaken — might have seen him another day, or going into another house — and transposed the memory in her mind, or been so accustomed to seeing him around that she imagined the whole thing. Any random snapshot of Weston Hathaway, either mental or photographic, was likely to have him in it. He was one of the fixtures.

What was it the Reverend Whittaker had said — something about how she'd been in the butcher's? Amos took off his cap and scratched his head with the same hand. Why had he noticed that last bit? Had Amos imagined that part because, logically, it was the only place she could have been in order to see someone going into Brenda's? Unless she'd been going past the house, in which case where to? Or maybe it was the reverend who'd assumed that was where Irene must have been.

Reverend Whittaker would be walking his Jack Russell down by the river about now. Amos could do with a breath of fresh air himself — it might clear his befuddled brain. He took his stick and set out.

Yes, there he was, admiring the cowslips. Amos hobbled across the meadow to him. 'Bit late this year but aren't they wonderful, Reverend?'

'I was just thinking that — you know I'd never seen red ones until I came here.'

'Not many people have — they were quite rare at one time, killed off by pesticides and other pollutants. Did you know there are over a hundred different varieties of wild flowers in this meadow? That's why it has a preservation order on it.'

'Well well. No, I didn't know that, Amos. And here was me thinking it was just red cowslips. I must learn to be much more observant, I can see.'

They stood together in the May sunshine — two middle-aged men, one in his dog collar, one with no collar at all — admiring the wild flowers while the terrier chased butterflies.

'Where were you before?' Amos asked,

half-remembering what Ma had mentioned.

'Cornwall, on the north coast.'

'Good sheep country,' commented Amos, tempted to say he'd been there recently. 'Why did you leave Cornwall, then, Reverend — nice place like that?' Amos was curious.

'Oh,' sighed the reverend. 'Mother had been ill for a long time and the bishop had been very kind, so when she died I needed a bigger benefice, more to do . . . and so I came here.'

Sometimes accused of being insensitive, nevertheless Amos declined to pry any further into what appeared to be a painful subject for the reverend. Instead he said: 'Actually I wanted to ask you about Irene Squires. She told you she'd seen me going into Brenda Smith's that day.' Amos was treading carefully, to avoid putting words into the reverend's mouth. 'Did she say anything else?'

Reverend Whittaker considered the question. 'Not that I recall. She just said she'd been in the butcher's and had seen you . . . either going in or coming out. I really can't remember.' He turned to face Amos. 'But you said you hadn't been there that day?'

'Exactly. That's why I'm asking what Irene Squires thinks she saw. Since I'm the only one who categorically knows it wasn't me, it seems I'm the only one interested in finding out who this man was.'

'I see what you mean.' Gently the reverend went on, 'Forgive me for asking such an obvious question, but why don't you ask Mrs Squires?'

'Ah, that's a long story I'm afraid, Reverend.' They started back up the hill. 'Did you notice if Napoleon had been injured that day when you found him at Brenda's?'

'Er . . . I . . . n-no, Amos, I'm sorry, I don't recall. I don't think he was limping or anything.'

'No, he's got a gouge out of the back of his head — trouble is we're not exactly sure when it happened.'

'I'm sorry, no. I was too shocked at finding Brenda to take much notice of Napoleon, I'm afraid.'

'But he was in Brenda's kitchen? That's what you told me the day after.'

'Um . . . er . . . y-yes, y-yes I think so.' He answered so vaguely that Amos found himself wondering why this was such a difficult question for the reverend. If you had just discovered a dead body would you then miss a large black pig in the same small room? Amos honestly didn't know.

'Thing is . . . ' Amos went on, 'the police

think he may carry a forensic clue to the killer, especially if the killer struck him — could even have the killer's DNA on him. They came to take traces from him, which he didn't enjoy much.' Amos chuckled, then, noticing the look of astonishment on the reverend's face, he added: 'Don't worry. They know lots of people pet Napoleon but if, say, they arrest a stranger then it could prove useful. Anyway, who knows?'

They continued their slow climb up the hill away from the river. 'All I remember is him coming down the road with you. I didn't notice his wound when he came through that barrier the police had erected, but I couldn't swear it wasn't . . . ' Amos clapped a hand loudly to his brow.

'I knew something didn't fit. I knew in the back of my mind. At the barrier — I've just remembered. Irene Squires was yelling that she 'must get to the butcher's' because she was having a dinner party that night — needed the meat for dinner! Yet she told you and the police she'd already been to the butcher's that day.'

'Is it important?' asked the reverend, as they reached the lane. 'Forgive me, Amos, but shouldn't we rather be asking ourselves who on earth might want to harm Brenda?' He showed no understanding of just how important it could be to Amos, which persuaded Amos not to make too much of it, at least not for now, not to the reverend. Equally Amos would have liked to confide in Reverend Whittaker about the possibility that someone might have killed Brenda at her own request. But he daren't do that either, in case the rumours Ma had heard were true and he had indeed helped his own mother. So instead Amos asked:

'Did she ever mention her sister to you?'

The reverend thought for a moment. His answer was guarded. 'Yes, she mentioned her.'

'You know the story, then?'

'Not really, no. I only know she hadn't seen her for a great many years — she regretted that. Why, you don't think Catherine had anything to do with this do you?' The reverend's eyes widened.

'No no. Just trying to answer your question.' Amos was aware that his political mind would seek connections with Phyllis Arbuthnot and Cyril Quartermaster where none existed. Would Phyllis have actually killed Brenda to get back at Brenda's sister after all this time . . . or asked Quartermaster to do it in return for agreeing to stand for the council? Now he really was being fanciful, yet he struggled to prevent his imagination from plunging down these byways.

'We will have to trust in the Lord, Amos. He'll sort it out. Now, I must hurry or I'll be late.' So saying Reverend Whittaker clipped the lead to his dog's collar and hurried on up the lane, leaving Amos leaning on the gate gazing out over the river.

Amos stayed where he was for some time with the May blossom sweet in his nostrils and the insects darting back and forth in the late-afternoon warmth. This was all Quartermaster's doing. Amos felt as though he was being watched all the time. People noticed where he went . . . yes, and even made it up when it suited them. He had absolutely no idea why Irene Squires had said what she'd said. He could have understood it better if he'd caught her sons stealing cars before the murder, but that escapade had been weeks after Brenda's death.

He was sure all routes led to Quartermaster. Squires wanted to do the building so maybe that was it. Irene Squires, in league with Quartermaster, was using her consummate acting skills to help discredit Amos.

So he could safely dismiss her evidence then. Except . . . Jack hadn't dreamt what he'd seen.

* * *

Unless it were the work of some random maniac, in which case the villagers were in even greater danger, there was a specific reason for Brenda's death. Could Quartermaster really have gone to such lengths? One minute Amos believed it possible but the next dismissed it as blinkered, berating himself for seeing the puzzle solely from his own viewpoint. Yet he felt certain the solution lay in local knowledge — the police couldn't solve this without help. Amos needed the chief inspector on his side. Which meant he must conclusively prove his own innocence, remove that nagging doubt so evident in Linklater's behaviour.

'How much do you know about sheep, Chief Inspector?' he asked without introducing himself — a pause occurred at the other end of the phone line while Linklater identified the voice.

'Not as much as you, Councillor.'

'I want to show you something.'

'I've seen the one in the Tate . . . if that's what you intend for my education.'

'Ah, but this one's alive.'

'Is this relevant, Councillor?'

'I think so. Come to the cottage — we'll go from here. Half an hour?'

Stephen Linklater arrived with his brows raised in question marks, and had to endure the Land Rover's filthy conditions as they drove out to Long Cast Meadow.

'How long did it take us?' Amos asked as they breasted the rise where the lane began.

'I didn't realize it was still Weston Hathaway right out here?'

'Strictly speaking it isn't but it's no closer to anywhere else. How long did it take us?'

'About ten minutes — mind, you were keeping to the speed limit with me on board. What's all this about, Councillor?'

'I want you to understand what I was doing when Brenda Smith was murdered and why it took me so long to come out here and fish a sheep out of the river. And I want to show you something else.'

Amos clambered out and opened the gate, just as he had that other day. They drove along the lane and turned into Long Cast through yet another gate.

As they started across the field Amos gesticulated at the sheep now running towards them, attracted by the sound of Amos's truck. 'All these in this field are mine.'

Once they had driven beyond the entrance-way and the churned-up earth of the feeding station, Amos remarked: 'No sign of other tracks today — there was that day.' Linklater said nothing. 'This field leads to the river, so usually you get other tracks only when there's a fishing competition.'

The sheep followed the Land Rover down the hill. Amos alighted, studying them carefully; Linklater joined him.

'What are we looking for?'

'There she is, see her.' Amos pointed, then, wading through the milling sheep, managed to grab the one he wanted. 'Look, no tags.'

'Probably lost them, I expect it's easily done. Look, what are we doing here? I enjoy a stroll in the country as much as the next man but I have work to do.'

'This is the sheep I rescued that day but when I counted them she was extra, didn't have my mark on her. As you can see there aren't any in the neighbouring fields — no other flocks she could have strayed from.'

'P'raps she swam, got carried along by the river?'

Impeccably dressed for this environment, Amos hobbled nimbly to the bank. The chief inspector was forced to take much greater care of where he put his feet.

'If you were a youngster wearing a fur jumpsuit, how far d'you think you could swim in here?'

'The current's swift, I'll grant you — but doesn't that make my suggestion more plausible?'

155

'She'd drown pretty quickly is what'd happen. And the current wouldn't carry her into the bank here where I found her, either. This isn't tidal, you know.'

'Mmm, I see. Well, this must've happened lots of times before. I'm sure it's not an earth-shattering mystery.'

'Look at the bank,' Amos persisted. It was still intact. 'What do you think the bank looks like after a sheep falls down it? That sheep was thrown in. Thrown in purposely — in a field farthest away from the village, one where I keep sheep.'

'So? Why not throw one of yours in?'

'Good question. Probably thought it'd be easier to bring one than try and catch one. Makes me think it wasn't a farmer.'

'But why?'

'To lure me out of the village, of course. I got a message on the answering machine telling me my sheep was in the river.' Amos saw Linklater's expression change from one of mild irritation to one of interest in a possible lead. 'Before you ask, no, I haven't got the tape any more — or if I have I've overwritten it.'

'Convenient.'

'Not very, no.'

'So you're still telling me you were down here at the time of the murder?'

'Yes, I'm showing you how long it took and why . . . and that it wasn't an accident.'

'Can anyone back that up?'

'Look around you.'

'So let's just revisit this for a minute.' Linklater unwisely leaned against the Land Rover. 'You say you were lured down here. At about what time?'

'I'd dropped Jack back around eleven forty-five to give him time to change before the lunch crowd started to arrive at twelve. Then I listened to my messages, one of which was this one, then I came straight back out. So I guess I left the cottage about twelve, got here about twelve ten or so.' The times he'd gone through this in his head lately.

'And how long were you here?'

'Well, just opening and shutting two sets of gates twice takes a while as you saw. Finding the animal took a few minutes — I went over to the island there before I spotted her — then I had to get her out. Oh yes, then I walked along in the river trying to find the place where she'd fallen in because I knew it'd be easier for me to get out that way, but I had to give that up and wade through the reed-bed. Then I went across and counted them all — twice, to make sure I hadn't imagined she was surplus. All in all, by the time I got back it must've been about one fifteen, I'd say.' Amos felt he'd forgotten something but didn't have time to explore the thought before Linklater accused him of a discrepancy:

'You told me one o'clockish before.'

'Well it's not far out is it — one or one-fifteen?' Amos was pleased it all fitted so neatly; Brenda must've been killed deliberately between twelve and one, while he'd been away.

'Brenda Smith was murdered at one o'clock.' The words hung there. 'And you've just taken me through a step-by-step account which easily places you in the vicinity at that time.'

13

'How do you know? Bit precise, that, isn't it? I'm surprised they can pinpoint it that accurately?' Amos was thinking fast. He'd sought to exonerate himself by demonstrating the validity of his alibi; had hoped to extract some new information out of Linklater through sharing his theory of having been lured away. Instead he'd incriminated himself even further.

'Mrs Smith's clock must have been knocked off the cooker by her or her assailant — it stopped at three minutes past one. And that's extremely confidential information — please keep it to yourself.'

Amos kicked at the front tyre of the Land Rover. 'So why lure me away so long before they killed her?' His theory suddenly looked silly. And why was Linklater trusting him with vital information — was it a lie to trip him up? Amos couldn't understand this at all now; he'd been so sure he'd been purposely distracted.

Linklater studied him closely as if weighing up whether or not to divulge something else. Amos was clearly a suspect but they'd not even cautioned him, so what was stopping them — surely not his position? Councillors don't have diplomatic immunity.

'Pr'aps you weren't lured here,' Linklater said quietly.

'But I've just shown you — '

'Coincidence? You must get a lot of calls to say your sheep are in the river.'

Amos felt deflated. Two steps back and none forward — except he now knew at what time Brenda had died . . . maybe.

'We've a witness who saw you in the village at one.'

'Mrs Nosy Squires, I know — thinks she saw me going into Brenda's. Well I can tell you something about that.'

'No, not her.' Linklater interrupted.

'They're all in it together. Can't you see they're all trying to get me off the council — so they can build their houses and make money.'

'Calm down, Amos. Why do you think we haven't arrested you?' He paused for effect. 'It was Mrs Pearson — she says you took her some wood.'

'Oh, my God, how did I forget that?' Amos felt warm with relief. 'I did, I often do. I get it on my way back from here — along that lane. Why on earth didn't you tell me before?'

'You didn't ask. I wasn't exactly hounding

you, was I? I assumed you'd probably remembered about her.' Linklater wasn't entirely convincing. 'Anyway, she said she knew it was one o'clock because she'd just started eating her dinner. She was adamant she always sits down at one on the dot, and that you were one of the very few people she'd have opened the door to then.'

'Lots of country folk do,' muttered Amos absent-mindedly. 'You can tell the time by them — comes of looking after animals — you have to have a routine, see. Same as children, makes them feel safe.' Amos rambled on while his mind was elsewhere.

'I knew there was something else, when I was telling you about the sheep. I'd forgotten about Mrs Pearson, but I also rang Fergus McAllister at DEFRA about the tags. He might know what time it was.'

'Even better. So you see, you were in the village at one, which is good because you have at least one witness who saw you . . . spoke to you even. Which proves you weren't at Brenda Smith's then.'

'But what about Irene Squires — when did she see me?'

'Since you know most of it I guess there's no harm in telling you — she originally said it was about half past twelve.'

'Did you ask Harry about that?'

'Of course,' Linklater said, visibly controlling his irritation. 'From what I recall, without consulting the notes, he said it must have been about then because he shuts at one.'

'So you don't believe her either?'

'She may be a bit muddled.'

'That was the other thing I meant to tell you. Later that day she was demanding to be allowed through the barrier, desperate to go to the butcher's because she was having people to dinner. You ask your constable. Sounds odd, don't you think — if she'd already been there earlier?'

'You'd be surprised what people think they've seen sometimes. What I'm looking for is a reason — who would want to harm Brenda Smith?'

'Still no further forward?'

'Not really,' Linklater admitted, belatedly removing his jacket and suspending it from his finger in an effort to keep it clean, as he draped his other arm along the wooden railing on the side of the trailer. 'We've ruled out robbery — at least the obvious kind. But of course the motive could still be money.'

'The will you mean. News has travelled remarkably fast, I hear. Anyway, I've renounced it — if that's the right word. What would I do with money, take to drink?'

Linklater smiled. 'You could have a more comfortable life.' He surveyed the acres of lush green pasture, the hedgerows teeming with wildlife, the sheep grazing peacefully, the dancing river. 'No, I s'pose not.' Amos thought the remark genuine, that Linklater might understand why he didn't need Brenda's money.

'Have you talked to her sister? She may have been expecting something, I imagine?'

'What sister?' Linklater stood up straight, clearly surprised.

'Ran off with Phyllis Arbuthnot's husband — ooh, thirty years back.'

'Not *the* Mrs Arbuthnot?'

Amos hoped he was proving his worth. 'Seems no one's seen or heard from Catherine since — not even Brenda.'

'So this sister will be the next of kin. How old would you say she is?'

Amos scratched his head. 'Well if she ran off thirty years ago, she'd have been about twenty-six then I'd say — so she's about fifty-six now. Ask old Sam, gets in the pub every day, he'd maybe have a better idea. It wasn't a woman though, surely?'

'Probably not — but a woman could be behind it. Did Brenda Smith have any enemies?'

'Not to my knowledge. She hated what the

likes of Cyril Quartermaster do to the village
— don't we all? She and her husband were
well liked. No, I can't think she'd have
enemies in the way you mean.'

'What about friends then?'

'Lots. She had lots of friends, me included
— but we wouldn't hurt her.' Linklater's face
clouded. 'By the look of you you've been
listening to tittle-tattle.'

'Well, it was well-known she was in the
early stages of Alzheimer's.'

'Rubbish. Is that what her doctor says?'

'No, but people round here — '

'Let me tell you about villages, Chief
Inspector. One tiny thought becomes an
immutable fact quicker than I can say Weston
Hathaway. If I were being generous I'd say
it's because they're all deaf, so what they
can't hear they invent. In my opinion Brenda
no more had Alzheimer's than I have — and
I'll have none of your jokes about that either.'
He caught the quick smirk crossing Linklater's face and added: 'I'm well aware you think
me pretty forgetful lately.'

'So what was wrong with her, then?'

'Nothing — except old age and loneliness.
She missed her old man dreadfully and she
couldn't do all the things she used to do any
more.'

'Somebody said she rambled and was apt

to say all sorts of things that didn't make sense.'

'Not to me she didn't. Who told you that?'

'You don't think she needed to go into care?'

'I didn't say that. She deserved to be looked after if that's what she wanted. I'm just telling you she was all there — she wasn't senile. Why?'

'Just wondering if it was a motive for doing away with her. These care places are very expensive these days. Someone who stood to gain from her will wouldn't want to see their legacy disappearing in care fees.'

'You mean me,' Amos said sadly.

'No, I mean somebody who thought they would inherit. A sister for instance, or one of her husband's nieces or nephews.'

'Are you serious?'

'It happens. Got any better ideas?'

Linklater's phone rang and he walked a few yards away to take the call. After finishing his conversation he dusted himself down ineffectually before getting back in the Land Rover. Amos turned the key in the ignition.

'John Wilkinson's your solicitor too, isn't he? Did you know before her death that Brenda had left you some money?'

'Certainly not. John is a man of great integrity and Brenda never mentioned it to me.' Amos was rattled. Just when he and Stephen Linklater were beginning to understand one another, one phone call had wrecked things. 'Your boss, was it — on the phone? Wanting to know what progress you were making?'

'The chief superintendent thinks you're mixed up in this.'

Amos whipped the key round and the Land Rover juddered as the engine shut off. 'What! He's being leant on from above.' Amos swivelled in his seat to look at Linklater. 'Your suspecting me is a criminal waste of time while the real killer is at large.' He sat back in his seat. 'I didn't want to tell you this because you'll think me paranoid but now I'll have to. Cyril Quartermaster badly needs to build those houses up at Hunter's Farm. I'm sure you've heard all about it.' Linklater nodded. 'He's well-connected with the local politicos through his generous donations, so he thinks it's only me blocking his planning application; get rid of me and it'll go through on the nod. You'll remember how he tried to discredit me over his aunt's gift.'

'That might be a reason for killing you . . . but why Brenda?'

'To make it look as though it was me.' There, he'd voiced it.

Linklater digested this slowly. 'But he's not

166

been around lately — we've been ringing his home. He's one of the few we've yet to interview. Actually we weren't too bothered because he's so rarely here.'

Amos shrugged. 'You're the detective — I'm just telling you who's behind this vindictive behaviour. What did your boss say exactly?'

'That you are an obnoxious man with no respect for your betters and who can't be trusted.'

* * *

After he'd dropped Linklater at his car Amos set off along the road again, drawing up at Harry's as he was closing for the day. He needed to know what Harry made of Irene Squires's story.

'You wouldn't credit it but trade's been noticeably down since Brenda's death — it's as though folks don't want to walk past her house,' Harry grumbled, as he stowed away the awning in front of his shop.

'That's true of the whole village, every-where's very quiet. We've got to find out who did it, Harry, we stand more chance of figuring it out than the police.' Harry gave him a strange look. 'I wanted to ask you about that day again. About what Irene

167

Squires said she saw — and when.'

Harry blushed deep red. Concentrating on his shoes he said: 'I think we should leave it to the police, Amos, gives me the jitters it does, the whole business.' He shivered to illustrate his feelings. 'The sooner they take that tape away from the house the better, too, I can't see why they have to keep it sealed off after all this time. Then maybe your Napoleon'll stop sitting there waiting for her an' all.' Harry stopped for breath.

Amos hadn't expected this. 'I only wanted to ask you whether you remembered Irene coming here that morning? After they'd imposed the roadblock, she demanded to come up — to get the meat for a dinner party. Which doesn't make sense if she'd already been.'

'I'm surprised you don't leave it well alone, Amos, and that's the truth. Now I must get on, I've got to clean down yet.'

Amos put his hand on Harry's shoulder. 'Hold on, Harry. What's the matter, this isn't like you?'

Harry shook him off. 'You know full well.'

'No I don't. Tell me,' Amos demanded, completely lost.

Harry glanced around, the lane was deserted. 'I saw you,' he whispered. 'I know why you did it but I don't want to think about it. You're a good man, Amos, which is why I've not said anything to anyone . . . but I saw you. So don't come here playing games with me. Just leave it!' Harry turned abruptly and went back inside. Amos followed him, pulling the door behind him and setting the sign to 'Closed'. Harry started washing down the shelves vehemently.

'Harry, will you stop and look at me for a minute — please.' Amos leaned over the counter staring directly at Harry.

'You're the second real friend who has said a similar thing to me and I want to repeat what I said to him. I categorically was not at Brenda's that day. I absolutely did not kill her.' He waited for Harry to assimilate this before going on. 'Obviously someone who resembled me did go into Brenda's and may be the murderer. None of us is safe until we find out who that was. I'm not lying, Harry, believe me. I need your help to find this man, otherwise . . . well, I hate to think.'

Harry came from behind the counter and sat down on one of the two chairs he kept for the aged and infirm. Amos collapsed into the other.

'Can you tell me exactly what you saw?'

'Well, as I said to you when you first asked — and it was the truth — when the sun streams in I can't see too much out of the window there.' Harry indicated the display window, now cleared for the night, which faced Brenda's side door. 'But I must have been leaning in getting a joint for somebody when I noticed your head and shoulders above the hedge there. Whoever it was must have been about your height because that's exactly what I see when you go — used to go — there.'

'What time was it, do you remember? Close on your lunchtime, I bet.'

'I couldn't tell you, Amos, I really don't remember. But I know it was that morning because it was the first thing I remembered when the police cars piled up the lane and we found out what had happened.'

'Did you see his face?'

'No, but I never see yours when you're going there, unless you turn round, of course.'

'Can you remember anything else at all? Did you see him come out?'

Harry thought. 'I'm sorry, Amos, no I can't. I didn't think anything of it at the time, I'm so used to seeing you go up that path.'

'Don't be cross with me for asking, Harry, but could you have imagined it — because you're so used to seeing me there? Or could it have been another man my height but otherwise not necessarily like me — and you just assumed it was me?'

'No, it was the first thing I remembered . . . with some horror I can tell you,' Harry admitted. 'And no, it couldn't have been just anyone, he had your sort of jacket and cap on.'

'You mean these?' Amos pointed to his clothes.

'Aye.'

Having set out to discredit Irene Squires's sighting once and for all, instead Amos had proved her story. Now he couldn't put it down to Jack's eyesight or her spite; someone had definitely called on Brenda that day dressed like him — deliberately or otherwise.

14

Amos received an unexpected phone call from Stephen Linklater late on Friday night.

'Didn't know you fished?' Amos said as he joined Linklater on the riverbank the following morning.

Suitably attired this time, Linklater was sitting on the grass, staring intently into the murky depths. 'All the time, Amos.' He smiled. 'But I can only watch today, we're still in the close season, remember.' He sighed. 'Thought you might like a progress report but it would be unwise for folk to see us conferring.'

Pleased, Amos lowered himself on to the grass beside Linklater, wondering why he did this so seldom — sat on the riverbank and drank in the peace. 'It was just about here that a couple of fishermen had a fright last year.' Linklater turned to face him. 'They'd settled themselves down for the day, keepnet in the water, bait tin open beside them and their lunch behind. Imagine their surprise when they heard a snort and turned to find a ruddy great bull moving in on their tuna sandwiches. I'd only put Horace into the next field the day before — how was I to know there was an opening through into here?'

They fell silent, watching the flow of the water. Eventually Linklater said: 'We've been trying to trace Catherine Donoghue through Somerset House — Sam supplied her surname for us, saved us looking up Brenda's birth certificate.' Amos was pleased Sam was being more forthcoming with the police. He'd had a quiet word with him — explained that the sooner the killer was caught the better so he should be as helpful as possible.

'Have you any idea how many Catherine Donoghues there are? Anyway we believe we've found her birth certificate, thanks to you and Sam.' He took his eyes off the river for a moment to look at Amos. 'Thing is, she wasn't Brenda's sister — she was her daughter.'

'Well I never! I didn't know that,' Amos exclaimed, taken aback. 'What do you make of that then? Are you sure?'

'Fairly, yes. I think we've got the right Catherine Donoghue, the dates tie up, mother was Brenda Donoghue and she was born in Gloucester. Not that far away but far enough. No father registered.'

'So that was it. Brenda must've been about seventeen at the time — a mistake I assume — so she passes her off as her sister? Can't see why?' Amos realized how little he'd known.

'Not now perhaps, but things were different fifty odd years ago, weren't they? It would've been a big stigma, not only for Brenda but for the child as well. And presumably Brenda didn't meet Mr Smith until later, so it was better to make Catherine her young sister.'

'I wonder if Catherine knew? No one ever breathed a word of it in this village — I'm sure I'd have heard otherwise. Does this have to come out, Stephen? It doesn't seem fair somehow — Brenda is murdered so everyone must know her secret.'

'Not unless it becomes pertinent no, all we're doing at present is trying to find Catherine — for several reasons.' He went on. 'I went to see Phyllis Arbuthnot again; confronted her with what I'd found out and asked her why she hadn't thought to mention it.' He paused. 'She said it wasn't relevant.'

'Did she tell you where to find her ex-husband?'

'Said she didn't know . . . but I wonder. Mind you, I can't think what reason she would have to withhold the information, but I felt she was keeping something back.'

'Still in denial?' Amos replied. 'All these years she's been convincing herself it simply didn't happen. If she tells you where he is, supposing she knows, she's admitting to herself that he exists — him and his lady friend. But what about Phyllis's brother, have you asked him?'

'OK.' Linklater sighed. 'We didn't know she had a brother.'

'Mmm. Alan Tregorran saw him here not long ago.'

'Don't happen to know his surname, I suppose? I'd rather not have to ask Phyllis and forewarn him.'

'Nasty little devious mind you have, Chief Inspector,' Amos said with a twinkle. 'I'll ask Alan for you; if he doesn't know it shouldn't be too hard for him to find out.'

'Talking of nasty minds — we caught up with your Mr Quartermaster yesterday, in his London office. Nice amiable fellow isn't he?' Until he saw Linklater's grimace, Amos thought Quartermaster must at last have considered it prudent to be less aggressive.

The chief inspector continued: 'Didn't endear himself to us. Although we had an appointment he kept us waiting over an hour, then proceeded to harangue us about you. That's really why I wanted to talk to you this morning, I'm worried he might do something stupid and I want you to be on your guard. There's no doubt he holds you solely

175

responsible for the council's refusal to grant his planning permission and if he doesn't get it through this time — '

'Don't tell me he was making threats in front of you, of all people?'

'Yup. Stupid man, isn't he? Clearly doesn't rate us either. I had to be careful. From what the chief superintendent says, Quartermaster is still kicking up about you at County Hall. I'm glad I don't have your job. You can keep politics, give me good old-fashioned crime any day.'

'That's not politics, that's bribery and corruption — good old-fashioned crime. It looks like political influence but at bottom it's achieved through money — greasing palms, withholding preferment, blackening people's names — it's all the same thing just masquerading under different titles. That's the real reason he hates me, because he can't bribe me — or at least he hasn't the brains to figure out my price.'

'And what is your price?' Linklater asked slowly.

'It's no secret.' Amos smiled. 'It's whatever is best for the community I serve. If he builds the right houses I'll help him.'

Linklater relaxed. 'I'm afraid that's unlikely to be his approach.'

'What did he say about Brenda's murder?

Where was he that afternoon?'

'Says he was on a train to London, we're checking it out. He didn't have his ticket but those automatic barriers swallow them so that's not incriminating in itself. Says he'd been in Oxford which we can check . . . but unless he can prove departure and arrival times his alibi's wide open. But I still don't see why he'd kill Brenda. Did he even know her?'

'Probably not. Makes it easier for him doesn't it — much less likelihood of his being caught — since there's nothing to associate him with the victim. You know my theory, Stephen, he wants to incriminate me and he doesn't care how or about what.'

'Mmm. Well, I certainly wouldn't turn your back on him if I were you.'

They watched the river for a while longer. 'Best be off,' Amos said, struggling to his feet and looking around for Napoleon who was dozing in the shade of the Land Rover — his exercise unaccomplished.

'By the way, what did they find on Napoleon — your forensic people? You haven't said.'

'Haven't I?' Stephen was concentrating on the water just a shade too keenly. 'Lots of things is the answer, Amos, lots of things.'

'People's DNA, you mean?'

'Yes, but until we get a clue as to the killer's identity, it's not much use.'

'But we could use it as bait, couldn't we? As long as Napoleon isn't in danger — for all his faults I wouldn't want him hurt.'

'We've already taken the DNA evidence from your pig so there's no reason for anyone to harm him now — best thing we could have done for him in that sense.' Linklater looked up at Amos and gave a rare grin. 'You can even give him a bath if you want.' He turned back to the river. 'This trap — what did you have in mind?'

'We could tell everyone that the killer's DNA was on Napoleon and that the police are starting a programme of tests to try and match it. Whoever refuses has to be worth investigation.'

'But as soon as the killer thinks about it, if he's local he'll know there'll be lots of other DNA on Napoleon,' Linklater argued.

'Not male DNA, there won't. Napoleon likes the ladies. We could mention that too.'

* * *

'He's openly accusing me of murdering Brenda?' Amos couldn't believe what John Wilkinson had just said over the phone.

'I don't know yet, but surely even he's not

178

that stupid,' John replied.

'What's happened then?'

'At the moment all I know is he's taken this opportunity, as we thought he might, to have another go at you at the draft stage of the standards board report. You'll remember that this stage gives both sides the opportunity to point out major omissions and errors before the inspector's decision is finalized? Well, from what I can gather, Quartermaster's playing the 'new evidence' card. Obviously it's to do with Brenda leaving you that money. I know, I know you're not taking it, but with his contacts he was bound to find out sooner or later. He's not going to let that opportunity go, is he?'

Amos groaned. 'You mean it's new evidence of yet one more poor old lady I've diddled out of a fortune.'

'Something like that, yes. Though I must say, he's being extraordinarily vehement about it.'

'Saying I murdered Brenda, you mean?'

'Well, it's a short leap between the two for a mind like his, isn't it? I think he's been telling the board about you being seen going into Brenda's that day — just to prove you made a habit of calling on her — and is hoping that their imagination will fill in the gaps.'

'Him and Vernon Squires are in this Hunter's thing together. And this is Irene Squires spreading her malicious lies again — put up to it by Quartermaster I'll be bound. I've a good mind to go round there and — '

'Amos, Amos,' John interrupted, 'I strongly advise you not to do anything like that.'

'You know I think he did it, don't you?'

'We shouldn't be having this conversation on the phone. I'll come over.'

Thirty minutes later John Wilkinson arrived at Amos's cottage.

'Are you serious? Do you really think Quartermaster killed Brenda?'

'Yes.'

'Why, though?' John propped his long length against the wall, arms folded.

'To spite me — set me up — just like he is doing. That's what I told Linklater.'

John unfolded his arms and shifted his weight back on to his feet in surprise. 'You told Linklater that? What did he say?'

'Not much, what could he say? I think he put it down to the ravings of a village idiot. Either that or the 'he would say that wouldn't he' of a guilty man — me trying to shift the blame on to Quartermaster.'

'Slow down a minute. You're saying Quartermaster deliberately murdered Brenda in order to frame you for her murder?'

'We-ell, that's what I said, yes, but it could have been less premeditated — if it makes you happier. It wouldn't have been difficult for Quartermaster to discover that I was helping out other old folks round here — not just his aunt. But he needed proof, right? Proof that I've leaned on them in some way, forced them to give me things, vote for me . . . you know.'

'But he made that up about his aunt to cause trouble for you.'

'How long is it before liars start to believe their own lies, John?' Amos paused to give John time to accept this axiom. 'So he goes looking for more proof. Maybe he decides to do what he's accusing me of — lean on somebody vulnerable like Brenda, get her to say I've been extorting money, threatening her,' Amos went on. 'You never know, he could've been phoning her before that, asking her about me. Brenda wasn't daft despite what some said. It could've been what drove her to write me into her will, just to show him she couldn't be got at.'

John gasped. 'And when she wouldn't co-operate he lost his temper?'

'Yes, or put his hands round her throat as a threat and didn't realize his own strength. I don't know.' Amos flung himself into a chair, drained.

John was standing in the middle of the room now, alert. 'So, having murdered her he decides to pin it on you. Why not? So much the better. So he lets Irene Squires into his secret?'

'I doubt it. She's a vain, selfish woman but accessory to a murder? No, I don't think so. All Quartermaster had to do was suggest to her that telling a little lie would help to blacken my name and get me barred from office so her husband could go ahead and build all those houses for him. I don't suppose it occurred to the silly woman that her deception could waste enormous amounts of police time and hence prevent the real culprit from being apprehended . . . or get an innocent man convicted.'

For the moment Amos relegated Jack's sighting to his eyesight deficiency and Harry's to the fact that Quartermaster might look like Amos — from a distance, with the sun in your eyes — and mentioned neither to John. Nor did this scenario of death caused accidentally fit with luring Amos to Long Cast . . . which would indeed mean Quartermaster had killed Brenda deliberately. John would have found that even harder to accept.

'I grant you it sounds feasible — just. But

182

let's not get carried away, Amos. We're talking about a respectable businessman here, not some lowlife!'

'Are we? What does he do in the City but take risks? He's a risk-taker, John, who cares only about winning.'

'OK, but you're suggesting some Machiavellian plot where he sets out to discredit you through a rumour.'

'And what does the City work on? What's its currency, eh? Rumour, that's what! That's how he operates every day. The tiniest whisper here, a nuance there and the stock shoots up or dives. That's how men's fortunes are won or lost in a moment. Sleepy old Weston Hathaway is a veritable pushover in comparison. Or so he thinks.'

John retired to his post against the wall — his hand to his forehead. 'So what do you want me to do? How do you want me to respond to the standards board?'

'After we've denied it, you mean?' Amos crossed the room to John. 'I'll tell you one thing we can do: play him at his own game. There must be some sort of financial standards board which regulates people like him. Could you find out how we go about lodging a complaint — so we can have him investigated?' Amos was already thinking about Alec and whether he'd heard any more about the spread-betting subject. Maybe they could use that.

'This is dangerous talk, Amos. Are you sure you want to get into this? Why not just — '

'I'm sure I don't, John, but what choice have I got? The man'll have me hanged unless I fight back.'

15

Amos and Jack were driving from field to field, checking the flocks. Amos had told Jack about his conversation with John Wilkinson and his growing conviction of Quartermaster's guilt.

'Jack, you're the one who saw him. Could it have been Quartermaster in Brenda's that day?'

Jack took a while to answer. 'Surely someone would've seen him walking either up or down the road, and nobody's mentioned it.'

'On the contrary, even the police neglected to interview him in the belief that he's so rarely in the village he couldn't possibly be of any help. But don't you see, that's what's so clever about it. He was purposely dressed to resemble me, either in case he was seen — and the sight of me is so common I'm damn near invisible — or deliberately to incriminate me.'

'Either way you're saying he committed murder, just so he could build a few houses. I could go along with your idea that he went there to intimidate Brenda — get some

185

evidence against you — but I have a problem with him murdering Brenda in cold blood.'

'OK, so he disguised himself so he wouldn't be seen going to threaten her. What I want to know is how much of a disguise was it?'

'How do you mean?'

'Well, you were without your glasses and you were looking through bottle glass. Perhaps more important, when you saw a male figure there you expected it to be me . . . either me or the reverend. So maybe he wasn't disguised at all?'

'What does Harry think?' Amos had told Jack what Harry had seen.

'I haven't asked him yet. Harry said it was someone my height.'

'Well, that fits. Quartermaster's tallish, about six foot like you.'

' . . . and that he was wearing my jacket and my cap — admittedly glimpsed from the back, from a distance, head and shoulders only.'

'Put like that it could've been anyone.' Untethered in the back, Napoleon grunted as they bounced over the hummocky ground and Jack swung in his seat to make sure he was all right — catching a profile view of Amos in the process. 'That's it! I was about to say there must've been something deeper, something subliminal about the figure — how it acted or looked or moved perhaps — that made Harry and me immediately think it was you. Now I think I've got it. You wear your cap pushed up on your head. Even when you start off with it straight like everyone else, you soon push it back and up again.'

Amos pulled his cap down flat. 'Do you think so? Do you think that's what made both of you think it was me, from just one glimpse?'

'Yes I do.'

'Which proves my theory that Quartermaster set out to impersonate me.'

'I've just had another thought,' Jack said. 'Would Quartermaster go to all that trouble? I don't know why but I've always had the impression he's a lazy bastard; it would be more in character for him to hire someone else to do it.'

'Now that is stretching it — hire a hitman to attack an old lady!'

'Who says she was meant to be attacked? As you said, maybe it was meant to be a warning that went wrong and the guy panicked and killed her.'

Amos pulled the Land Rover on to the verge and he and Jack alighted to lean on the field gate, counting the sheep. A large tractor came round the corner with a grinning Alan

Tregorran on board. 'Nothing better to do, you two?'

'Just the man,' Amos replied wading across the grass to him. 'Been meaning to ask you about Phyllis Arbuthnot's brother.'

'William Hornby-Smythe you mean?' Alan leaned down and switched off his engine.

'Ah, so that's his name. How well do you know him, Alan?'

'Only by sight really, seen him at the odd function. The family had the drapers in Warwick, a large department store. Sold out to one of the chains years ago.'

'So that's where the money came from. And he ran the store? I imagine he's retired now.'

'Oh no, he's an actor, or certainly was — stage actor, character parts, that sort of thing.'

★ ★ ★

For when Jack was too busy to help, Amos had devised a number of stratagems for accomplishing two-man tasks on his own; one of them for feeding the sheep at Long Cast. It had been a dry spring and he still needed to supplement their diet until more of the new grass came through. Yesterday he and Jack had loaded a heavy bag of feed on to the back of the Land Rover so that, today, Amos had only to set the motor in a low gear at the top of the field and let it crawl along while he distributed the food. That way he could spread it around without having to carry the bag.

His mind on other things, principally Quartermaster's latest poisoning of the standards board, Amos must have set the gear too high. Standing on the back forking out feed, he sensed the Land Rover gathering speed. For a second he thought he'd simply reached a small downhill section but the vehicle kept accelerating.

Gauging the manoeuvre as best he could, he clambered awkwardly over the side nearest the cab. Retaining his grip on the side bars with one hand, he stretched his right foot on to the driver's step and managed to grab the door handle. He heaved himself into the driver's seat as the Land Rover careered down the steep slope to the river . . . thinking himself lucky to have averted a possible catastrophe.

He stamped on the brake pedal. It failed to connect. The vehicle hurtled on. He tried again. Still no effect. Refusing to believe the brakes weren't working, he pummelled the pedal while the Land Rover continued its now headlong plunge down the field, like a horse that's slipped its halter, unrestrained. Amos flicked off the engine and yanked at the handbrake with both hands, afraid the cable would snap and the handle come away altogether. As the vehicle began to check, he used his right hand to steer directly for a low shrub. They pitched through the front part of it but eventually came to a halt when the gorse's prickly fingers grabbed the chassis, subduing the momentum.

The collision with the shrub threw him forcefully against the steering wheel, winding him and bruising his ribs. Amos stayed where he was while he recovered his breath. He could hear rushing. It wouldn't be the sheep, they'd have fled in the opposite direction as soon as the Land Rover had begun its unnatural descent. Had something happened to his ears?

Lifting his head to better test his hearing, he saw faces appear at the window. Rarely had he been so pleased to have company, even Jem and his minder. For one fleeting second it crossed his mind to wonder why they were here. What had they been up to? But even in his befuddled state he realized they'd hardly show up now if they'd caused the accident . . . unless they'd come to finish the job.

'You OK, mister?'

Jem opened the door gingerly and helped Amos out, supporting his arm until he regained his balance. Still shaky, Amos opted to sit on the grass for a minute or two. Jem crouched beside him, looking concerned. The minder opened up the bonnet.

'What happened?'

'Brakes, the brakes didn't work.'

'We saw you manage to get in — but then it speeded up. Black out, did you? Hit the wrong pedal?'

'I don't know. They just didn't seem to work.' Amos stared at his feet as though his boots might have been at fault.

From inside the bonnet came: 'Jem, come and look.' Jem went over to the vehicle while Amos stayed where he was, already feeling more himself. Both gypsies came back to Amos.

'This a new motor?'

Amos could forgive the uncertainty, his was a working vehicle — now with a redesigned grille. 'Insurance company loaned me a brand-new one. Why?'

'You've no brake juice.'

'I've never bothered checking that.'

'Emptied on purpose. Aaron here thinks so too.' Jem indicated the minder who was lying on his back on the grass sidling his way underneath the Land Rover. It didn't take

191

him long to find what he was looking for. A muffled shout came from below the vehicle.

Jem interpreted: 'They cut a hole in the pipe — so the fluid drained out.'

Amos tried to digest this news. 'You mean someone doctored my Land Rover to make the brakes fail?'

'Yeah.'

Quartermaster, thought Amos immediately. Jack was right, he's hiring people to cause trouble. As the thought sank in he asked: 'How did they know when it would happen?'

'They didn't. The brake fluid would leak out — you might have seen a black stain in the road?' Jem looked at Amos enquiringly, then shrugged, presumably accepting this as an unlikely proposition. 'Any remaining fluid around the system would soon be used up . . . and then your brakes would fail.'

'You mean it could've happened anywhere?' The enormity of what they were telling him surged through Amos. 'I could have mown over the kiddies going down that steep hill into Stratford with the infant's school at the bottom; or ploughed through the cows crossing to the milking sheds on the top road; or just driven off a cliff somewhere?'

'Yeah.'

Accepting Jem's proffered arm, Amos levered himself up off the grass and hobbled round, inspecting the Land Rover. He looked ruefully at the bodywork, the dented front, the scoured sides. It would have to have been a gorse bush. It was easier to contemplate the damage to the vehicle than dwell on what might have happened to him . . . and any number of innocent bystanders. Whoever had done this didn't give a toss for anyone else.

'They must have disconnected the alarm, otherwise I'd certainly have heard it in the cottage. So it must be someone who knows their stuff about cars.' Amos wasn't deliberately being accusatory but the remark hit a sensitive spot. Jem said coldly:

'Not really, mister. You're always leaving it unlocked. When you're in the pub, when you park it outside gates and go off over the fields — you even leave it in the middle of Stratford with the keys in the ignition. Anyone could have taken their chance, you gave them plenty.' He paused, 'And anyway, they could have cut that pipe without triggering the alarm.'

'I see what you mean,' Amos said, chastened. 'Widens the field, doesn't it?'

'We'll go and get our motor, tow you out.'

'I'd be very grateful for that later, but first I'd better tell the police. I expect they'll want to see where it actually happened. Don't want them accusing you guys of tampering with the evidence, do we?' He grinned at Jem and drew out his mobile.

'We'll get it this evening, then. Do you want us to put it right for you?'

Amos hadn't thought of that. He didn't want to go anywhere near Squires's garage now he knew that Bruce and Keith were car thieves, if as yet unconvicted by due process of law. His alternative was one of the Stratford garages or the one at Broad Farthing — but why not give these lads a try? 'Yes please. I'm stuck without it.' He hadn't time for the insurance company to bugger about again.

'It'll be outside your cottage in the morning. Can't do the dents in that time, of course, but we can reshape the grille and sort the brakes out.' Jem and Aaron melted away while Amos rang the police.

'Stephen, now he's trying to kill me.'

★   ★   ★

'You're convinced it was deliberate,' Linklater said when he arrived, more as a statement than a question.

'I can't see why or how a brand-new Land Rover would lose its brake fluid otherwise. It's not hot enough for it to have evaporated, is it, Chief Inspector?' Amos's sarcasm

194

masked the growing shock that someone had tried to kill him. Tampering with his vehicle could easily have led to death — not only his own but very possibly other people's too. 'I suspect you'll find that the pipe underneath has a cut in it.'

Linklater went over to the police mechanic, who was already extricating himself from underneath the Land Rover; they stood conferring while the fingerprint men started work. Amos wandered down to the riverbank where Linklater joined him five minutes later, frowning. 'You don't think this could have been kids — a prank perhaps?'

'Do you?'

'In the circumstances, no I don't. Our people say it was definitely deliberate . . . and more certain to cause serious damage than simply slicing the brake cable. You'd probably have discovered that soon after you set out, without suffering too much harm. Or if they'd sawn through it but left a few threads there's no telling whether the brakes would ever have failed before it was discovered at your next service. No, this had the best chance of maximum impact.'

'So you agree, someone tried to kill me?'

'It looks that way, I'm afraid.'

'And there's only one man with a strong motive for wanting me well out of the way

'. . . Cyril Quartermaster.'

'No one else?'

'Not enough to kill me — no.'

'We'll bring him in. But unless we come up with something to tie this, or Brenda's murder, to him, I won't be able to keep him.'

'Which means he will try again.'

Linklater gave an unwilling shrug. 'Maybe.'

'I was afraid you'd say that. By the way, while I think of it, Phyllis's brother is William Hornby-Smythe. Apparently he's an actor — lives near Warwick.'

'Thanks for that. He might just recollect where her husband and Catherine fled to originally — if he ever knew.'

Linklater started back up the hill. Amos followed him 'Was there anyone else around this afternoon?'

'No.' Why make trouble for the gypsies unnecessarily. 'I was with the Land Rover the whole time, so no one could've got at it here.'

'Pity you haven't a guard dog, Alsatian or something, instead of that damned pig of yours. I think you should get someone to go with you on your rounds — just for a bit — until we get to the bottom of this.'

So that's what it had come to. He could no longer go about his daily routine in safety.

★ ★ ★

Jack was on the doorstep waiting for him. Amos had called him from the field to explain what had happened.

'You don't have to follow me absolutely everywhere you know.'

'I know — and by the way, you can put the Land Rover in my outhouse at the pub when you get it back. Mine can stand in the drive — it's yours they're after.'

'Thanks for reminding me.'

'Anyway, I didn't come about that. I wanted to show you this. I think the council have messed up their paperwork.' Jack waved a letter from the District Planning Department.

'Mind if I get in first?' Amos was feeling the strain of the day and its implications.

'Who's mending it, Amos?' Jack followed him into the cottage.

'A couple of the gypsies from Broad Farthing,' Amos answered quietly.

'Are you crazy? Those devious bastards — it's probably them who nobbled it in the first place.'

'Why should they come and help me if they'd been trying to harm me? They could've finished me off in the field — pushed me in the river. And why would they want to, anyway?'

'Their sort don't need a reason — probably

197

still bear a grudge after you made them pay for your tup that night.'

'So why did they tell us about the car stealing changeover point and what night it happens?'

'Because it suited them. They were getting blamed.' Jack sighed. 'So you've let them have the Land Rover so they can wreak all sorts of mischief with it. I call that dumb, Amos Cotswold.'

'Mmm . . . well, I don't think they will, somehow. I can do with some allies looking out for me right now, Jack. I know, I know you do, as does Alec — warns me when he hears anything — and John tries to keep me out of legal hot water. But someone tried to kill me, I can't get over that. And those devious bastards, as you call them, are the most likely to detect that trait in someone else. If Quartermaster has hired someone . . . then the gypsies are the ones most likely to sniff him out.'

'But why should they help you?'

'What was it you wanted to show me?' Amos took the letter.

'If I've understood it correctly it says they've referred my application to the conservation people and to DEFRA.' Jack twisted his neck to check the letter Amos was still reading. 'I reckon they've got their paperwork mixed up, don't you?'

'This is a standard referral letter by the looks of it. Which is why they talk about sending your application to Uncle Tom Cobley an' all — but I don't see why.' Amos dialled the deputy chief planning officer. 'Brian? One of my constituents has put in an application for change of use . . . yes that's the one, paddock to garden.' Amos listened. 'You've had what?' He listened some more. After he'd hung up he turned to Jack who was swaying from foot to foot in curiosity.

'It's not a mistake Jack . . . seems there's been an application for a preservation order for your paddock.'

Jack spluttered. 'Why? What does that mean?'

'Someone thinks it should be preserved as a site of unusual natural phenomena. Apparently a particularly rare moss likes your paddock,' Amos explained, as mystified as Jack. 'And who do you think suggested this?' He paused. 'None other than our friend Vernon Squires.'

'Oh, for heaven's sake! What's got into that man? He was furious that day he saw the notice, if you remember. What was it he said again — something about altering the village? Yes, that was it: 'churning up our country-side'. What's his game?'

'Blessed if I know — but like you, I don't believe it's rare mosses.'

'I reckon he's found out I was with you that night when his son was caught and he's doing this out of spite.'

'I don't see how he could know you were there — and anyway — Squires was funny about your application before we went to Cornwall.'

'What'll happen now?'

'That's what I was trying to find out. It actually goes to DEFRA, and they decide whether or not to support the suggestion. I imagine they'll come and see you.'

'Yes, but what if they do issue a preservation order or whatever they call it? Surely it wouldn't be for the whole paddock? And would that mean I couldn't turn it into a garden?' Jack scuffed his feet on Amos's already threadbare carpet.

Amos was thinking. 'It also means you can't build on it.'

'Do you think that's what this is really about? We thought about that before, didn't we, but he's a builder. It still doesn't make sense.'

'All I can think is he believes your application is the first move in a plan to demolish Moon Cottage and maybe build three or more properties on the site — a trick his dad missed forty years ago. Maybe he's just being a dog in the manger.'

'But I don't want to build on it.'

'I suggest you go and convince him of that. By the way, I've a shrewd idea I know where this preservation order thing came from.'

'Not from you, I hope!'

'Maybe — indirectly. It's a bit coincidental that I was talking to the Reverend Whittaker about preservation orders on fields just last week.'

'It's hard to imagine Vernon Squires chatting to the reverend.'

'No, but Mrs Squires could be making a habit of it.' Amos glanced at his watch. 'I might just catch him before evening prayers.'

Amos crossed to the phone and dialled. 'Reverend, a quick question. You'll remember I told you about the preservation order on River Meadow — did you by any chance mention it to anyone else?' He held the phone outwards so Jack could hear too.

'Umm, yes, I do remember mentioning it. I have to confess — after you were asking me about Irene Squires and what she'd seen, I happened to bump into her.' The reverend paused, as though he'd lost the thread.

'Go on, Reverend, about River Meadow.'

'Oh, I just told her what you'd said, that

there are over a hundred different varieties of wild flowers in that field, so many in fact that they'd had the foresight to preserve it. She said she hadn't realized you could do that. Well, frankly neither had I; I must say Amos, you really are a mine of information.' Jack moved away, mouthing words Amos could only guess at.

'She didn't by any chance mention Moon Cottage?'

'No . . . why should she? But I did tell her you'd been asking about what she'd seen the day Brenda died.'

Amos groaned audibly.

'Have I done something wrong Amos? Only you seemed reluctant to ask her yourself, yet you were wondering why she'd wanted to go to the butcher's twice and whether she could tell us any more about what she'd seen. So I asked her for you.' Amos held his breath. 'But she just said she'd told the police all she knew and didn't want to think about that horrible day any more. I was only trying to help Amos.'

'Yes, I know, Reverend, don't worry, it's all right. Thank you.' Amos hung up.

'So she went home and told her old man about preservation orders on fields.' Jack voiced Amos's own conclusion.

'Yes. He'd probably come across it in the

past — it'd be something to avoid if you're buying land you hope to build on. This simply came as a timely reminder. I'm sorry, Jack.'

'No use crying over spilt information. The question is, what do I do now?'

'Presumably it's untrue — there is no rare moss in your paddock unless . . . no, I can't see that.'

'What?'

'Well, I suppose if he's gone this far there's nothing to stop him planting some?'

'Over my dead body.' Jack realized too late. 'Just an expression Amos, just an expression. Boy! What is going on around here? Come to the country for a peaceful life, the advertisement said — you remember, that big pointing finger.'

'That was 'Your country needs you'.'

'I knew it was something like that.' Jack subsided into despondency. 'They could get in from the back very easily — across Alan's fields; could climb through the post and rail fencing, plant their moss and be away again. With this dry weather they'd leave no tracks. Mind you they'd have to put it at the house end, under the willows, where the moss is now. It's got to be somewhere feasible, hasn't it?'

'Look I've about had enough and you've a

pub to open. One more day won't make much difference — it'll be there already if that's what he's up to. Let's go tomorrow — see what we can find.'

16

Amos borrowed Ted's pick-up for an hour. He'd told Alec on the phone that Quarter-master had been back to the standards board with fresh evidence; drawing their attention to a legacy Brenda had left him.

Alec was waiting for him on the steps in front of the house. He led Amos around the corner of the building, through the exotic colour of the azalea shrubbery, and on to the back terrace. Cold lager in misted glasses stood ready on a small cast-iron table. Amos admired the view across the parkland — a quintessential Victorian landscape, down to the Scottish longhorns, brushed by willows, grazing by the brook.

'That's what I feared would happen,' Alec sighed, ushering Amos into a cane chair. 'But he's forfeited all the goodwill he built up by throwing his money around . . . and has completely misjudged the high regard people around here have for you — irrespective of their party. He gambled we'd be only too pleased to destroy your reputation.'

Amos had guessed what Quartermaster had been up to behind his back, trying to turn others against him. 'I appreciate what you say Alec, and believe me I'm very grateful to you. He's certainly twisted events into a very black picture for me.' They supped their beer in silence for a minute, drinking in the evening sounds along with the perfidy of Quartermaster's behaviour. Somewhere in the park they could hear a cuckoo.

'Something happen to the Land Rover?' Alec enquired.

'Somebody cut the brake pipe.'

'Accidentally I trust.' Alec liked to live in an ordered world, where deliberate vandalism represented an unthinkable departure from civilized behaviour. He had once told Amos he'd never sit as a magistrate lest he lose his good opinion of human nature.

'Chief Inspector Linklater thinks that unlikely.'

'What!' Alec banged his glass down on the table in shock.

'Luckily I was in Long Cast Meadow when it happened but the brakes could have failed anywhere — killed anyone. And who is it hates me enough to do that?'

'You can't think that was Quartermaster, surely?' Alec's eyes were wide with disbelief.

'I wouldn't put anything past him now. I hardly know the man but I'd supposed him to be the usual greedy outsider who sets out to bully us rural simpletons into submission. Now I don't think that at all — I think he's an out-and-out crook!'

'He certainly seems unprincipled — his father would turn in his grave.'

'For all we know young Cyril was the one who put him there.'

They drank in silence again.

'Do you know Phyllis Arbuthnot's brother?' Amos asked.

'Hornby-Smythe? Yes . . . but not well.'

'Do you think Quartermaster knows him?'

'I don't know, it's possible . . . why?'

'Just thought he might, seeing as it was Quartermaster who leaned on Phyllis to stand against me in the elections.' Amos decided not to upset Alec further by telling him that Quartermaster . . . or an accomplice, might have murdered Brenda to get at him.

'William's never been involved in politics to my knowledge.' Alec sat on the edge of his seat. 'What do the police think about this brake incident? What are you going to do?'

'There's not much I can do except be vigilant — and figure out who killed Brenda.'

'You're convinced the two are connected?'

'I'm not sure of anything, no,' Amos confessed. 'But I have a gut feeling they are — maybe not directly, but someone's out to get me one way or the other.'

'Could it be more than one person?'

'You mean Quartermaster hired someone who killed Brenda and then doctored my car himself?' Damn, now he'd said it.

Alec stared at him, then into his beer. He looked up and out at the countryside, before turning his eyes back to Amos. Drawing a deep breath, at last he said, 'No, though that's obviously another possibility. I meant two unconnected people — one who killed Brenda, for whatever reason — and one who tried to kill you?'

'All I know, Alec, is that Quartermaster is in this somewhere, so I've decided to turn the tables, so to speak. I'm going after him now.'

'Is that wise?'

'I don't see why not. I can't just sit here like a frightened rabbit dazzled by the glare of all these attacks, I've got to act.'

'P'raps you'd better not tell me any more.'

'Oh, it's not a secret. I'm going to report him to the Financial Services Authority, if that's what they call themselves — the FSA.'

Alec's face cleared. 'Do as you would be done by, eh? Then I think I may be able to help you. I made a few phone calls before you arrived — and received some intriguing answers.' Amos was listening.

'You'll remember me telling you there were rumours circulating in the City about him being in hot water?' Amos nodded. 'Well, it seems he's had a lot of problems from gambling on the stock markets and, like most obsessive gamblers, decided to solve his problems by upping the stakes. But unlike betting on horses or cards, with this spread-betting you can lose more than your original stake if you're not careful.'

Amos was intrigued. 'Surely there must be a safeguard against doing that?'

'Yes, there is. It's called a 'stop-loss'. But, to use betting parlance, you don't get such good odds if you apply a stop-loss; and our Mr Quartermaster is a greedy man. And that's not all . . .' Alec paused to sip his beer.

'It seems he's also been involved with what they call Contracts for Difference or CFDs for short. They're a way of profiting from a rise or fall in a stock's value without actually owning it. Again, it's possible to make big money from a small stake and that might be what he did — initially — but then over time he got too greedy and lost it again. One big difference is that with CFDs you are liable for Capital Gains Tax.'

'You mean you think he lost all he'd gained before he'd paid the tax on it . . . so had nothing from which to pay the tax?'

'Certainly worth looking at, I'd say.'

'Would you mind explaining this to John

Wilkinson for me, to be sure we're saying the right thing. I'd hate to miss the point, they wouldn't believe us a second time.'

'I'll do better than that, I'll ask my accountant to explain it; hypothetically, you understand.'

★ ★ ★

Amos never knew who'd be standing on his doorstep next, day or night. He'd taken the truck back to Ted and stayed for a coffee so it was gone ten o'clock and nearly dark as he swung round the corner, colliding with a shadowy figure bent over Napoleon — the Reverend Whittaker.

'Sorry, Reverend, are you all right?' Amos grabbed the cleric before he lost his balance. 'Didn't see you there.'

Reverend Whittaker straightened his jacket and ran a finger round the inside of his dog collar as if it were too tight or somehow twisted. 'I'm fine, Amos, should've heard you coming. I'm surprised you don't fall over Napoleon here more often.'

'I used to but he knows to keep out of my way these days. You must have distracted him,' Amos said, chuckling.

'I wondered how he was? You said he'd been hurt?'

'Oh yes, he's much better thanks. Look you can see, it's healed nicely. He met a lovely young lady who made it all better, didn't you, boy.'

'Was that the police DNA people?'

'The DNA people? Oh yes, I mean no, it wasn't. I'd forgotten I'd told you about them.' A thought suddenly occurred to him. 'Did you tell Irene Squires that too?'

'I really can't remember — I — er — I might have I suppose. Does it matter?'

'No, no, in fact I think it's pretty much common knowledge, I don't think Chief Inspector Linklater is keeping it quiet. He's launching a programme to test everyone, well, the men anyway — you know, just for elimination purposes. Other than you, very few pay him any attention.'

'Actually I'm glad I bumped into you . . . or rather you . . . never mind.' Reverend Whittaker was never a man for lighthearted humour even when he saw the joke. Life was a serious business for him. 'I wanted to ask you something.'

'Do you want to come in?' Amos invited grudgingly, wanting only his bed.

'No, no, I was just after your opinion really. I've been thinking about our conversation in the meadow that day. Oh, and I am sorry if I caused you any trouble with Mrs Squires, only I happened to see her and I thought I'd try and help.' Amos shook his head to indicate it didn't matter, his tiredness must be evident. 'No, well, as I was saying, I wondered . . . could someone strangle themselves?'

Amos was taken aback. 'Did Brenda commit suicide, you mean?'

'It could have been an accident, couldn't it?'

Amos wondered if the reverend was thinking of Brenda's burial — perhaps the church still refused to bury suicides in hallowed ground.

'You see, I think that's what happened to Mother.'

Amos waited for him to go on but he didn't.

'You'd have to ask Chief Inspector Linklater but my guess would be no. People hang themselves of course. You found her — did it look as though she'd tried to hang herself?'

'I don't know. I suppose not . . . but what if someone cleared up afterwards, not wanting it to look like suicide.'

Amos was far too tired for whatever it was Reverend Whittaker was trying to tell him, although tempted to mention the theory that someone had assisted Brenda — at her request. Maybe that was what the reverend was getting at. 'Reverend, I can't help you, I'm far too tired, I'm afraid. Could we talk about this some other time, do you think?' He regretted being rude and felt there might be something important here, but he couldn't stay awake.

'Of course, I only wondered. 'Night, Amos, and . . . thank you.'

Amos fell asleep wondering how long it had taken for Irene Squires to tell Quartermaster the two other facts that Reverend Whittaker had given her: that Amos had been asking questions about what she'd seen, and that the police were interested in the DNA found on the pig. He missed the stealthy approach of the vehicle with its engine cut, as it drifted to a halt outside his house; missed the shadow of the driver against the window as he crept away.

★ ★ ★

Walking across the paddock at Moon Cottage took him back years. It had a rectangular shape and was edged with large horse-chestnut trees down the left-hand side and willows on the right. From here he could see across Alan Tregorran's fields to the river in the distance.

The original Moon Cottage had been a tiny fifteenth century thatched dwelling gaining its name, so it was thought, from its special positioning. In the nineteen sixties Vernon Squires's father Frank had bought it as a hovel and replaced the old building with a chalet bungalow. Shortly afterwards, when Frank committed suicide, to avoid bankruptcy Vernon had been forced to sell the new house along with this back field which he'd fenced off from the garden. Six years ago Jack and Marion had bought the place for their retirement.

Privately, Amos was extremely surprised that Vernon Squires had chosen rare moss with which to challenge Jack's request. He was surprised Squires was objecting at all — but a much more likely prospect would have been the existence of Roman remains. Over the years Alan Tregorran had ploughed up literally bagfuls of Roman coins in the field next door.

'There you are.' Out of breath, Jack came hurrying down the lane and across to Amos. 'I saw your motor outside, so I assume they brought it back all right, then?' Amos glared at Jack, cross with his lack of faith.

Unabashed Jack went on. 'I wasn't sure if you'd come down here or had wandered off somewhere else.'

'I was early. I haven't been here for years . . . and Napoleon was already ahead of me so I thought I'd better follow him in case he trampled over those rare mosses.' They both chuckled.

'I've just passed him, rooting around in the corner there where the lane comes out into the paddock. Who knows, maybe it's truffles I've got here, not mosses.' He glanced in Napoleon's direction. 'Have you found what Squires is talking about?'

'No, I've been busy day-dreaming.'

Jack pulled his features into a frown. 'You know, one thing's so obvious yet it didn't occur to me until this morning — how does Squires know there is rare moss here?' Amos went to reply but Jack stopped him. 'I know it's probably a fiction anyway but this is private land so how does he know — unless he's been trespassing?'

'Good point; it's not as though it's a commonly accepted fact in the village — like something that's been talked about for years.'

'Having said that I expect he'll say his father told him when he owned the property, except that's a bit thin. If so, why hasn't he mentioned it before?'

'The answer is because you're the first to apply to change the use.'

'Oh come off it, Amos. If you really cared

about a rare moss as much as Mr Squires suddenly seems to, would you leave it to chance?'

'We're not dealing with logic here, Jack. The DEFRA people will be concerned purely with whether the moss is a rare one and whether it is indeed here.'

'Let's see if we can find it, then.' Jack moved back towards the shaded area under the trees where it was damp and darker. 'Though I'm blessed if I know what I'm looking for.'

Amos toured the perimeter of the paddock, examining the trees. In one corner, next to a dyke, stood an old willow bent double with age; its green fronds trailing like lank hair on the ground. He parted the strands and entered its dank interior — where moss clung in abundance to its grizzled grey torso. But was it rare? Amos doubted it.

Thus occupied he'd not concerned himself with Napoleon nor heard anyone approach down the lane. Suddenly the peace was shattered by a loud squeal, a thunder of hoofs and a strangled shout. Amos was nearest and arrived at the paddock opening in time to see the rear view of Vernon Squires stumbling down the lane. Planted four-square at the field end, Napoleon was growling at the fleeing figure like a dog. Squires disappeared round the corner before Amos could call him

— then his car roared off down the road.

'What was he doing here?' Jack asked, catching Amos up.

'Coming to talk to us, I'd say — he must've seen my wagon outside and wanted to see me. Damn, that could have helped you.'

'More like creeping up trying to overhear what we were saying without us knowing. Did you hear him coming down the lane?'

'No, but I was some distance away. Napoleon reacted as soon as he smelled him, I'd guess.' Amos smiled. 'It's a long time since I've seen him behave like that, though.'

'Makes me even more certain Squires was creeping about. If he'd genuinely been coming to talk he'd have stopped at the end of the lane — once he'd put some space between him and Napoleon. Would have yelled at you to keep your pig under control. The fact that he ran away makes him guilty in my book. Do you think he's got some treasure buried in this field he doesn't want me to find?' Jack said, chuckling. 'Nah, he'd have fetched it by now.'

Amos went to calm Napoleon who hadn't moved from his 'on guard' stance and was still emitting low, angry noises. 'It's OK, old chap. You saw him off. Good boy.' He bent to stroke the pig, comfort him. 'Why don't you carry on with your scratching about — Jack and I would like truffles for our supper so don't eat them all, will you?' Amos glanced over to where Napoleon had been digging. Mildly curious he strolled across. Who knew, Napoleon might have nosed out the site of the freshly planted rare moss. If so, Amos sincerely hoped he'd eaten it.

The area was strewn with old bricks, now half-covered in ivy. The ground was hummocky under the trees here, probably the burial mound so beloved of builders too lazy to transport their rubble. Napoleon and Jack joined him.

'Find anything?' Jack asked.

'No, only rubble by the looks of it. You'll be able to make a rockery in this corner. What's he so interested in?' Napoleon had gone back to his digging with renewed energy, turning over rotting leaves, chunks of concrete, broken bottles. As a stray sunbeam pierced the canopy above them, Amos saw it, glistening. He dived to retrieve it before Napoleon's foot interred it again.

'What's that?' Jack asked, alerted by Amos's unusually swift reaction. 'A bracelet of some sort?'

Amos rubbed the blackened silver against his jacket. It was a name-plate bracelet, a style popular in the sixties, inscribed both inside and out.

'Probably belonged to that family I bought the cottage from. What does it say?' Jack asked, his eyes on the bracelet. He looked up. 'Hey, Amos, what's the matter?' Jack took a concerned step forward, his arm outstretched. 'You OK?'

' 'Mary.' It says, 'Mary'.'

17

Amos was back in nineteen sixty. He'd waited until she was sixteen, although her stepfather still refused to let her mix with people. Some days she'd have big bruises where she said she'd fallen over or walked into a door but they'd all known he abused her . . . called it discipline, reckoned she'd be spoilt unless he was strict with her. She'd been a headstrong girl, clever too, and devoted to her mother.

On her birthday Amos had met her off the bus from Stratford where she'd taken a job in an office, though she could easily have made it to university but for her stepfather. Amos had waited for her, walked home beside her and given her the bracelet, offering to take her away. It was so long ago now.

She'd laughed and tossed her head and thanked him very much, and called him her friend but declined his invitation. A month later her mother was diagnosed with cancer and Mary gave up her job to nurse her until she died two years later. Only weeks after her mother's death, Mary disappeared.

'Amos?' Jack pulled him back to the present.

'Did he find anything else?' Amos asked slipping the bracelet into his pocket. Napoleon appeared to have lost interest and had wandered off elsewhere.

'Doesn't look like it. No hidden treasure, not even an old coin or two.' Jack studied Amos. 'You look a bit off-colour — something the matter?'

'Just old ghosts, Jack, just old ghosts.'

'Don't you start — the witches' association'll be wanting to preserve this place next as one of their sacrificial spots. I'm surprised it's not littered with weird symbols or something — just to make their point.'

'You think it's not?' Amos said straight-faced.

'So what are we going to do, then? Say we've poisoned the ground, say there can't possibly be any rare moss? Should I get my own expert in first — just so's I know what the score is? Problem with that is, if he does find something I can't very well ignore it then, can I?' Amos wasn't listening. 'Amos? What's got into you?'

'Her name was Mary Walters and she was very beautiful.'

'It was her bracelet — Mary's?'

'Yes.'

'Come on then . . . who is she?'

'I need to think, Jack.'

'But what about my paddock?'

'That's what I need to think about.'

'I don't understand.'

'Ask Sam about Mary Walters. It's funny, you know, he mentioned her when we were in the crowd by the barrier, the day Brenda was killed. He said: 'There's not been a murder in Weston Hathaway since young Mary Walters . . . and they never did find her body'.'

Jack was motionless. 'Oh no, you're serious, aren't you? She's buried here in my paddock, isn't she?' Jack moved smartly away from the trees and the rubble heap, lifting his feet carefully and minding where he replaced them, as if afraid he might step on her. 'Good God, that's all I need, for it to become a famous murder site! Hang on, though — that means they'd have to dig it up, doesn't it? I'll go and ring the police right now.' Jack brightened instantly.

'No.'

'Amos, we don't have any choice. If there's a body here we have to report it — no matter how long it's been there. I remember a guy I knew who was digging out a swimming pool in his garden and found a skeleton with a knife in it.'

'No.'

Jack was clearly frustrated with Amos's stonewall approach. Hazarding a motive he said: 'You're not worried about the planning department, are you? Oh, for heaven's sake, Amos, you can't be afraid they'll think you dreamt this up to get round the preservation order? No one would do that.'

'You of all people should not be surprised at what they throw at me. One whisper of my doing this purposely for you, my friend, and the standards board will be down on me like a load of manure.'

'But it's not a trick. We've found her bracelet.'

'Yes, and that's all.'

'What do you mean, 'that's all'? We haven't started digging yet.'

'Neither should we. People lose bracelets all the time. I know why you're keen to get the diggers in, Jack, but if I were you I wouldn't. Actually I wouldn't be surprised if they found some Roman coins and then declared it an important archaeological site — then where would you be?'

That knocked Jack back for a second or two. 'Yes, but you seem so sure this particular bracelet belonged to this Mary Walters.' Amos nodded miserably. 'In which case we can't just ignore it, can we? What was it doing here?'

Not so fast, thought Amos, slow down. He wasn't referring to Jack's entreaties but to the revelations bombarding his brain. Why was her bracelet here? Had she herself been here — and if so, how come? He needed time to assimilate them, understand their meaning — and their consequences.

'I don't know, Jack, we need to tread carefully.' Both men looked back at the mound. 'It won't pay us to go off at half cock, there could be all sorts of repercussions, we must think this through. Anyway, don't you have a pub to open?' A cowardly way out, Amos admitted, but he knew Marion had gone into Stratford and he needed time to think without having to explain himself to Jack.

Jack glanced at his watch impatiently. 'You're right, I must go.' He started walking towards the lane, then, when he realized Amos wasn't following he turned irritably:

'Aren't you coming?'

'If you don't mind I'd like to stay here for a bit. Don't worry, I promise I won't do any digging while your back's turned.' Jack shrugged. 'And Jack, please don't mention the bracelet to anyone, will you? Not just yet.'

'And don't you go telling Marion about this . . . this . . . body. She'll have a fit. You owe me an explanation, Amos Cotswold.' Jack pointed his finger at Amos, turned and marched out of the paddock, his back straight, chin in the air.

Having spoken to the district licensing people at the council offices in Stratford, Amos rang Stephen Linklater. He had to know how he was getting on with Quartermaster. Linklater had said he intended to bring him in for questioning but that had been twenty-four hours ago and Amos had heard nothing since.

'Did you get hold of Quartermaster?'

'This is a bad line, Amos, where are you?'

'Waterside.'

'Buy you a pint in the Dirty Duck at six.'

'All these ruddy steps,' grumbled Amos, ten minutes later, as he climbed the steep ascent to the pub across the road from the river, fifty yards along from the theatre.

They settled outside with their drinks.

'So? What about Quartermaster?'

'We don't have much to go on except his dislike of you, and that's not against the law. Don't forget he's got friends in high places.'

'Far fewer than he used to have.' Amos told Linklater that part of his conversation with Alec.

'He still hasn't proved where he was on the afternoon of Brenda's murder — but on the other hand we haven't had any reports of him being seen in Weston either.'

'What about my Land Rover? I'm sure it

was him — or at least he was behind it.'

'We didn't get any clear fingerprints off it, only lots of yours and lots of smudged ones. Neither does he strike me as the type who'd indulge in amateur mechanics.'

'I thought that, yet I understand you wouldn't need to know much about cars, someone could easily have told him what to do. Anyway, Jack Ashley reckons Quartermaster hired someone else to do it.'

'It's still not enough to go on, Amos, we need something more concrete.' A pile of rubble, bricks and pieces of mortar covered with scrubby grass and mosses flashed across Amos's mind.

Linklater went on. 'But I do have news of sorts. I don't think I mentioned it but when we did the house to house enquiries in Weston we asked everyone if they'd seen any strangers — a standard question, obviously. Well, one or two said the same thing — that they'd seen someone they didn't know but who looked familiar.'

'I know, someone dressed like me going into Brenda's.'

'That's what you think Irene Squires saw?'

Amos let that go, he wasn't about to tell Linklater he didn't believe a word Mrs Squires said, but that two of his friends had said the very same thing.

'No, I don't think this was about that. This was someone who looked familiar but whom they couldn't place. So who's that likely to be?' asked Linklater.

'I don't know — usually happens to me with people who work in shops or garages or as doctors' receptionists. They become very well-known faces but out of context you have a job to remember who they are.'

'Round here,' Linklater executed a theatrical sweep of his arm encompassing the immediate environs, 'It's actors.'

'So you agree with Jack — you think Quartermaster hired an actor to dress up like me?'

'I didn't say that. We've nothing to place this familiar stranger at Brenda's — at the moment they're two disconnected subjects. But there was a stranger about that day. And thanks to you we've discovered who it was: William Hornby-Smythe — visiting his sister, according to him.'

'There, what did I tell you! So Quartermaster does know Hornby-Smythe, I thought he might. And of course, Hornby-Smythe would be keen to avenge his sister.' In his eagerness to position this exciting new development Amos grabbed wildly for the conclusions he wanted.

'Hold on, Amos. On your behalf, I asked him if he knew Quartermaster. He said 'vaguely'.'

'He's not going to tell you Quartermaster hired him, is he!' Amos suddenly registered Linklater's tone. 'You don't think he killed Brenda?'

'I don't think he was hired by anyone. He's not the sort — far too arrogant to be someone else's lackey.'

Amos sagged, deflated. 'That fits, knowing his sister. But does he know where Arbuthnot went, his ex-brother-in-law?'

'Still his brother-in-law apparently. Said his sister and Arbuthnot were never divorced — something to do with money, I gather. When I pushed him about the man's whereabouts he muttered 'Abroad, I suppose'. I've got our people trawling through the ports information for that time to see if that's true. As you'll realize, records of all departures from the UK thirty years ago are not the easiest things to come by, let alone search . . . and yes, I can see what you're thinking. Brenda Smith's daughter, stroke sister, can only be a suspect if she hoped to gain by the death, and only a credible suspect if she was in the country at the time. The problem with that is, she could have come back months or even years ago.'

'National Insurance records, Inland Revenue?' Amos suggested.

'No sign. There wouldn't be unless they

were working or claiming benefit here.'

'Drivers and Vehicle Licensing Authority?'

'No record — only record is for him in nineteen fifty-eight when he passed his test. Maybe she never learned to drive.'

'Medical records — maybe Catherine signed on with a doctor?'

'We traced her old surgery — doctor was long dead, and they reckoned they still had her records, though they haven't produced them yet. No record at all for him.'

'Didn't mean to be found from the start, did they? Then neither would I if I'd been married to Phyllis Arbuthnot.'

★ ★ ★

Amos took the Land Rover back up to Jack's garage as Jack was closing up. He felt foolish going to such extremes but Jack had insisted and until he could be sure who'd tampered with his brakes he had reluctantly agreed it made sense. It was either that or a full-scale check every morning, which his knees couldn't contemplate. He was also trying to remember not to leave it unattended in lonely field gateways. Jack was out in the yard taking the air while Marion cashed up.

'I asked Sam about your Mary Walters.'

Amos had known he would. He'd wanted

Sam to tell the story rather than do it himself.

'I can't do Sam's accent but he said she was a pretty lass, a real sweetheart but not one to cross. Said her stepfather used to lay into her and her mother died of cancer and soon after that Mary disappeared without trace. Sounds to me like the stepfather did it — hit her a bit too hard one time, p'raps,' Jack reasoned.

'I think that's what the police thought . . . dug up his garden, and his allotment, if I recall.'

'Maybe she just ran away?'

'Her stepfather said she took nothing with her — that incriminated him even more, yet he could easily have lied. No one else would have known what she had or hadn't taken.'

'What happened to the stepfather? I don't know of any Walters round here now.'

'His name was Stubbs. He married her mother when Mary was about ten, I think, then adopted her against her will; she refused to use his name. Once the police let him go he left. Had to; everyone thought he'd done it, so there wasn't much future for him here. I don't know what happened to him after that, I didn't like him.' To avoid being quizzed any more Amos said:

'I've been thinking about your paddock.'

That much was true. Amos knew he had to flush out Vernon Squires, find out what all this was about — particularly now they'd unearthed Mary's bracelet.

'Good. It's a bit late to ring them now but I'll ring the police first thing.'

'I don't think that's a good idea, Jack, but I have another proposition I'd like to put to you.' Amos moved down into the front garden of the pub. It was dark but the light streaming out from inside, together with the fairy lights strung around the eating area, was enough for the purpose. 'The play's usually held here?'

'Yes, you know it is, on Midsummer night, two weeks from now.'

Amos ruffled the grass with his feet. 'New turf, isn't it?'

'Done in early spring. Yes. It's OK now though. You can walk on it.' Jack was evidently becoming more and more exasperated with every sentence off the subject.

'I was thinking there's never enough room here, and more people come to the play every year. You could do without them churning up your nice new lawn.' He watched Jack's face. 'Why don't you get a one-off entertainment licence to hold the play in your paddock?'

Jack was speechless while this settled in his brain. 'They wouldn't let me,' were the first words that came out. 'They'd say it could endanger the moss.'

'Different departments — don't talk to each other. Fire exits and safety is all you need worry about. You'll have to light it, of course.'

'Light what?' said Marion coming down the path.

Recognizing a likely ally, Amos awarded her his best smile. 'I'm trying to persuade Jack to hold the play in your paddock. There's more room and you'd avoid spoiling your front garden here.'

'But the leaflets have already been sent to the printers. Mind you,' she realized, 'it just says Weston Hathaway, we always assume people will know where.'

'Good, then that's settled. All we have to do is provide a few big direction signs on the night.'

'Hang on a minute — I haven't finished thinking about this yet,' Jack remonstrated. 'What's this all about, Amos? What are you up to?'

'I'd have expected you to jump at the chance. Just think, all those people might accidentally trample on the rare moss without it being your fault.' To stop Jack arguing further, Amos glanced pointedly at Marion behind her back. 'Don't you think it's a good idea, Jack?'

'Put that way, yes, I guess it is,' Jack agreed

but his glare at Amos said in big letters — *And what about that poor girl who's buried there?*

'Marion?'

'I like it — gives us much more room, and people could bring a picnic. Well done, Amos — can you really get the licensing people to agree?'

'Consider it done.' He'd already checked it out with them that afternoon.

Amos strolled back down the road in that half light peculiar to June. Somewhere an owl hooted and was answered by its mate — both drawing gradually closer, pulling the net tighter, reeling him in. In the lime boughs above him tiny black bats flitted in flocks and nearby the crickets unwisely exercised their hoarse throats. Instead of going straight home, almost unconsciously he detoured around past Moon Cottage, aiming to cut down the lane and back across the corner of Alan's field. Being there might jog the memory that gnawed away at him, help him remember, help him understand.

It had been earlier in the year than this and colder — but the same sort of night, when you felt anything could happen. He'd been out burying a sheep savaged by a stray Alsatian — had driven back past here on his way home. Even after all these years he vividly remembered the night, probably because of its horrors, but what else had happened? What was it he couldn't remember?

He drew level with the house; everywhere was very quiet. For several years Jack and Marion had let the cottage but it was empty at present while they did it up for themselves. Not one for fanciful thinking or imaginative sightings, nevertheless Amos felt a faint stirring of unease as he turned into the lane. Perhaps he was being foolhardy, wandering around alone at this hour. He'd never had to worry about it before, but two days after someone had seriously tried to harm him, well . . .

Then he remembered, remembered seeing a figure that night she'd disappeared. He'd driven past the end of the lane and just caught a glimpse, yet he hadn't considered it out of place which was why he'd thought no more of it. Days later, when they couldn't find her, he'd not thought twice about seeing Frank Squires that night. But now he'd found Mary's bracelet in Frank Squires's paddock that sighting had become significant.

Halfway down the lane with the blackness of the paddock opening up in front of him Amos felt the hair on his neck bristle. Turning sharply he saw two men — five yards behind him.

18

They held their cudgels loosely, meaningfully. Held them as professionals carry weapons — balanced, ready. A cold wave washed through him.

'Sorry to startle you, mister. We didn't expect you to come down here . . . and well . . . we thought we'd better catch you up, like.'

'Why are you following me?' he heard himself snap, automatically adopting aggression as his best chance of survival but unsure how many more shocks his ageing heart could take without retaliating.

'Ma's orders.'

He was being slow but he was struggling to understand what was going on here. Undecided what to say he concentrated on controlling his breathing and kept quiet, conscious that his stroll had been ruined but prepared to accept it might be for good reason.

'She told us to make sure no one got a second chance . . . after the other day.'

'And you thought — '

'We saw you headed this way and it didn't

look too clever to us. Thought p'raps you'd been lured down here at this time of night.'

Amos felt he owed them at least the simple explanation, though underneath he wasn't at all sure why he'd decided to come here. He couldn't remember ever having done so before, certainly not in recent years. 'I was just taking the air, too awake to turn in.'

He retraced his steps back up the lane with Jem beside him and Aaron as the rear guard a pace or two behind; unsure whether to be grateful, curious or worried. A ludicrous thought struck him. Were the gypsies up to some illicit activity in the paddock which they hadn't wanted him to discover?

Maybe they'd been there as lookouts . . . not self-appointed bodyguards at all. Oh no, don't say they'd found out about the bracelet and decided to dig up the paddock themselves for some obscure reason. He knew better than to ask himself how they could possibly know — these people were unnervingly telepathic. The real puzzle was why.

'Why is Ma so concerned about my health?' The minute the words were out he knew it was a waste of time. The reply would be utterly predictable.

'You'd have to ask her that.'

The tranquillity of the evening lost, he allowed himself to be escorted home — his companions vanishing at the gate without a goodnight between them.

Deep in thought he lifted the latch on his front door and had shuffled halfway across the threshold before he sensed that the evening wasn't yet over. She sat in deep shadow, her eyes the only thing he could see in any detail. With exaggerated precision he completed his entrance, turned and closed the door behind him. He walked a few paces towards her, came to a halt in the middle of the room and looked down at her. Although she'd never been here before, it felt perfectly natural to find her there in his seat by the fireplace.

'I owe you an apology,' she said softly.

'You owe me a ruddy explanation,' he replied without raising his voice above that of hers.

'Naomi stole your telephone tape because I asked her to.'

This wasn't at all what he'd expected. He'd forgotten about the tape, had convinced himself he'd thrown it away. He had little choice but to indulge Ma and her riddles.

'Are you going to tell me why?'

'Only that we guessed it could be key and wanted to make sure it was safe.' He could hear her smile in the dark. 'I wasn't sure you'd look after it. But I didn't like having to steal it.'

'Why didn't you ask me for it, then — or tell me why it was important?' Even now Amos was far from understanding the real implication of that tape. Someone had tricked him into going down to the river — presumably because they wanted him out of the village when Brenda was killed. But why?

'You can have it back if you like, now I think you realize its importance.' She put the little Perspex box on the mantelpiece with the alacrity of a recently confessed Catholic relieved of her sin.

Tired of the shilly-shallying Amos turned the lamp on, symbolic of the light he wanted shed. 'Why did you have me followed — and what, if anything, has that got to do with the tape?'

'Because I worry about you.'

He was immediately disarmed. Of all the possibilities he hadn't considered that one. His favourites had been that the gypsies, as so often these days, were simply seeking to avoid the blame landing in their lap or . . . were seeking to deflect him.

'Not for any altruistic reason, I'm sure. What are you afraid I'll find out?'

She left an uncomfortably long pause before she answered, so long that Amos suspected he'd come close to the truth. 'You could say we have a vested interest in you remaining on the council. We need you. Someone's trying to kill you, Amos, can't you get that through your thick skull? And that wouldn't do us any good.'

'Quartermaster?'

She frowned. 'Why him?'

'He's the only one who stands to gain by my death. Did you know he's virtually told the standards board that I murdered Brenda, or at least that I benefit greatly from her will. Not that I do, I've turned it down. With me out of the way he thinks he'd be able to build whatever he likes here.'

'If we knew who it was we wouldn't have to follow you to protect you, would we?' she said with faultless female logic. 'But who killed Brenda may not be the important point. Why does he want you blamed? Why you, why not . . . say . . . the Reverend Whittaker?'

'I've just told you — to get me out of his way. And because no one would ever suspect the reverend, that's why. And anyway, how do you know someone's trying to frame me?' Amos didn't believe that either Jack or Harry, and certainly not Linklater, would have been talking to the gypsies.

'Why else would they trick you into going to some lonely spot where you wouldn't have an alibi? What other possible reason could there have been? Normally you'd also have been the unlikeliest suspect.'

After she'd gone Amos sat for a long time in the dark, wondering whom he could trust. How did she know he'd been lured to Long Cast Meadow? Had one of her people seen the lamb put in the river deliberately? Or was it the gypsies who'd lured him there themselves — which would explain why they'd wanted the tape — but not why they'd brought it back or why they'd wanted to kill Brenda in the first place, let alone frame him for it . . . except perhaps to get at him, just out of spite. Stop, enough. Wherever the truth lay he had to go along with them — for now.

★ ★ ★

The following morning, as he and Jack battled to move one of his flocks to a new pasture, Amos said nothing about his adventures of the previous night. Nor did Jack appear to be in any mood to discern that something untoward had happened. Instead he was bursting to know why Amos suddenly wanted the play to be in the paddock.

'You blighter, you knew I couldn't quiz you in front of Marion, you planned that purposely. Now she thinks it's a done deal.'

240

'Isn't it?'

'No, it damned well isn't. Not until you tell me why. Trouble is the whole blooming village seems to know already — and thinks it's a good idea.' Good old Jack, open as ever.

'What, even Mrs Squires?'

'Especially Mrs Squires, surprisingly — something to do with her entrances. She can make them much grander with the extra space — sail in with her entourage. Whereas in the pub yard she'd just have to squeeze her way on to the stage like everyone else.'

'Which means her old man is less likely to go bleating to the conservation people.'

'Exactly. Which is the bit that was worrying me. So now will you tell me why? Is it so we can say the moss was killed accidentally?'

Amos still hadn't thought his idea through completely — his reticence was therefore partly due to lack of precision. 'You remember last year, when you wanted to find out how the cows were escaping from the field up the Stratford Road, to find the loophole?' Jack nodded impatiently. 'And you rattled a feedbag from outside the fence?' Jack said nothing, still visibly displeased. 'Well look on this as rattling a feedbag.'

'You mean it's a feint — a trap of some kind?'

'Yes.'

241

'Which will show if there's rare moss there?'

'No.'

'Which will show if there's a dead body there?'

'You're getting warmer.'

'For God's sake, Amos, I've had enough of your brainteasers. I would really like to turn that paddock into garden. I will even agree to open it to the public every year in aid of your favourite charity. I am also happy to hold the play there this year — but what has any of this got to do with whatever you're up to?'

'I'm sorry, Jack, but I'm not sure I can tell you. Let's just say I'd like to play a hunch and that hunch entails staging the play in your paddock this year — if that's OK?' He knew he was being overbearing and hoped their friendship could take it. He wasn't playing games, this mattered very deeply to him, so deeply he couldn't explain it, not to himself and certainly not to Jack. All he needed now was a young lady.

★ ★ ★

It was a measure of how much his behaviour had changed that he took the trouble of manoeuvring the Land Rover into and down the narrow passageway which led to the car

242

park at the back of John Wilkinson's offices. A week ago he'd have left it on the double yellow line outside with the engine running.

Amos clumped up the worn stairs, rattling the banisters with the purchase he exerted on them. Thus alerted, John was waiting for him at the top.

'How do I get hold of a coroner's report, John?'

'The one on Brenda?'

'No, one from nineteen sixty-two.'

'What on earth would you want that for?' John's face creased in puzzlement — adopted a 'has the man gone completely barking' look.

'I want to know what they reckoned about Frank Squires's death.'

'Who was Frank Squires when he was at home?' Of course, John had been in Stratford only twenty-five years so wouldn't remember the case.

'He was Vernon Squires's father. It was Frank who founded the building firm. Hanged himself in one of his barns, as I recall.'

'Well, I can get you the coroner's report if you like. But you might get more from the library — the back numbers of the local paper. Do you want me to send my clerk round to see what he can find.'

'Do you trust him? I'd go myself, only

that'd be bound to set tongues wagging and I don't want this getting out. I just want to refresh my memory, that's all.'

'Implicitly. He knows more about the goings-on in this town than most people.'

'Could he do it today?' Amos was pushing it now.

'I expect so.' John gave a long-suffering sigh, 'What exactly are you up to this time, Amos?'

'It's vague — I'm not sure myself.' He was at a loss as to how he could explain to John the issue with the paddock. It was probably nothing . . . and he didn't want to talk about the rare moss in case John felt obliged to lecture him on exactly what Jack was and wasn't permitted to do in these circumstances. No, it was best left buried at present.

'I'd say you've got enough on your plate right now without going off on some tangent. I've been speaking to the standards board.' Amos sat down heavily in a creaky old carver. 'I was going to call you.' John paused, clearly unhappy. 'They've decided to review the new evidence because it is relevant to the case.' Amos leaned forward, face scowling, mouth open to remonstrate. 'No, don't say it, I know — but they have to look into it. I'm seeing them on Thursday to tell them the circumstances of Brenda's will, how she saw her bequest to you and why she did it.'

'They don't seriously think I leaned on Brenda, do they?'

'Let me give my evidence, then let's see.'

'Did you talk to Alec's accountant?'

'Yes, all under way. I must say it sounds as though Quartermaster has been playing dangerous games where money's concerned. Alec's people have been enormously helpful, even drafted some of the submission to the Financial Services Authority for us. We could send our findings to the Inland Revenue as well — just for good measure. Of course they can ignore it if they choose.' John's worried eyes belied his matter-of-fact tone. He went on:

'I haven't sent anything until I checked again with you. I mean this sounds good in my office here in broad daylight, but do you know what you're getting yourself into, Amos? It might seem like fair retaliation to us but . . . well, whistle-blowers rarely fare well, do they? You could be escalating things out of control.'

Amos interrupted him: 'And who was it cut the brake-pipe on the Land Rover and why? Maybe it'll be my windpipe next time, do you think? Ma said . . . ' Amos stopped, thinking it unwise to fuel John's concern any further even though he'd probably be dismissive about a gypsy's opinion; would bracket it with fortune-telling and tea-leaf reading in his legal lexicon.

'Believe me, John, I'm a lot more worried about it than you are — it's my neck remember. I even parked at the back today to lessen the chance of anyone seizing their opportunity to have another go at the motor. And now I put it away in Jack's shed at the Hathaway Arms overnight.'

John looked suitably surprised and impressed and then even more worried. 'And the police still have no idea who did it?'

'It's unfair to think they could. I wasn't a random victim, this was a personal attack. So I'm the one most likely to know who it was.'

'And do you?'

'It's Quartermaster, or someone in it with him. I know, I know. Why go looking for trouble? Because I've no intention of giving in and letting him do as he likes with our village. I will not be intimidated by the likes of him. He knows I can't be bribed or bullied so he's try-ing to frighten me. John, the only way to deal with people like him is to come out fighting.'

'Oh, so you think cutting the brake pipe was just trying to frighten you, 'not attempted murder, your honour', no, of course not.'

'Just take it as my way of being able to accept it, will you — or you *will* frighten me.

Quartermaster's not short of brains, he just thinks understanding people is irrelevant. He may have realized that we would discover his little financial irregularities sooner or later and has planned his attack to have just the effect it's having on you. He hopes we'll think reporting him not worth the trouble it would cause, that he can tell lies about me with impunity, safe in the knowledge I won't retaliate. Well, he's wrong.' Amos ran out of breath. 'Get on with it John, submit our complaint to the FSA.'

'Made your will, have you?'

A cold shiver ran through Amos. He respected John and it was evident that his solicitor wasn't joking.

★ ★ ★

On his way home Amos received a call from Linklater — causing him to divert to Long Cast Meadow. He'd been here every day since the 'Land Rover mishap' as he chose to call it, but never without first checking his brakes.

'Thought you might like to hear the news.' They stood companionably on the riverbank in the early evening sunshine, watching the fish jump.

'We've found Catherine Donaghue, or Arbuthnot as she calls herself — in Oxford.'

19

'That's not far away.'

'No, we actually traced her through the deed poll people. We had to break the news to her, she said she didn't know.'

'How'd she take it?' Amos asked.

'Coldly I'd say. But she was forthcoming enough. Said she'd been to see her mother that week.' Amos gasped in surprise. Linklater went on. 'Oh yes, she knew Brenda Smith was her mother — apparently she'd known since just before she left. It was one of the reasons she went the way she did, abruptly, and the main reason why she never contacted Brenda afterwards. She was furious with Brenda for not telling her before, though what difference would it have made I wonder?'

'Does she know who her father is?'

'I didn't ask her, why?'

'Grasping at straws, that's all.'

'I was much more interested in why the change of heart just before Brenda was killed — why go back after all these years? And what's the link between that and Brenda Smith's death?'

'And?'

'Well I told you she was forthcoming — candid even. It seems she'd found out, apparently from the previous solicitor, that Brenda had changed solicitors. We need to check that out because it's the only fishy piece in her story. For some reason she thought this was sinister and decided to have it out with her mother. Maybe the previous solicitor was a friend of Catherine's . . . maybe Brenda knew that so went to John Wilkinson when she decided to alter her will, to avoid news of her changes getting back to Catherine. Who knows? It should be easy enough to find out.'

'So what happened when Catherine went to see her? It must have been a huge shock. When did she go? Did Arbuthnot go too?'

'Hold your horses a minute and I'll tell you what I know. Catherine said she went alone to see Brenda — the night before her death. She parked at the pub and walked down. Ten o'clock at night she said, so it would have been dark. No one mentioned seeing her, that's for sure.' Linklater paused, getting back into the flow. 'She said they had a row and she left about thirty minutes later.'

'Some reunion; poor Brenda. It would be enough to give her a heart attack.'

'Yes. Of course I asked her what the row

was about and she said: 'Because she left me out of her will'. Which we know is true.'

'Neatly disposes of any motive Catherine might have had for killing her mother,' Amos said in case Linklater hadn't thought of that. 'Unless of course she went back and killed her out of spite. And what about Arbuthnot?'

'I was coming to him. Arbuthnot's in an open prison, North Sea Camp in Lincolnshire.'

'What?'

'Been there three months, got another eighteen to do. Went bankrupt and unable to pay his debts — ripped a few people off along the way.'

'Might explain why Brenda didn't want to leave Catherine her money — because she knew he'd get hold of it. Do you think Phyllis knows?'

'She may, some well-wisher will doubtless have told her!'

'Talking of prison sentences, any news about young Keith Squires and his hobby?'

'Well, it's a joint operation between our lot and the Cornish Constabulary — because the thefts were in the two areas, as I think you know already.' So Linklater had figured out that Amos must have followed Keith to Cornwall.

'Between you and me we've been holding

back, trying to trap the receiving ring. We know the cars from Keith's place were going abroad and that he wasn't their only supplier.'

'So when is it likely to come to court?' Amos asked.

'Oh, not for a while. Why?'

'It's just that I expect they'll want me to testify and I'd rather not have to do that over the next couple of weeks.'

'Expecting to be busy? I thought the lambing was over. By the way, how's that pig of yours? I hear you've been spreading tales that we're going to test everyone's DNA,' Linklater said shortly.

'We discussed it. I thought you'd agreed. Just because the police resource is scarce doesn't mean you won't start soon, does it? Just mention of it might spook the killer into revealing himself.'

'That's what worries me. The incident with your brakes happened soon after we took the DNA from Napoleon — which doubtless you broadcast even before we talked of deliberately using it as a trap. Maybe you've already frightened the killer into taking direct action; which means he'll probably try again. We haven't the manpower to give you twenty-four-hour protection, not with the life you lead.' Real concern came through in Linklater's voice.

Amos hadn't the heart to tell him what a good job the gypsies were doing in the absence of the police. 'That doesn't make sense though, does it? You'd expect whoever it is to leave the country or panic in some other way but why should your finding the killer's DNA on Napoleon make him want to kill me?'

'Presumably because you're the link. Unless the culprit turns out to be a complete stranger to Weston, we wouldn't know whose DNA it would be unusual to find on Napoleon, but you would. And don't forget they probably intended your failed brakes to look like an accident — to prevent us from making a connection between your untimely death and any DNA found on the pig.'

Amos breathed in. 'At least that makes me feel safer. It takes time and effort to set up a convincing mishap — they can't just jump me in the dark.'

They lapsed into silence, Amos wondering how to ask for Linklater's help on the subject of Frank Squires without explaining exactly why. A look at the police file might be enlightening — that's if they could find it from forty years ago. If he was right then he would need a way of persuading Linklater to get involved anyway. Can I ask you a favour, Stephen?'

'Something to do with Brenda Smith's murder?'

'Not that I know of, no. It's something that happened here over forty years ago, nineteen sixty-two to be precise. A man called Frank Squires — you know Vernon Squires the builder, his father — hanged himself in his barn and I just wondered if there was anything in the police file that might suggest why.'

'Can I ask why you want to know that — after all this time?'

'Just a thought I had, nothing more. Any chance you could have a look?'

'Have you any idea how much work that involves?'

'Well, obviously don't bother if it's a lot of trouble. I just thought if it was relatively easy — not like a murder inquiry is it — a suicide I mean? It's probably only one slim file, may not even be that much.'

'All right, all right, I'll see what I can do. But I'll tell you now, it's unlikely it'll have anything but the bare facts. They didn't go in for opinions when they had to bash everything out on temperamental typewriters.'

★　★　★

Sunshine spilled over the altar, through the chancel, and along the nave; as though the

Almighty had bowled a tin of primrose paint down the wicket of his church. It had rolled on unimpeded into the slips. Catching Amos as he passed by, the tumbling yellow wash drew him back to his unfinished conversation with the reverend.

Removing his cap he stepped through the doorway. Reverend Whittaker rose stiffly from the altar steps where he'd been kneeling and with a swish of black cassock came down the church to greet him. He looked at Amos questioningly.

Amos propped himself against the end of a pew crossing one foot over the other in front of him. The reverend mirrored his position against the opposite pew, arms folded lightly.

'The other night when you asked me if Brenda could have strangled herself . . . were you saying maybe she accidentally killed herself? I didn't quite follow you.'

'I'm not sure I do either, Amos.' Reverend Whittaker swung himself into the pew seat as if his legs could no longer support this conversation. 'I think what happened to Mother, and how I feel about it, still clouds my thoughts.'

'What did happen?' Amos asked softly.

The reverend took a deep wavering breath like the prelude to a sob. 'Oh, she took an overdose of sleeping tablets — by mistake I'm sure and . . . well, I was pleased for her. She's at rest now, with our Lord.' He stopped but forced himself to go on. 'I've never told anyone this before, but I do wonder if I left those tablets there on purpose. I knew she was apt to get muddled and when she couldn't remember whether she'd taken her tablet — she'd take another one. I knew that.' He wrung his hands, twisting his wrists over and back repeatedly.

'But you also wonder whether she did it knowingly — decided to end it all herself? And both would be wrong . . . in the eyes of the Church?'

'Yes.'

'So you think someone might have helped Brenda commit suicide? Or, finding that she had, altered the scene to make it look like murder — so no one would think ill of her . . . or start looking for whoever had helped her, which is a criminal offence of course.' Amos glanced at the reverend, wishing he hadn't put it so bluntly. 'Whoever that was, wanted the police to look for a murderer. Of course they should have faked a break-in or a robbery or something to give credence to that conclusion, but they were probably disturbed and had to leave quickly.'

'Something like that,' Reverend Whittaker whispered.

'What gives you that idea?' Just supposing Brenda had asked others beside himself to kill her if she did have Alzheimer's, he was sure she wouldn't have included Reverend Whittaker. On the other hand someone she might have spoken to may have felt the need to discuss the proposition with the reverend — to help them understand what they should do.

'Several reasons.' The reverend hesitated. 'But mainly because she was very upset the night before.' Another deep shuddering breath. 'You know when you asked me if I knew about her sister? Well yes, I did.'

'You knew Catherine was her daughter?'

The reverend looked up sharply. 'Yes, but I didn't know she'd told anyone else.'

'She didn't, I found out. Go on, why was Brenda upset?' Amos asked.

'Her daughter had been to visit her. But what should by rights have been a joyous reunion was a scene of bitter recrimination — at least on Catherine's part. It seems there was a big row. Catherine was extremely angry when Brenda told her she'd left her money to the village.'

Amos was careful not to admit he'd already been told this by the police — nevertheless it was useful corroboration. 'So you wouldn't have been surprised if Brenda, who thought she might have Alzheimer's anyway, was so distraught at finally seeing her daughter again in such a distressing way . . . she decided she'd had enough.'

'No, I wouldn't.'

'How do you know about this, Reverend?'

'Oh, Brenda rang me as soon as her daughter had left, she was in a dreadful state. I went straight round.'

'Well, I don't think she did — commit suicide, I mean. The police haven't mentioned it and I'm quite sure with today's post mortem methods they could tell if she'd tried to hang herself first and then someone had tried to cover that by strangling her.' A little of the tautness went from the reverend's face.

Amos went on: 'OK, someone could have strangled her at her request but I can't think who — and there are much easier ways.' He glanced at the reverend, realizing too late that he'd touched a sensitive nerve again.

'Have you told the police about her daughter's visit?' Amos knew the answer.

'No, not yet. But you're right. I must . . . now. You don't think she did it, do you?'

'I don't know, Reverend. I hope not. Matricide is a partic . . . ' Amos moved his weight back on to his feet, stamping them to get the circulation going again and cover up his gaffe. Smiling weakly, he walked awkwardly back out into the morning.

★   ★   ★

Amos's door was open as usual but Linklater tapped on it anyway.

'Isn't it too obvious, you coming to the cottage? Got my information, have you?'

'I thought once in all these weeks wouldn't be remarkable. In fact it might look odd if I didn't call on you now and then.'

Linklater perched himself on the arm of an easy chair. 'You'll remember the one part about Catherine Arbuthnot's story I wasn't happy with — about her calling on her mother because she'd got wind she might be rewriting her will? Somehow it didn't gel?' Amos nodded, interested. 'Well, contrary to your opinion of us, we have been following up all the loose ends, one of which was our friend Quartermaster and his alibi.'

At last, the police had realized he was right about Quartermaster: 'What's he got to do with Catherine and her mother?'

'Who knows, but that's where he went that afternoon. Oxford. To see Arbuthnot.'

20

'What? Well, well, who'd have thought there was a connection there?' Amos couldn't understand the ins and outs yet but he was sure this would help to tie Quartermaster to his crime. 'But Arbuthnot's in prison — unless he's been tagged and released? What's the connection between Quartermaster and Arbuthnot? Arbuthnot's old enough to be his father.'

'If you'll let me I'll tell you.' Linklater indicated Amos's armchair, which Amos obediently sat in.

'When we questioned Quartermaster again about that afternoon he said he'd been to see someone about some money they owed him. It was only when we insisted on a name or we'd arrest him on suspicion of murder that he told us who it was.'

'Why so shy?'

'That's what we wondered. But Arbuthnot's a shady character, which Quartermaster must realize, so maybe he didn't want us to know they were doing business together.'

'What sort of business?'

'That we don't know — except that it involved a debt.'

That would figure, thought Amos, since he's hard up. 'So how come they know one another?'

'The City's a small place. They both have political connections, they both have links with Weston Hathaway, and they both like the prospect of a quick buck. It wouldn't surprise me to find they had several mutual acquaintances.'

'So, while Arbuthnot's in jail, Quartermaster needs to collect his debt. So he phones Catherine and leans on her like the bully he is. Maybe he gives her forty-eight hours to come up with the money — saying he'll be up to collect it.'

'And she goes hotfoot to the one place she hasn't already tapped for money — her mother,' Linklater finished.

'Who was having none of it — hence the row.'

'So why lie about it — why not say that's what happened?' Linklater asked.

'Don't know.' Amos's mind was working fast. 'Unless she actually didn't know what was in the will, that Brenda didn't tell her . . . so she returned the following day to finish her mother off and inherit her mother's money — as she thought. And only afterwards discovered she'd been disinherited.'

'It's possible,' Linklater said. 'Except she has an alibi for the following day.' He held up his hand, 'And yes, we're checking it. Nor did anyone report seeing a strange female in the village that day.'

'I hate to even voice this possibility, Chief Inspector, but I do just have to ask,' Amos said. 'You are sure you've got the time of death right, aren't you? Is there any possibility that Brenda could in fact have been murdered the night before?'

'You mean could Catherine have killed her mother on her first visit?'

'Yes.' Except the reverend said he'd gone round after Catherine had left. 'Or later that same night?'

'No.'

Linklater paced the room for a minute while Amos digested the news about Catherine's connection with Quartermaster. Abruptly he stopped. 'You asked if I'd found the information you wanted on Frank Squires — well, I found the file.'

Amos wrenched his attention back from the contemplation of Catherine Arbuthnot murdering her mother. Linklater went on: 'But there's hardly any information in it.'

'Indulge an old man, Stephen, refresh my memory.'

'Were you here then?'

'Yes I was, but like most young men I wasn't paying too much attention to the case of a grumpy old bugger who'd hanged himself. It actually wasn't that uncommon. Maybe it was the wars that did it, most of the people his age had been through both and those who got gassed in the first lot were never the same again. I didn't like him and I liked his son Vernon even less, so no . . . I don't remember it very well.' He omitted to tell Linklater he'd been so wretched at the time that Frank Squires's death had hardly registered.

'He was found hanging from a beam in his barn by his son, Vernon. By then he'd been dead a few hours. He was known to have money worries and, as you mentioned, to suffer from bouts of depression — and drinking. He'd consumed a great deal of alcohol just prior to his death. The coroner brought in a verdict of suicide whilst under the influence.'

'Nothing else?'

'No.' Linklater stroked his chin. 'What's this about, Amos? What are you looking for?'

'I don't know, Stephen, I just have this very strong . . . call it a pointer. A strong feeling that I should look in this particular corner.' Linklater raised a sceptical eyebrow. 'OK, OK. There have been some strange goings on lately over Jack Ashley's paddock.' Linklater breathed out again. 'And without boring you with all the details I just had this idea it might have something to do with Squires senior's suicide.'

'But that was nowhere near Moon Cottage.'

'No, but he built Moon Cottage.'

'I didn't know that. You think maybe that's what put him in financial difficulties?'

The phone rang. 'Yes? Ah it's you . . . No, it's fine, fire away.' Amos signalled to Linklater to stay and then returned to his listening for a couple of minutes. 'That's all? Mmm, interesting remark though. Please thank him for me, won't you? Thanks again.'

Amos turned back to the chief inspector. 'I thought you might be interested in what the *Stratford Gazette* had to say on the occasion of Frank Squires's death. Apparently there's a short piece about it — since he owned a local building firm and was an old boy of the Grammar School, that's not surprising. It says most of what you already know, except for the editorial comment at the very end where it remarks on their having been: *two serious events in as many days, Frank Squires's suicide and the disappearance of Mary Walters, in the otherwise unremarkable village of Weston Hathaway.*'

'No talk of witchcraft?' Linklater asked. 'From what I can gather all unexplained occurrences around here are attributed to that particular phenomenon.'

'People always fear that which they can't explain — you and I are no different, Chief Inspector.'

'So what do you make of it?' Linklater yawned, making little attempt to conceal his waning enthusiasm for the subject of a forty-two-year-old suicide case.

'Me? Well I think it might help if we could see the police file on Mary Walters — don't you?'

21

Amos knew Quartermaster would make a move as soon as he guessed who'd reported him to the FSA. So he continued to stow the Land Rover in Jack's garage. Having supped the obligatory pint, it was getting on for half past nine and growing dark as he left the Hathaway Arms to walk the 300 yards to his cottage. Making his way slowly through the drinkers in the front garden he eventually extricated himself from their jocular banterings and set off down the lane.

Unheralded, an idling engine sprang to life and a large flashy sports car thundered up the road towards him. The vehicle was coming straight at him, he could sense the malice emanating from the roaring ton of metal. Unable to move, he remained nailed to the ground, mesmerized; his only conscious thought being for Napoleon, who, thank God, was nowhere to be seen.

With a sickening scream as the road peeled the skin off its tyres, the car lurched at the last moment, ramming its front offside wing into a hawthorn hedge, clawing and bouncing its way to a halt. Amos still hadn't moved but now he snatched a breath.

The driver emerged physically unscathed, a look of undiluted hatred etched into his puffy face. He crossed the road to Amos, fists clenched ready. 'What the hell do you think you're playing at, Cotswold?' Cyril Quartermaster was pink with rage, like a spoilt child singularly unprepared for being treated the way he treated others. 'How dare you pry into my private affairs, how dare you!'

'Only following your example, Quartermaster.'

'My affairs are none of your bloody business. You're jealous, that's your trouble. Hate to see someone else making good through their own hard work.'

In other circumstances — if this hadn't been the man who'd driven his aunt to an early grave and might well have murdered Brenda Smith — Amos would have laughed. 'I knew your father, remember. What you've inherited was down to his and your aunt's efforts, not yours.' He could hear the wise counsel of John Wilkinson in his head as he said it but he couldn't help it. He should have kept quiet, let Quartermaster get it out of his system. Now he'd made things worse by challenging him.

Quartermaster raised an arm to strike but halted it in mid air as the crowd from the pub emerged into the lane. 'You're a money-grubbing shifty-eyed bloody yokel who thinks he can get rich by threatening old ladies and bullying people. Don't think I don't know what you've been up to. You're the most twisted bloody councillor I've ever come across and I'm going to make damned sure you suffer for this. You mark my words. I'll get you when you haven't got your cronies with you!' He stopped short of actually spitting at Amos but the bile seeped from his lips.

Amos's mind was whirling. Should he accuse Quartermaster of Brenda's murder here and now? Did he have any evidence?

Quartermaster strode back to his car, reversed it violently, and roared back down the road in a shower of gravel; the bent metalwork sorry testament to his unbridled rage. Amos apprehensively watched him go, wishing he'd been able to stop him and knowing he'd exacerbated things by piercing the man's self-delusion. Who else was he going to hurt?

Jack had arrived towards the end of Quartermaster's tirade. 'It wasn't until the garden suddenly emptied that I realized something was up!' he said, breathless from hurrying. 'I'll walk down with you, just in case.'

'I'll be fine, Jack. Don't worry, he's not

267

going to try anything tonight — not with all these witnesses.' But beneath the sangfroid, Amos felt shaken.

'I didn't even know he was in the village. Shouldn't we tell the police?'

'Tell them what? That Quartermaster can't drive. That he lost his temper?'

'That he threatened you.'

'Almost goes with the territory, wouldn't you say? I'm not going to be popular with everybody, am I? Wouldn't be doing my job if I were.'

22

Napoleon often stayed out all night in the summer — usually because he'd worn himself out gorging on someone's compost heap then snoozed where he was, too bloated to make it home. But when he wasn't there first thing in the morning, demanding his breakfast, it was odd. Napoleon always knew when food would be on offer and Amos was a creature of habit. He'd opened the back door half an hour ago, when he first got up, but still no sign of the pig.

He whistled. That usually bore results after about five minutes — but not today. Amos felt uneasy. It was nearly six o'clock, the sun was shining brilliantly, the birds were still in full morning song. What sounded like a bird scarer boomed every few minutes in the distance, one of Alan's probably. Everything appeared normal except . . . no Napoleon.

Annoyed, because he had a lot to do today, Amos set off to look for him. Starting with the back lane he walked briskly, calling as he went, until he came out into Alan's barley field. He scanned the crop and the hedgerows and was just about to turn and head back when he heard a distant grunt — over on the far side. Was that something black near the copse?

Full of concern as to what might have happened to the old boy, Amos hurried as best he could around the perimeter of the field, calling all the time. He could see him now, twisting, grunting, obviously trying to respond but failing. Was he injured?

The pig was up on his feet all right. From a distance, all four legs seemed OK but he was straining against something. Oh no, not a trap. Although Amos couldn't see his feet the old boy didn't look to be in pain. Then he saw it — a rope anchoring Napoleon to a tree on the edge of the small wood.

'What the blazes?'

Amos couldn't believe his eyes. The pig looked none the worse for his ordeal, thank goodness, but who would deliberately tie him up out here? He'd tan their backsides for them when he caught them, that was for sure. He fondled Napoleon's snout and backed him up to the tree to slacken the rope, make it easier to untie. As he bent over the pig a shot rang out.

Amos reeled backwards, his ear stinging. Napoleon shrieked and danced on his rope, a tethered target. Wood pigeons rose, scream-ing, into the air, crashing through the upper canopy in their bid to escape and a chestnut streak of fox tore out from the trees and hared along the boundary. Amos threw himself to the ground and lay there panting, wondering what would happen next.

Peace descended on the wood. Amos felt his ear, it was still there but pouring blood. Cautiously he raised himself to a sitting position the better to examine Napoleon, who was shaking and whimpering. If Amos could have knelt properly with his bad knees, he'd have prayed for the first time since Christmas.

'What's the problem, Nap old boy? What is it then?' Like master like pig — shot had grazed the pig's ear too. 'Does it hurt anywhere else?' He ran his hand over Napoleon's considerable girth but received no warning grunts or signs of other damage.

Try as he might he couldn't think this an accident. A warning maybe, rather than a direct attempt on his life? Yes, he could believe that, otherwise why had the gunman stopped?

From the other side of the copse he heard shouts. Amos kept very quiet and very still, wishing he had a gag for Napoleon. Only when the voices grew closer did he recognize the guttural tones and realize they were calling to him. He struggled to stand, one hand clamped to his ear to staunch the sticky flow, the other using Napoleon, still tied to his tree, as a prop.

They burst through the greenery at a run. Jem brandishing a twelve-bore, Aaron his trusty cudgel. Amos wanted to know whether the gun had been fired . . . but then, they could have been out after pigeons.

'You don't go until six-fifteen, Mr Cotswold. You never go before then.' Amos could tell he wanted to add *What do you think you're playing at, leaving home without our permission.* As usual with this pair, reciprocal aggression would be the best policy.

'So where were you when I needed you?'

Noticing his ear Jem asked: 'You OK?'

'Napoleon's worse.' He indicated the pig. 'Did you see who was shooting?'

'No, nothing. But we were on the road, on our way to you when we heard the shot. Somehow it didn't sound like someone shooting pigeons, so we decided to come across country to investigate and that's when we heard the shrieking. Whoever it was had plenty of time to escape over the next field when he heard our fourtrack.'

'Is Naomi at home?'

Jem showed surprise at the abrupt change of subject until he followed Amos's gaze to the injured pig. 'Yeah, back at the camp. Hang on a minute. Aaron . . . ' Tossed the keys, his minder fetched their vehicle and transported them all to Broad Farthing.

* * *

'Whatever's happened now?' Ma came bustling out of her wagon, already dressed even at this hour. Taking one look at Amos and judging his condition able to wait for a minute she attacked Jem.

'I thought I told you to watch him! He could've been killed!' Amos felt like some precious but unloved commodity. He consoled himself with the thought that it was the shock talking.

'Don't blame the lad, Ma, it was my fault. I have this notion I can just go wandering anywhere I like, when I like. Silly, isn't it? We came to see if Naomi could . . . ' He hadn't finished the sentence before the girl magically appeared, like a genie ahead of her summons. She went straight to Napoleon, who whimpered for sympathy.

Ma didn't say much, just cooked breakfast and sat looking at him thoughtfully while he ate it. Amos said even less, grateful for the lack of questions while he tried to figure out what to do . . . and how much to say.

'It wasn't a coincidence, was it?'

'I've got to catch him red-handed, Ma. I

should have at least seen him instead of taking cover as I did.' Amos still couldn't credit that someone, Quartermaster or his hireling, was seriously trying to kill him . . . in broad daylight, in Weston Hathaway. And through not taking the threat seriously he'd not only endangered his own life but put Napoleon at risk too, a dumb animal.

After last night and the brake-tampering episode he didn't want to think about Quartermaster; refused to succumb to the welling fear he knew would be there if he let it. He'd just had a rough few days, that was all. He preferred to distract himself with a much less dangerous problem — Jack's paddock. Reluctant to reveal too much of his hand, he said, 'Meanwhile I need your help with something else . . . or rather, I need Naomi's. I want her to do some acting for me. All the village girls are busy in the play and I need a young woman just to help me for five minutes that night.' Conscious of the gypsies' wariness of the villagers he added hurriedly: 'She won't have to talk to anyone else, won't have to say any lines and she won't be in any danger. Jem can come as well if he likes.'

'Try stopping him. He's sticking to you like glue until this Quartermaster business is finished.'

'I should be flattered, Ma, I know, but something tells me you've an ulterior motive.'

'What's this thing in aid of that you want Naomi to do?'

'That would spoil the surprise, Ma, now wouldn't it. There's just one other thing . . . '

She waited.

'It would help if Naomi were dressed as though it were the late fifties or early sixties . . . you know, hairstyle and dress.' He stopped, embarrassed. 'You'll have much more idea about that than me.' He improvised hurriedly. 'The play's being done in that sort of costume this year. She needs to blend in.' What else could he say, it sounded so bizarre?

'The play starts at seven-thirty so everyone will be in their seats by then. If she comes to my cottage at eight she won't run into anyone.'

★ ★ ★

At his request the gypsies dropped Amos and Napoleon at Alan Tregorran's. Amos didn't mention the morning's events, though out of sheer curiosity and the desperate hope that there might still be an innocent explanation he asked: 'Were you or your sons out shooting pigeons this morning?'

'No, why?'

'Oh, I could have sworn I heard some shots coming from your copse.'

'Funny you should say that. Marge said she thought she heard something over that way. They're supposed to ask me but some of 'em just do as they please these days. It'll be that lot from Broad Farthing, I'll be bound.' He paused. 'What happened to your ear?'

Amos touched his sore ear and winced. 'Alan, I wonder if you could lend me some ammunition, your gun takes the same as mine.' He might refuse to admit he was scared but it would be foolish to be totally unprepared and he hadn't time to go shopping. A well-timed shot in the air might be sufficient to deter a would-be assassin.

23

John Wilkinson stood with his back to the fireplace, looking deeply troubled. He'd clearly come on a mission — which Amos must resist. He had to convince John he was right to fight — so he told John about Quartermaster's attempt to run over him, and this morning's shooting.

'This is exactly what I feared, Amos. I did warn you. This man is desperate and you're standing in his way. When does his application come in front of the committee again?'

'This week — day after tomorrow.'

'I'm not sure when he's at his most dangerous — now, when these attacks might be warnings to tell you to back off, or if the committee decision goes against him, when he'll come looking for revenge.'

'You make it sound like a third-rate Western.'

'You may well joke but this is no laughing matter, Amos. For heaven's sake, man, it's only a few houses, it's not worth dying for. There, I've said it, that's what I think.'

How to answer that? John was concerned for his safety, so was he! But he couldn't let

Quartermaster do as he liked simply because he was the more ruthless. 'Put like that I'd agree with you but it's not that simple, is it, John?'

'No, because you're pig-headed and you hate losing. Isn't that what this is about now? You don't want to be the one to back down, you want the village to expand in the way you prefer. And you don't want to give in, as you see it, to a bully.' John would have made a good barrister, he could make things sound so plausible when he wanted to — even when they weren't true.

'Do you think I haven't accused myself of all those things? Do you think I find it amusing to know I was driving a car whose brakes were useless, to be almost mowed down, to be shot at . . . especially when I can't run away?' For the first time he voiced his loathing of his own incapacity, his physical weakness. More calmly he said, 'I know what you're trying to do, John, and I thank you for it, but I can't do anything else.'

'Not even if it costs you your career as a councillor?' The cruellest barb saved for last.

'What?'

'The standards board, they're very concerned. Come on, it is unusual for two elderly ladies to leave a councillor what are regarded as significant legacies, within weeks of one

278

another.' Looking at Amos's furious scowl Wilkinson went on. 'Yes, yes, I told them you turned it down. I even told them that it was Nellie's legacy that had given Brenda the idea. They've never seen it before because there aren't many councillors like you. I told them that too. But they judge by the norm, what else can they do?'

'So Quartermaster wins anyway.'

'Not entirely, no. You see, if you were to drop this campaign against his application then he might agree to drop his complaint to the standards board.'

Anyone but John and he'd have shown them the door for that. He took a deep breath. 'John, I'm not giving up now. I cannot stand idly by and let Quartermaster ruin this village — and that's what fifty houses would do, swamp us. If I drop the campaign, Weston Hathaway will be changed for ever. Do you want that? And if the standards board choose to believe that lying cheating scum rather than me . . . well I can't help that. I know I haven't done anything wrong.' Even as he said it he thought, neither had Brenda and look what happened to her.

'What about withdrawing the report to the FSA? You don't need to antagonize him any further.'

'Absolutely not, John. Look, I haven't got

time to argue with you. I hear you but I have no choice.' If only he had, could back down as John suggested. For the first time Amos felt the full import of what he was doing. Up until now he'd chosen not to think too hard about it or had told himself he could always change tack later; now, while he'd been explaining to John, he realized he couldn't. He had to put a stop to this, and the only way was to get Quartermaster. He had the blackest feeling of signing his own death warrant.

Amos pushed the subject aside, he had other work to do before the play tomorrow night — had to see Stephen Linklater; get him organized.

★ ★ ★

'Did you find the file on Mary Walters?'

'I see you've had an accident.'

Amos put a hand up to his ear self-consciously. 'Occupational hazard, I don't notice most of the time.'

'You noticed the other night though. I hear Quartermaster tried to run you down. Why didn't you call me?'

'What could you have done?'

'We're going to charge him with dangerous driving — there were enough witnesses and they're queuing up to testify for you.'

280

Amos remembered John Wilkinson's warning about not antagonizing Quartermaster any more than was necessary but he said nothing. The man had been driving dangerously, why should Amos deny it?

To escape the rain, they were sitting in Amos's Land Rover outside the council offices in Stratford; Amos had spread a newspaper on the passenger seat as a concession.

'I hope this clears up for tomorrow night, it's supposed to,' Amos said, frowning at the weather.

'Oh yes, the play.'

'Did you find the file?'

'Yes, I did,' Linklater swivelled in his seat to look at Amos. 'Stunning girl, wasn't she? You must have known her.'

Amos was prepared for this. 'Yes, everybody thought so.'

'So what was all this about her old man beating her?'

'Stubbs was her stepfather, and she was a clever, wilful girl who'd been used to having her own way before he came on the scene. Now you stop beating around the bush and tell me what the file says.'

'Most of it's about Stubbs — statements from the neighbours, from his employers, that sort of thing — nobody liked him. Then

281

there's a lot about the search for the body. The police were convinced it was him but they couldn't find sufficient evidence to make a charge stick. They dug up his garden and his two allotment holdings.'

'I know, even his asparagus beds. Have you any idea how many years it takes to establish an asparagus bed?'

Linklater raised his head at this outburst. 'You don't think he did it?'

'What do you make of that comment in the *Stratford Gazette* about her disappearance and Frank Squires's suicide being in the same fortnight, in the same village?' Amos asked.

'If I had your sort of country logic I'd probably be looking for the third thing.' Linklater chuckled. They fell silent and watched the rain for a few minutes.

'I told you there'd been strange things happening about Jack's paddock behind Moon Cottage. It all started when Jack applied to change its use — he wants to turn it into a garden,' Amos explained.

'Where you're going to hold the play, I gather.'

'Yes, tomorrow. Anyway, Vernon Squires has kicked up an enormous fuss about it — out of all proportion, you'd think. He's even told the conservation people there's a rare moss there which must be protected. I ask you.'

'So?'

'So when Jack and I went to try and find this rare moss, Napoleon dug up an old bracelet, one of those identity bracelets common in the early sixties, with the name 'Mary' on it.'

'Coincidence? What's the paddock got to do with Squires?' Then Linklater remembered. 'Oh yes, Frank Squires built Moon Cottage, didn't he?'

'In nineteen sixty-two.'

'I see.' Linklater was quiet for a minute or two. 'I think we'd better have a chat with Vernon Squires. These old cases are never closed and if he knows something that can help us establish what happened — '

'I was hoping you'd say that,' Amos said, adding quickly: 'Tell you what — why don't you do it after the play tomorrow. Better still, come to the paddock about nine o'clock . . . and, er . . . bring your sergeant, will you?'

'What exactly are you up to, Amos?' Amos didn't answer. 'And can I have that bracelet?'

'I was afraid you'd ask that. I can't find it. I'm sure it'll turn up, probably fallen out in the truck here somewhere. Jack can verify what we found, he saw it too.' Amos leaned first one side of the steering wheel, then the other, peering intently amongst the assorted debris on the floor, pretending to search.

24

If all went to plan, tonight would tell
— would finally clear up the mystery of Jack's
paddock. For Jack's sake, and his own, he
hoped to frighten an explanation out of
Vernon Squires. Why was he making this fuss?
And what was Mary's bracelet doing here?
Amos sat on a stool at the paddock entrance,
Napoleon at his feet. Not that Vernon Squires
arrived from that direction. As Marion had
prophesied earlier to Amos, he drove his wife
down to avoid her hair getting windswept,
and came in the back way from the
temporary car park in Alan's field. Just as
well, judging by his last encounter with
Napoleon . . . but Amos had counted on
hearing Irene arrive.

He wasn't disappointed. Her imperious
tones carried across to him as she swept into
the cottage. The queen had arrived. Careful
to take Napoleon with him, Amos left his post
and pointedly traversed the length of the
straw-bale seats on the left-hand side of the
paddock, chatting to the picnickers. He had
banked on Squires sitting near the front to
get a good view, and by this method ensured

he would sit to the right of the stage, near the willows.

At just after 7.30 the players mounted the improvised platform and a hush fell on the crowd. Unobtrusively Amos strolled slowly back up the lane towards the road.

At eight o'clock Naomi and Jem tapped on the door. She looked wonderful in a pink checked dress, but it was her hair that stunned Amos — dark and straight to her shoulders with the ends flicked out, a long fringe at the forehead.

'Will I do?' She gave a nervous twirl.

Speechless, Amos nodded and gestured for them to come in while he explained what he wanted them to do, and waited for dusk to fall.

Amos gathered that the interval would run from 8.45 to just after nine, probably ten past by the time the audience had settled down again. The play would re-open with the second part of Act III where Puck gives Oberon a progress report on their trick on Titania: '*My mistress with a monster is in love.*'

By about half past nine they would be starting on Act IV, one of Irene Squires's big scenes where she falls in love with Bottom complete with his ass's head — ironically symbolic of the misleading nature of outward

285

appearances, Amos thought. Vernon would be paying attention and the light would be fading.

On such a still night the sound of 200 voices, suddenly released, easily carried as far as Amos's cottage, signalling the beginning of the break. A minute or two later Stephen Linklater drew up, accompanied by both a detective sergeant and a detective constable. 'Shakespeare fans,' Linklater explained.

Jem had already left to take up his position in Alan's car park and Naomi remained in the kitchen until the last minute. Amos hadn't enquired where Aaron was but he suspected not far away.

'So are we going to catch the second half then?' The detective sergeant was without Linklater's patience. They waited for the hubbub to subside gradually into silence again and then the three policemen set out for the paddock. Amos and Naomi followed a few minutes later.

All eyes were on the makeshift stage, the lighting for which served to throw the rest of the auditorium into even greater shadow. Amos had suggested the sergeant might like to position himself just beyond the trees, the burly constable could remain at the lane entrance and Linklater and he would shelter beneath the willow fronds — as close as possible to Squires.

Their timing was perfect. As they reached their respective positions, the third act was coming to an end. Naomi started to tremble and Amos put his arm around her.

'Are you cold sweetheart?'

'No, just nervous. There's something about this place.'

'No one's going to hurt you, don't worry,' he whispered.

As Act IV began, Titania and her entourage made a grand entrance from the far side of the stage. Squires was watching carefully. As Amos had hoped, the man occupied a bale on his own, few people were that friendly with him and there was no sign of either of the sons. Amos gave Naomi a little push. At the same moment he threw a clod of earth up into the willow branches to draw Squires's attention from the stage towards the advancing girl.

Concentrating on his wife's scene, Squires glanced momentarily to his right, returned his gaze to the stage, then appeared compelled to look again at the spectre advancing towards him. Even seen through the gloom the changing expressions on his face were worthy of several Oscars — had he been acting.

Naomi was halfway towards him, looking directly at him — gliding across the turf soundlessly, unsmiling. The scream started as she approached to sit beside him on the bale. His mouth opened and out came a spine-chilling primeval sound. Squires leapt from his seat and blundered backwards, scattering other people's picnic things, stumbling blindly, gasping to escape.

Outclassed by the drama unfolding among the audience the action on the stage stopped. Briefed by Amos earlier, the lighting man swung the farthest arc light on to Squires as, still shrieking, he fled into the arms of the constable stationed for the purpose at the paddock entrance. Before hobbling after Linklater and the sergeant, Amos stayed to see Jem vault the fence behind the stage and hurry towards Naomi.

Squires was thrashing about, red-eyed, shouting. As soon as he saw Amos he pointed wildly, held back by two policemen:

'OK, he did it. It was him.'

'Who did what?' Linklater asked.

'My father — killed Mary Walters.'

★ ★ ★

The after-play party was held in Moon Cottage. Cast, playgoers and most of the imported choir from Stratford were squeezed into the tiny lounge, spilling out on to the

288

small patio and the cottage garden.

When most of the people had dispersed, and they could talk privately, Marion said peevishly: 'If it hadn't been for the spotlight some people might not have noticed anything.'

'I was afraid he'd get away amongst all those people and I thought what he said in that state would be the truth,' Amos explained. Marion was looking at him strangely but he couldn't help it. He was still in shock, couldn't understand it, not yet. After all this time, to find that . . .

'What if he'd had a heart attack?' countered Marion. Jack and Amos shrugged simultaneously.

Jack took Amos aside: 'So what do you make of what he said, that his father killed Mary Walters?'

'The local paper must have been right,' Amos said, 'her disappearance and his father's death were connected.' Was that why Frank committed suicide?

Jack ran his hands through his hair. 'Oh no, I don't think Marion can take this Amos — not a dead body in the garden. Come to that I'm not sure I can either. Not to mention what it'll do to the value of the house. We'll never be able to sell it after this.'

'Slow down, slow down. Who knows what it all means?'

'But you must have known. Otherwise why did you think he'd react to that young girl the way he did. By the way, who is she?'

'Oh, she comes from another village. All our youngsters were tied up in the play if you remember.'

'So explain. How did you know he'd react like that.'

'I didn't, not exactly.' Amos sat down on the low patio wall and gazed out across the dark paddock. 'For weeks we'd been trying to catch a stray Alsatian which had been preying on the lambs up by the Stratford Road. So two other chaps and I took it in shifts to lie in wait for it. The night Mary Walters disappeared the early shift man had gone home and I arrived too late.' He sighed. 'By the time I'd put the injured ewe out of her misery and buried her, it was gone midnight. I drove home past here, nearly cannoned into Frank Squires's vehicle which was parked outside and spotted him running down the lane.'

'Did you tell the police that — at the time, I mean?'

'Of course not.' Catching sight of Jack's quizzical expression he went on, 'Don't look like that. It was so commonplace it never occurred to me — he'd been building the place for months. His car was always outside

290

during the day. I thought nothing of it.'

'Not even when they couldn't find her?'

'Why should I associate Mary Walters's disappearance with Moon Cottage? The police came asking if anybody'd seen anything unusual — answer, no, I hadn't. Anyway they were convinced her old man had done it. I didn't like him.'

'But what about when Frank Squires topped himself.'

'I didn't connect the two, neither did anyone else that I know of . . . except some smartass on the *Gazette* it turns out.' Again, Amos omitted to say he'd barely noticed the suicide at the time. 'Us youngsters had neither the time nor the money to go buying papers and anyway, maybe it takes an outsider to spot the obvious. Old man Squires had always been a miserable old bugger — we thought he was better off out of it.'

'So when did you . . . ?' Jack didn't have to finish.

'When Napoleon dug up that bracelet.'

'Where is it, by the way? Linklater asked me, said you'd lost it.'

'That was the first time I connected Mary's disappearance with Frank Squires. Even then it was mainly because Vernon was making such a fuss about your paddock. Rare moss indeed — he's hardly the environmentalist's friend now, is he? And if he simply wanted to stop you building on it why didn't he suggest there were Roman remains here?'

'Because that would have entailed an archaeological dig?'

'Precisely.'

'So what'll happen do you think?' Jack stopped looming over Amos and sat down beside him, sipping his Scotch. The sounds of Marion and Lindsay clearing up, drifted out from the cottage behind them.

'Depends what Vernon has to say, I imagine. It may be that he only suspects his father. He could even say we planted the bracelet. I don't know. It's not much to go on.'

'But his reaction tonight was charged, like he'd had an electric shock. What made you think to flush him out like that?'

'Well he was hardly going to open up otherwise, was he? Not to us and not to the police. Stands to reason, otherwise he'd have come forward years ago with his suspicions. It was your application to change the use which resurrected it all — but he didn't go to the police then either. Instead he comes up with all sorts of spurious reasons why you shouldn't be allowed to dig up the paddock.'

'And that's why you were so reluctant to go to the police when we found the bracelet

— because you thought he'd deny all knowledge?'

'Mmm. I knew we had to really frighten him somehow — and I thought tonight might be our opportunity.'

★ ★ ★

Stephen Linklater rang Amos's cottage about midnight. 'How did you know?'

'You first.'

'Well, by the time we got him down to the station his wife had appeared and demanded we send for his solicitor — which seemed a bit over the top seeing as how we only wanted to ask him a few questions. Anyway when the solicitor finally arrived, our friend Squires had had time to cool down. Mind you, he's still shaken.

'Dinsdale, the detective constable who apprehended Squires by the entrance, said the man was petrified. He'd stopped screaming but was gibbering. Kept saying: 'Why is she doing this?''

'So what's he said since?'

'Not much really. Reckons he suddenly had some sort of fit — wait for it — reckons you slipped something in his drink in the interval.'

'But I wasn't even there!'

'I know, you were with me. He's obviously

trying to throw enough confusion around to cover up what happened. We questioned him about Mary Walters and asked him why he thought his father had killed her — which is what he said at the gate, if you remember.' Linklater took a breath. How could Amos forget.

'After he'd conferred with his lawyer he said that the young girl who approached him tonight was dressed as though she'd come from that era. He said it was simply that association, together with his 'drugged, hallucinatory state' which had made him think of Mary Walters at that moment.'

'And do you believe him?'

'We asked him all the usual questions about how well he'd known Mary Walters. He said not very well. Then we asked him again why he'd said his father had killed her. That caused another conference with the lawyer after which Squires said he didn't recollect saying that at all.'

'But we all heard him.'

'Yes, I know. But since you haven't told me what you know I could hardly take it any further tonight. As it was, I was in danger of an entrapment charge — the chief superintendent's in the same Masonic lodge as Squires.'

Amos took a deep breath. 'Frank Squires's

truck was parked outside Moon Cottage the night Mary Walters disappeared and I caught sight of Frank in the lane. He was often there, I thought nothing of it.'

'You never associated Frank with Mary's disappearance?'

'No, never. Not until Vernon started being so damned peculiar about the change of use application — and then of course we found the bracelet.'

'Well, it looks as though Jack's going to get his place dug over at police expense.'

'Do you have to? I mean, it's not very nice for Jack and Marion, is it?'

'Thanks to you, Amos, we are on the verge of solving a forty-year-old crime and now you say, 'Do we have to?'.'

'But Frank Squires is long gone — what good will it do digging up the past?' Amos asked.

'Not quite the point, is it?'

Amos tried again. 'Why didn't Vernon come to you with his suspicions — and why is he denying them again now?'

'Family honour — something like that, I imagine.'

'Or there really is nothing in this. Shouldn't you wait, at least ask him again when he's calmed down — explain it won't be any reflection on him. Then you could be more certain before you go causing people further upset — and spending the taxpayer's money.' Amos felt wretched. Instead of helping Jack as he'd intended, his meddling was going to cause more trouble. Unlikely to be content with digging up just the paddock, there'd be police trampling all over Marion's prized house and garden.

25

Alec FitzSimmons was waiting for him on the steps of County Hall. 'I saw your wagon so I guessed where you'd be coming. Saves me a phone call.' Alec was beaming.

'You look pleased. What's happened?'

'Bengy Pargitter just phoned, has those pudgy fingers of his in all sorts of police pies, has Bengy. Models himself on the Scarlet Pimpernel, you know — complete idiot to the untrained eye but underneath . . . ' They went into the marble entrance hall and stood to one side, out of the way of the constant comings and goings. 'Cyril Quartermaster was arrested for fraud last night.'

'Arrested . . . for fraud!' Amos couldn't believe it. 'Are you sure?'

'Oh, positive. They're keeping it quiet until they've got hold of all his documents and computer files and the like. They'll have been into Hunter's by now I expect.'

'But someone would've . . . Oh of course, it was the play last night and the whole village was busy watching that. They couldn't have picked a better time to go unnoticed. What sort of fraud? Was it what we thought? Was this because of what we sent to the FSA?'

'Yes, at least partly. It sounds big. It'll be in the nationals I'm sure as soon as they release it to the press. Apparently he's not in it alone.'

'They won't be able to keep him for long though, will they?' Amos was wondering how this might affect this evening's planning committee meeting and the decision on Quartermaster's planning application.

'Not without charging him, no . . . but Bengy reckoned they'd charge them today.'

'He'll get bail?'

'Apparently not. I asked that — wondering how he might react to you.'

Amos felt immensely relieved. 'Surely it wasn't just what we said to the FSA?'

'I shouldn't think so. Looks as though they've had him in their sights for some time — but I expect every bit of evidence helps.'

'I can't get over it. It's almost too good to be true, isn't it? What'll happen to his planning application, I wonder?'

'You'll have more idea about that than me. Explains why he was so determined — he obviously needed those expensive house sales to buy his way out of trouble. Without them he's been caught.'

★ ★ ★

298

'Amos . . . Amos!' The voice came from behind him as he walked across the road to the district council offices. Turning he saw Linklater striding to catch up with him. 'Glad I caught you — something's happened.'

'Vernon Squires has remembered what his daddy did?'

'No, I haven't seen him yet. I've just had a call from Scotland Yard — the Fraud Squad. They've arrested your friend Cyril Quartermaster.'

'Yes, I know. Good, isn't it.' Amos grinned.

Linklater stopped, hands on hips. 'How do you know?'

'Will they keep him in, do you think?'

'I'm glad you don't know everything. The Yard have opposed bail. We often do in fraud cases because we're afraid these characters will skip the country and live off the funds they've salted away offshore. But once I found out, we added the dangerous driving charge . . . and other suspicions. So, they'll keep him in a remand prison for the moment.'

'Thank you.' Amos meant it. With Quartermaster behind bars he felt considerably safer — could stop jumping at shadows.

'There's more.'

Amos sat down on the low wall outside the council offices.

'Remember I said Arbuthnot was in an open prison in Lincolnshire?' Amos nodded. 'Well, they let them out sometimes, to do useful work in the community or for various other reasons. It's a day release — they're not considered a threat to public safety, you see.'

'Don't tell me he's escaped.'

'No, but he was out the day Brenda was murdered — and, it seems, unaccounted for for most of the day. We're still trying to pin down exactly what happened. The warders have all clammed up because someone there's going to get the blame. He probably told them his wife was in a highly distressed state and they took pity on him — it'll be something like that.'

'Well I'll be . . . So you think he did it?'

'Certainly has a motive. As we said before, perhaps Quartermaster gave Catherine an ultimatum, say forty-eight hours to get the money. She goes to see Brenda, who refuses to give her any. So she rings Arbuthnot in jail who decides — and here we assume they didn't know Catherine had been disinherited — that one way out is for him to go and threaten Brenda . . . or murder her for the money.' Linklater explained.

'But why didn't anyone see him? I don't think people were very vigilant that day.' Amos said it quietly, aware for the first time that no one had mentioned seeing Jack Ashley visit Brenda's either. Then another problem occured to him. 'If Quartermaster's alibi is that he was with Catherine at the time Brenda was killed . . . but Arbuthnot did it . . . '

'You mean Arbuthnot left it a bit late. Didn't have much choice, I expect. Quartermaster was going to have to wait for his money anyway, but perhaps Arbuthnot needed to be able to show it would be there, in Brenda's will.'

'If that is the case it's not surprising Quartermaster was so put out when he found out what the will contained. He virtually told the standards board *I'd* murdered Brenda. Have you spoken to Arbuthnot?'

'On my way up there now — I caught sight of you as I left the police station.' Amos followed Linklater's glance down the road to the police car with its patient driver propped against the door, waiting. 'But it means I won't have time to come over and question Vernon Squires today after all.'

'I don't suppose there's any hurry about that. Let's just hope friend Arbuthnot hasn't decided to go walkabout today, too!'

For a few minutes after Linklater had left Amos remained where he was on the wall, cogitating. So it looked as though Quartermaster hadn't killed Brenda after all — but if

Linklater's theory was right, he had been the cause of her death.

So far today he'd heard of Quatermaster's arrest and the likelihood that it was Gordon Arbuthnot who'd killed Brenda — for her money. What was the third thing going to be?

★ ★ ★

Amos made it back from the planning meeting to the Hathaway Arms before closing time.

He couldn't prevent the chuckle escaping as he lifted the latch into the bar. The news was good and they'd all be agog to hear it. Sure enough, the minute he crashed open the door the bar held its breath. He pulled up his half-mast trousers and adjusted the string around his jacket to permit this procedure, playing for time — enjoying the moment. He heard Marion give a little gasp — she knew it was Thursday night and by his dramatic entrance must have guessed what he had to tell them.

Incapable of saying anything quietly he yelled: 'Hunter's — we did it. It's been rejected!'

★ ★ ★

Having had only two pints he drove back down the lane, albeit slowly enough for

Napoleon to lumber along beside him. Tired of leaving the Land Rover in Jack's shed, Amos felt thankful he no longer needed to indulge in such precautions.

He had to hand it to them, they were efficient. He'd been back in the cottage only five minutes when Jem tapped at the door. 'We were wondering if you were going out again mister — you not putting the motor away like.'

'It's not public knowledge yet, Jem, but they've arrested him — Quartermaster — for fraud. And they're not letting him have bail either. Go home, you two, get a good night's sleep for once. Tell Ma I'll be up to see her in a day or two — and thank you.'

The call came at two in the morning. A penetrating shrillness roused him from the first relaxing sleep he'd had in months, its unrelenting urgency a siren of foreboding. At this hour phone calls always heralded bad news.

26

'Come quick Amos, there's a dog rampagin'
among your sheep at Long Cast — like a
bloodbath it is and I can't do nothing to stop
him on my own.' It sounded like old Ned
Trumpington who often fished in the next
but one field in the summer. Whoever it was
was very out of breath but then they would be
if they'd hurried to get to a phone.

Amos knew he could ignore it; let it
happen; go back to sleep — pretend he
hadn't had the call. After all, what could he
do? He sat on the side of the bed trying to
regain command of his head — and his
senses. It was chilly and he shivered
involuntarily. It would be dark and nasty out
there. Daylight would be a better time to
tackle it. He knew all that but all the same he
couldn't refuse. He had to go — it wouldn't
go away otherwise.

Thank goodness he'd left the Land Rover
outside. He grabbed a flashlight, a stout
walking cane, the twelve bore and a handful
of the ammunition Alan had given him
— little had he known what he'd need it for.
He could've done with another gun but there

was no time to waste in rousing anyone.

He drove the Land Rover at breakneck speed out to Long Cast. But instead of taking the direct road from Weston he cut up the Stratford road and circled round and down the old drovers' track and back across the river that way so as to approach Long Cast from the opposite direction. Before he topped the rise he cut the engine and his lights and coasted silently down the hill to the field beside Long Cast so as to retain some element of surprise. He could hear nothing as he pulled off the road into the gateway of this neighouring field — a gateway he wouldn't normally have passed coming from Weston. And there, tucked well off the road into the trees, was an empty BMW. So this was about the car theft after all.

Amos pulled the Land Rover on to the verge, blocking the BMW's exit. He dialled Linklater.

'Where are you?' he whispered, fingers crossed that Linklater was back from Lincolnshire.

'What's the matter?'

'I'm at Long Cast. Someone rang to say there was a dog here slaughtering my sheep . . . but I moved the sheep out of here days ago.' In the dark, Bruce Squires must have assumed that the flock was down by the river.

'For God's sake make yourself scarce. Repeat, do nothing. I'm on my way.'

Amos let himself out of the Land Rover quietly, landing softly in the grass and leaving the door open. He crept up the road towards the first gate into the lane which led to Long Cast. It had been left invitingly open. Creeping back to his vehicle he stuffed a feed bag into his string belt and loaded the shotgun. Better safe than sorry. He reasoned that the first gate had been left open to entice him in — and that whoever was waiting for him would be inside Long Cast Meadow, somewhere near the second gate.

They'd reckon he'd alight from the Land Rover, open the second gate, drive the Land Rover through then, being a careful shepherd, get out again to shut the gate. That's when they'd strike — waiting until the Land Rover was well inside the field and thus less available as a means of escape. They knew he couldn't run.

What was the plan? To knock him over the head then drop him in the river, making it look as though he'd fallen in in the dark and drowned — with any luck the autopsy would conclude he sustained the blow on the head as he fell. He had to admit it was neat. He would bet the call had been made from a mobile which was now on the riverbed and hence untraceable. People might wonder what he'd been doing out there in the dark but then he was known for wandering around at night. They'd just put it down to a final fatal eccentricity — or, worse, guilt because he'd strangled Brenda.

All this and more shot through his head as he crept slowly and carefully past the BMW and on into the field beside Long Cast. He could do as Linklater said and just sit tight and wait for the police to arrive. The BMW was blocked in anyway, all he had to do was hide. Yes, and let Bruce Squires get away, down the field to the river path and then in any direction he chose. He could even walk home to Stratford that way and when questioned as to why his car was pulled off the road near Long Cast he would say it had been stolen. Amos smiled in the dark. It was ironic if nothing else.

And then what? He'd have another go and another until one day Amos's luck would run out. Ma always said he lived a charmed life but he'd ticked off about eight of his nine, he reckoned. No, he had to make sure Squires was caught.

He climbed awkwardly over the gate into the field, fearful lest its creaking were heard in Long Cast. Between this field and Long Cast there was a small copse, more like an overgrown thicket. After Horace's attack on the fisherman's lunch last year, Amos and Jack had blocked the gap with a couple of hurdles on this side. If he could manage to move those on his own, he had a chance.

Bruce would be expecting him to have arrived by now; would be concentrating on the Long Cast entrance, straining to hear the Land Rover's approaching engine. But the more time that elapsed the more Squires would become alert to his own danger. Amos must work extremely quietly, couldn't afford a single grunt, wheeze or cough to escape as he struggled with the fencing. His eyes were popping with the effort and he nearly fell over with the second one as it gave way unexpectedly, catching him off balance.

By now Squires must be anxious. Then Amos heard the engine, about half a mile away, he'd say, coming from the Weston Hathaway direction. He hoped it was a four-track, preferably a police four-track. The timing was perfect. Squires would think it was Amos coming at last, and be positioned near the second gate. If Amos could force him out into the lane by blocking his escape through Long Cast, then Squires would run straight into Linklater as he turned into the lane — if. If not, as soon as Squires saw the police car he would run for it. They'd never get him in the dark.

Amos glanced across the field where an infinity of blackness stared back at him. Long Cast was a huge field and Amos might not be able to run — but he did have a trump card.

Just as he was thinking this he felt hot breath down the back of his neck and sensed he was no longer alone. He looked up at the enormous black shape towering over him . . . Horace had come to investigate. He hadn't realized how close the bull was and hadn't wanted to attract his attention until he was ready but, just as he'd been fishing out the feed bag to rattle gently, here he was. Amos had never felt quite so pleased to see him.

Thankfully tiny sounds would now be drowned in the noise of the Land Rover engine, which had grown very close. Still quietly, Amos enticed Horace through the thicket into Long Cast. As they reached the other side, the Land Rover was turning into the lane. Any second now Bruce Squires would see it was not Amos and run. Amos could just make him out from this distance, crouching behind the hedge near the gate.

Promising to make it up to him later, behind Horace's back Amos pointed the gun in the air and fired. The bull let out an ear splitting roar and rushed forward. Catching sight of the astonished Squires and forgivably assuming him to be the cause of the disturbance — he charged.

Squires had no choice but to run for the gate. He dived headlong over it. Inches behind him Horace thundered into the flimsy wood which splintered ominously yet held. As Amos retreated into the thicket, he looked over his shoulder to see Squires in a heap at Linklater's feet.

He didn't bother replacing the hurdles. Horace could enjoy both fields for a while as his reward. The bull would deter any chance passer-by who might take a fancy to the shotgun, which Amos buried hurriedly in the undergowth.

By the time Amos regained his Land Rover more policemen had arrived to recover the BMW. 'You got him, then?'

'Vernon Squires, yes sir.'

'Vernon? But this is Bruce's car.'

'Yes, Councillor, *Vernon* Squires.'

27

Leaving his cohorts to deal with Squires, Linklater followed Amos back to his cottage.

'I could have sworn I heard a shot as we drove down the lane.'

'I was too busy keeping out of Horace's way to hear anything,' Amos replied.

It was Linklater who put the kettle on — and found the Scotch bottle. Amos sat in his chair gazing straight ahead, stunned. 'It was Vernon then, not Bruce.'

'Yes. Why did you think it was Bruce?'

'Because I recognized the BMW. It had Bruce's number plates. The whole thing makes sense now.' Amos sat on the edge of his seat, leaning forward as the enormity of it all became clear. 'I only assumed it was Frank.'

Linklater looked as though he thought Amos had finally flipped, sustained one shock too many and reverted back into the past. 'Drink your tea,' he said soothingly.

Amos ignored him. 'All those years ago, I assumed it was Frank because it was his truck parked outside and I was used to seeing it there during the day. The same thing's been happening here recently; people have assumed they saw me going into Brenda's — because I often did and because someone resembling me went in there.'

Linklater stared at him.

'I did the same — assumed it was Frank I saw — without thinking about it. Now I know it wasn't. I can see him as clearly as if it were yesterday. It was Vernon I saw that night, not his father. And Vernon knew I'd seen him.'

'Which explains why the man was frightened out of his life the other night — thinking he'd seen the ghost of the girl he'd murdered. I thought his reaction extreme for a crime his father had committed.' Linklater relaxed at another mystery solved. 'And it means Vernon Squires had a pressing reason for wanting rid of you. You're the one person who can place him at the scene of the crime.' Linklater sighed. 'As soon as we find her body your evidence will clinch it.'

Amos wasn't listening. In a trance, he said, 'It's like before, don't you see? Everyone was so convinced it was Stubbs they never suspected Squires; never searched the paddock because they'd no idea she'd been anywhere near it. I've been so obsessed with Quartermaster, I failed to realize that Squires had a motive. Forty-odd years ago it was just one hack on the *Gazette* who remarked on the strangeness of two serious events in one village happening within days of one another. Was he suggesting they might be connected? We've had that too — the attacks on me and Brenda's murder.'

The furrows on Linklater's brow deepened, but before he could respond Amos remembered the trip to Lincolnshire. 'How did you get on with Arbuthnot?'

'He denies it, of course — says he had to go and comfort his wife, says she was in a state because of the row with her mother. We're going to check his DNA against that on your pig; I said it would come in handy if we suspected an outsider. According to him he hasn't been anywhere near Weston Hathaway since he left thirty years ago — so we'll see, won't we.'

'What if it was Squires?'

'You're not seriously suggesting he murdered Brenda as well.' Again Linklater considered Amos as though the old boy had had too much excitement for one night.

'It's not so far-fetched. The more I think about it the more — '

'Don't go jumping to conclusions Amos. Vernon Squires has a solid alibi for the time Brenda was killed. He was at a Rotary lunch — even introduced the speaker who always starts promptly at one o'clock. He has twenty-seven witnesses.'

'I can't help that. Hear me out. Once this paddock business flared up, Vernon Squires must have been petrified that Mary Walters's body would be found and he knew I might remember seeing him there that night. But if I'd been so discredited no one would ever listen to me — '

'And I guess he daren't simply move the body then in case he was seen. But why not just kill you? Why Brenda, of all people?'

Amos had asked himself that before — about Quartermaster. 'Because it was easier to kill Brenda?' Amos stopped, his whole face clearing. 'That's it! That's it! I've been so stupid. She told me!' Amos leapt up scarcely able to speak.

'Told you what?' Linklater sat down, his shoulders slumped, visibly resigned to hearing that yet another vital piece of information had been kept from him.

'Brenda told me she knew about the shady dealing both Quartermaster and Squires indulged in — from her days as the bookkeeper at the garage. She offered to tell me so I could use it against Quartermaster when he was blackening me over Nellie's will. Again I was so busy concentrating on Quartermaster that I'd forgotten she'd said it about Squires as well.' Amos's words were

314

spilling over one another as his thoughts ran faster than his tongue. 'And Keith, that night in the shed in Cornwall, what was it he said? 'Brenda didn't mind'. She knew things, Stephen, I'm telling you she knew things which could've damaged Squires. Oh, he had a motive all right — he had to keep her quiet.'

'OK, maybe. But she'd known these secrets for some time by the sound of it. Why did Squires wait until now? Did he fall out with her? Why was she suddenly — '

Amos waved at Linklater, afraid the insight would disappear, desperate to hang on to it. 'They were in the bar that night. They were there — Vernon and Bruce — round the corner. They'd have heard the whole thing.'

'Now you've lost me completely.'

Amos sat down again but this time on the bitter edge of his seat, leaning towards Linklater. 'One night, Reverend Whittaker . . . ' Amos stopped, considering. 'I'll come back to him, remind me. Anyway, he was in the Hathaway Arms and we were discussing Brenda's deteriorating condition and whether or not she had dementia — and that Vernon Squires had told people she was capable of saying anything these days. Then Jack asked if it was all right to commit euthanasia in such cases and I said I didn't see why not.

'Squires would have heard all that. In her

supposedly declining state, he was evidently already afraid she might talk — give one or more of his little games away, whatever they are — hence his telling people she'd gone ga-ga. Plus I know Brenda was that furious about Quartermaster's building plans and his treatment of me that I wouldn't be surprised if she'd threatened to expose Squires and Quartermaster. Anyway, that's why he finally had to kill her: he could no longer trust her to keep quiet. And now he could justify it to himself by pretending he was doing her a favour — putting her out of her misery. Who knows, he may even have been one of the people she'd asked to do just that in the event that Alzheimer's was diagnosed. She wasn't daft, you know — she might have reckoned he'd be more likely to go through with it than the rest of us.

'Only a day or two later, Squires saw Jack's application for the paddock and presumably began to fear exposure from me. So what really sealed Brenda's fate was the idea of framing me for her murder.'

Linklater was quiet, sifting all this new information and sipping his tea. He had dark rings under his eyes. 'And I suppose that negates any evidence from Mrs Squires?'

'About seeing me? The time wasn't right anyway, was it? I tell you what though, it

316

might explain why people thought it was me. Squires is about the same height but more important, with his history in amateur dramatics dressing up to look like me would've been simple. He'd overheard the conversation in the Hathaway Arms as had plenty of other people, where it could be said I'd publicly supported the idea of mercy killing. Oh yes, framing me was child's play, wasn't it . . . except he hadn't bargained for folk's loyalty. By killing Brenda and making it look as though I'd done it, Squires could solve two problems at a stroke.'

'It wasn't just something Irene Squires made up, then?' Linklater wasn't slow.

'She might have . . . but there were other sightings. I definitely believe there was a character dressed like me, who called on Brenda that day.'

'You mentioned the Reverend Whittaker. Was he one of them?'

'Er . . . oh, I remember, yes — no he wasn't or . . . not to my knowledge. I had a long conversation with the reverend, one or two actually, mostly about his old mum. He's been bothered that, believing she had Alzheimer's, Brenda might have committed suicide; even asked me if someone could strangle themselves.'

'Actually it has been known. They do it by

inserting a spoon or similar implement in the garrotte and gradually twisting it. Pretty rare though.'

'But I'm wondering now whether it wasn't the other way round with Frank Squires. He'd been a miserable old sod for as long as anyone could remember; I daresay they'd call him a depressive these days. So no one was surprised when he hanged himself; but did he? Or did Vernon kill his father and then make it look like an accident — justifying it by thinking he'd be better off dead?' Amos reasoned.

'But why?'

'Because Frank suspected Vernon of killing Mary Walters? That reporter was right, the two events were linked.'

'So you're suggesting Vernon killed his old man too?'

'Maybe.'

'Go back a minute. If Vernon murdered Brenda because he was afraid she'd spill the beans about the irregularities in his business affairs, and attempted to frame you for it, to discredit you — in case you remembered seeing him by the paddock the night Mary Walters disappeared — why the subsequent attempts on your life?' Linklater had a point.

'Oh, because by then he thought she *had* spilled the beans as you put it. He also knew, from Reverend Whittaker, that I'd been asking questions about what Irene had really seen and no one else had owned up to sighting me; the frame wasn't working. And he thought you were going to compare everyone's DNA with what you'd found on Napoleon. So he had to eliminate me quickly. Apart from anything else, I was the link, you said it yourself after the brakes incident. Only I could be sure of Napoleon's antipathy towards Vernon Squires, which means he'd most likely come across him at Brenda's — the connection Vernon couldn't afford for us to make.'

Amos carried on, he'd remembered something else. 'And how come Squires senior didn't come storming in here, gunning for me as any irate father might, when I shopped Keith for car theft? I was very surprised he didn't. You told me yourself how he changed his tune when he found out I was involved. It's because he wasn't keen to advertise his motive for wanting Brenda out of the way. You have never suspected him of Brenda's murder because you didn't realize he had a motive — to keep her quiet. I should have done . . . because I knew.

'Vernon preferred to pretend the car theft hadn't happened because he was worried. He

thought maybe his worst fears had materialized and Brenda had told me all about it.
How else could I have known where to find
Keith? Oh yes, Vernon wanted to distance
himself from the garage in case we put two
and two together. So he came gunning for me
all right, but it was literally.

'And again, his action could have had more
than one benefit. Take the failed brakes
episode — which could have been meant to
look like suicide, or an accident. Either way,
with me dead you have to admit police
resources on Brenda's murder case might be
drastically reduced. It would just be assumed
I'd done it — for the noblest of reasons, of
course.'

'Haven't got a very high opinion of us, have
you?'

'Just being realistic, Stephen — you
yourself thought I'd done it at first, I'll bet.
Why wouldn't you?' Amos sloshed some
more Scotch into his empty coffee mug. The
strains of the day were beginning to tell and
he needed to keep going.

'I don't suppose he had to do much
persuading to get Keith to tamper with my
brakes either — sweet revenge for what I'd
done to him. By then the whole family had a
down on me. And I didn't tell you, but they
used Napoleon as bait for taking a potshot at

me; making it look like a shooting accident by someone out after pigeons — gypsies most likely.'

'How do you think we scrambled two patrols quite so quickly tonight? John Wilkinson told me. Don't look like that, he felt he ought to. He was only thinking of your safety, you know that.'

'Yes, I guess so. I didn't tell you because I thought the only way of catching Quartermaster was to let him try.' Amos reconsidered the wisdom of this. 'I know. If I hadn't already moved those sheep from Long Cast, I'd have walked straight into that third attempt.'

'Your bull won't be terrorizing the neighbourhood by now, will he?'

'Young Horace? No, he'll calm down and go back to his own field — when he realizes his grass was better all along.'

'We need to search that area, see if we can find what Squires intended to kill you with; he must have dropped it in his flight. My men didn't relish tackling the bull.'

'Will you look for Squires's DNA in the samples you took from Napoleon?'

'Oh yes, though Squires may still claim he petted the pig some other time.'

'As I said, it's unlikely . . . and he certainly couldn't now. Napoleon hates him, chased him up the lane at Moon Cottage the day we found the bracelet — ask Jack.'

'Because of what happened at Brenda's, you reckon?'

'I wouldn't be surprised — Napoleon isn't normally aggressive.' Amos got to his feet. 'What'll happen now?'

'First I'm going to get some sleep — Squires can cool his heels in the cells for tonight; we can hold him for trespass if his solicitor objects. Don't worry, I'm not going to let him out. We've got a lot of work to do tomorrow going over all the evidence in the light of everything that's happened tonight — and everything you've now told me.' He shook his head in disapproval

'We'll look into his affairs — see what Brenda might have known — take a closer look at that alibi — and of course now we've got two cases to look into, if not three counting Frank's death. I'm keen to get Brenda's cleared up, just in case the culprit is still at large. The older ones can wait but, as you've pointed out, maybe we have to go back to them to find the motive. And we'll have to excavate Jack's paddock.'

28

Amos told Jack his suspicions as they drove back up to Long Cast the next morning. It was only just light and on the pretext of making Long Cast safe for the police searchers, Amos had asked Jack to help him persuade Horace back into his own field. As Amos had predicted, they found the bull already returned, grazing gently on his side of the copse, they hoped tired out after his night's antics because they still had to re-erect the hurdles.

'You make a start, I won't be a tick.' Amos disappeared into the bushes emerging with the twelve-bore a few minutes later. Jack stared at the gun, opened his mouth then shut it again.

As they bent to their task Jack asked the same question Amos had asked only a couple of hours ago. 'What happens now? Do you really think he killed Brenda?'

'Yes, I do. All Linklater's got to do is prove it.'

'Pity you haven't still got that telephone tape — they can analyse things like that, you know — that would have proved it was

Squires who lured you down here that day. Hey watch out!' Amos had almost dropped the heavy fencing on Jack's foot.

'I'd completely forgotten about that. I have got it.' Jack wore an unmistakeable look of: *Why didn't you tell me that.* 'It just turned up, I forgot to mention it. Good, that'll help.'

His morning passed in a whirl of comings and goings, phone calls, discussions, sifting of ideas and standard police work. Amos handed over the tape to a quizzical Linklater who also requestioned the community. The police found a large baseball bat near the gate to Long Cast, which was sent for analysis.

John Wilkinson was one of the first on the phone — he'd been busy since the news of Quartermaster's arrest for fraud had become more widely known. This, he said, coupled with his previous explanations, had eventually persuaded the standards board not to pursue Quartermaster's allegations.

'So am I finally in the clear . . . or will they change their minds again?'

'You're in the clear, completely exonerated. They'll issue the final report by the end of the week.'

By early evening Amos was fit only to sit on a barstool in the Hathaway Arms, Napoleon at his feet.

'What'll happen to Hunter's then?' Marion asked.

'I expect it'll be sold to pay Quartermaster's debts. But don't worry. I reckon if we suggest there are Roman remains there, the conservation authorities will stop the planners having *carte blanche* over the site.'

'We'm seeing some changes round here, ain't we?' Sam pitched in. 'S'pect garage'll be up for sale and all. Can't see her running it.'

The Reverend Whittaker beckoned to Amos from the garden. Amos went to join him.

'I've been thinking about that day I found Brenda. My only defence is I was so shocked at finding her like that, it brought so many awful memories flooding back.'

Now what? Amos smiled encouragement.

'I remember now, I did pick the iron up and put it back on the stove, absentmindedly as much as anything, and I . . . I put the scarf in my pocket.'

'You've told the chief inspector this? You've given him the scarf?'

Reverend Whittaker nodded vigorously.

★ ★ ★

'What's the matter, couldn't you sleep?'

'Chance'd be a fine thing. No, I wanted to catch you before you did your rounds

325

— thought I'd cadge a cup of tea.' Linklater leant his lean frame against the kitchen doorpost, throwing a set of official-looking papers on to the table as he did so.

'I've brought you an application form for a gun licence.' They exchanged glances.

'We've charged Squires with attempted murder — it'll be murder later on this morning. We can now prove he killed Brenda. We've also picked up Keith in case you were worried about him, but I'm afraid Bruce has skipped the country — cleared out his bank account too.'

'I saw the Reverend Whittaker last night.'

'Mmm, not my favourite character at the moment — what on earth did he think he was playing at? Why didn't he come forward sooner?'

'He obviously had it fixed in his mind that Brenda had committed suicide — despite all the evidence to the contrary. He couldn't face it, thought it was his fault.'

'It might easily have been his fault had her killer gone free. Anyway, better late than never, I suppose. We've sent the scarf to the lab — I'm sure it'll have Squires's DNA all over it. Which reminds me . . . ' He looked down at the still sleeping Napoleon by the cooker. 'Did Reverend Whittaker tell you about the iron?'

'Said something about picking it up — why?'

'We think Squires hit Napoleon with it. You remember that wound . . . '

Amos boiled. 'The bastard. No wonder Napoleon went for him that day in the paddock. Pity he didn't get him.'

'Now we know the iron wasn't in its usual place, we're having it retested for prints, and we've already found Squires's DNA on Napoleon — but that isn't conclusive evidence in this case.'

'You will have enough for a conviction, though? What about his business dealings?' A shiver of fear ran through Amos, fear that Squires would get off.

'Oh don't worry — if you'll excuse the pun the iron turned out to be an important clue, an ironic one from Squires's viewpoint.' Linklater sat himself down at the table nursing his tea mug. Amos looked up, perplexed.

'You'll remember me saying I thought the sheep in the river was more than likely a coincidence?' Amos remained tight-lipped, convinced it hadn't been. 'Well, I have an apology to make, and not just because the specialists are ninety-five per cent certain it was Squires's voice on that tape — though that has certainly helped. No, we made a wrong assumption about the time of death.' Amos kept quiet.

'We assumed the clock had been knocked off in a struggle and it stopped at one o'clock or thereabouts. The time of death is notoriously difficult to calculate precisely, so it seemed like a good theory — ergo she was killed at one o'clock. Of course, when you told us yourself that you were back here by one, it could have looked black for you — but for Mrs Pearson. Prior to that, Squires's plan, to lure you away yet have you spotted going into Brenda's, had fallen apart anyway due to the villagers' loyalty to you; leaving only his wife swearing she'd seen you . . . at twelve-thirty.'

'But what made you realize it wasn't one o'clock?'

'The iron. We think Squires threw it at Napoleon knocking him out. Yes, that could've been at one o'clock, but it could have been earlier and then Napoleon knocked the clock off when he came round. He'd obviously be in a state — probably tried to rouse Brenda. The upshot of all this was, we rechecked Squires's alibi — carefully.'

Linklater smiled. 'Armed with our new information we dug a little deeper, asked if anyone had actually seen him at lunch. This time the caterer remembered clearing Squires's full plate when he didn't turn up. It's very unusual you see. Rotarians have this attendance ethic, if you don't attend and don't send your apologies you get blacklisted.

'After that it was easy to get those on either side of him to either remember or admit that Squires hadn't actually been there throughout, but had scooted in to the meeting just in time to introduce the speaker. They remembered he'd looked harrassed, assumed the cause to be some business affair and kept shtoom for him.'

'So when was she killed?'

'As you said, some time between twelve fifteen and twelve forty-five. Which gave him time to get into Stratford for one o'clock and was the time he'd arranged for you to be out at Long Cast — leaving you without an alibi.'

'So he did purposely dress up like me?'

'We think so, yes. Otherwise why go to the trouble of luring you out of the village? It's the only realistic explanation — and I certainly suspect some people saw him and might come forward now . . . ' Linklater let his sentence trail off, but Amos wasn't going to betray his friends. They could own up later if they wanted to.

'And of course he had a double motive for wanting to kill you. That Brenda had already told you his business secrets but, more important, that you could place him at the scene where we now believe Mary Walters was murdered. Especially after you set him up that night of the play. He must have thought you were taunting him — after all, he didn't know you hadn't realized it was him you'd seen that night.' Linklater frowned. 'Though one thing still puzzles me. Why did he kill Mary Walters?'

29

Amos glanced at the clock and rose from his seat. 'Let's see if Jack's up.' Taking his cap, his keys and Napoleon, he left the cottage and walked with his rolling gait down the path to the Land Rover. They drove up the lane to the Hathaway Arms from where Jack emerged unsurprised — until he caught sight of Linklater.

'Don't ask me, Mr Ashley,' Linklater said, answering the unspoken question as Jack opened the cab door. 'Councillor Cotswold just took off when I asked if he knew why Vernon Squires had killed that young woman forty years ago.' Linklater moved along the seat making room for Jack to climb aboard.

Concentrating on the road, Amos spoke without turning round. 'I'm not sure of the answer either, but we're going to see the only one who's likely to know — other than Squires himself, that is.'

Much to his passengers' surprise Amos turned abruptly into the gypsy camp at Broad Farthing. No one barred the way, Jem even raised a hand in greeting. The camp was well awake and bustling, the smell of barbecued bacon hung tantalizingly in the air.

Amos drew the Land Rover alongside Ma's caravan. Napoleon immediately leapt down and bounded round the corner. They heard a cry and as they clambered out a delighted Naomi appeared, Napoleon beside her. Linklater stopped in mid step, missed the tread and would have fallen in an ignominious heap on the ground had Jack not grabbed him. 'You're the girl who approached Squires at the play, aren't you? But in daylight, you're so like — '

At that moment Ma stepped out from her camper. 'Like that old photograph, Chief Inspector? Yes. I'm Mary Walters — Ma for short. And this is my grandaughter, Naomi.'

The kaleidoscope which was Jack's face, showed a succession of expressions — utter amazement, puzzlement, surprise, and finally relief as the implications of that simple statement sank in. He turned on Amos. 'You knew all along, and you would've let them trample all over my property. You let me go on thinking . . . '

'I'm surprised you didn't tell the police, we could have wasted a lot of time. What's this got to do with Squires, anyway?' Linklater was not amused either.

Amos held up his hand. 'Let's just say it wasn't my secret to tell, and I don't know all of it, anyway — I'm hoping I will now.' He gave Ma a warm smile.

'I've been expecting you since I heard of Squires's arrest and that it was him who strangled Brenda Smith.' Ma invited them in and dispatched Naomi to fetch breakfast.

At last Amos started her off. 'Ma, all I've ever known was when you tapped on my door that morning, the morning you disappeared. It was only just light and you were in a great hurry. You said not to worry whatever I heard, that you were OK but you were going away with Jacko Brown.' He could hear his voice becoming gruffer. 'I tried to stop you. I mean, Jacko Brown of all people.' It still hurt.

'Yes, a 'gippo'.' Ma smiled. 'I just wanted you to know I was OK. You'd always been so kind to me and I was afraid you'd kill my stepfather if I didn't let you know I was safe. I didn't want you to pay that penalty . . . and I trusted you not to tell anyone else.' She looked at the other two, then back at Amos. 'You never have.'

Jack and Linklater shuffled in their seats, obviously embarrassed by this unexpectedly personal turn in the conversation, this insight into Amos's past. Ma sat back in her seat. 'OK, I'll fill in the gaps — it can't do any harm now.' She turned to Linklater. 'Chief Inspector, you have to understand what my

333

stepfather was like.'

'I've read the file, ma'am. I gather Stubbs was a . . . disciplinarian.'

'Is that what you call it? I'd have done anything to escape, I couldn't bear to be under his roof a moment longer.'

'But I . . . ' Amos interrupted. He'd begged her to go away with him.

Ma put her hand on his. 'Yes, I know, dear Amos, but I didn't want you to leave. Your life was here.' She continued her story. 'After Mother died I went back to work in Stratford. One day, when I'd missed the bus and started to walk home, Jacko offered me a lift. I knew Stubbs would be furious if I was late and that I'd get another beating . . . so I accepted. Call it risk versus certainty if you like. Anyway, that's how we met.

'After that Jacko took to waiting for me at the bus stop and, well . . . he was wild and free and much older than me . . . ' She sighed. 'And most important of all, he could take me abroad where Stubbs would never find me. That's when I realized I could live with this man.'

Amos grunted, struggling out of his chair to pace the floor. Ma glanced across at him but said nothing.

'Why didn't you just run away?' Naomi asked.

'Where would I have gone? Don't forget I was under age, legal majority was twenty-one in those days, not eighteen. So I was bound to Stubbs by law . . . for another three years. I don't have to tell you how long that is at your age.'

Ma poured some more tea. No one dare speak, afraid they'd break the spell. 'The trouble started when Vernon Squires spotted Jacko and me together one day. Squires had pestered me before. I hated him, greasy stuck-up bully.' Ma shuddered. 'It was obvious what he was up to, thought he could get me through blackmail. Said if I didn't meet him that night he'd tell Stubbs who I'd been seeing — and I knew he would. He'd have taken great pleasure in knowing my stepfather had beaten me for it and that Stubbs would see to it Jacko and me couldn't meet after that.'

Amos threw himself back in his chair, felt himself gripping the arm, forty-two years after the event. 'Why didn't you tell me? I'd soon have sorted out Squires!'

'That's exactly why I couldn't. I knew you'd half-kill him, so would Jacko have done if he'd known. That and the stupidity of youth . . . I thought I was invincible. I could sort my own battles, thank you very much. Ha!' Ma slapped her thigh.

'Go on, what happened?' Naomi prompted, flushing pink.

'I know it sounds foolish now and it was, but I suppose I thought I could reason with him; use my womanly wiles to prevent him telling Stubbs until I'd had the chance to finish making my plans. Otherwise I'd be locked up and escape would be impossible.' She sighed.

'So I agreed to meet Squires late one night at his father's building site, Moon Cottage. I needed to spin him along — just to give me more time.' She stopped, surveying her feet. Amos wondered how far she'd been prepared to go — and why she'd never told him any of this before.

She again leaned across to Amos, touching his arm. 'I daren't tell you at the time, I didn't know what you'd think of me . . . and I'd no right to ask you for help when I intended to run away with Jacko. Afterwards it became a different matter — but I'll come to that.'

Amos looked across at Linklater and Jack sitting on the other side of Ma's big table, both quiet, mouths half open, concentrating. Linklater was obviously wondering why the police had never been told and Jack, as he'd said, was wondering why Amos had left him thinking Mary had been killed and buried in the paddock. He hoped they'd understand. It wasn't just because it was Ma's secret — which he'd sworn to uphold — but he too had wanted to understand what her bracelet had been doing in that paddock. Wanted to know about this connection with Frank Squires that she'd never mentioned.

'I'll not go into detail about the meeting with Vernon Squires except to say we ended up having a fight at the back, near the entrance to the paddock — yes, an ill-matched one. He pushed me and all I remember is falling . . . then nothing.'

Naomi gasped involuntarily.

'When I came to, I was very cold, my hair was sticky with blood and it was as dark as the devil and as silent. I'd fallen on a pile of builder's rubble, concrete slabs and the like and must have hit my head on one of them. I remember a dreadful pain.'

Ma paused for a minute, seemingly back in that paddock. 'I'm not sure which terrified me most — the witchcraft stories I'd heard about the place, that Vernon might be waiting to pounce on me again at any moment, or that Stubbs would find out what I'd been doing.'

'That's when I must have seen him coming out of the paddock — and you were lying back there injured and I'd no idea.' Mary must have fallen when he'd shot the ewe, he'd felt it. He still remembered all that blood hitting him, had known something evil had happened.

'So what did you do?' Naomi whispered.

'I walked all the way to the gypsy camp, which was near Stratford in those days, and asked Jacko to take me away, there and then. It wasn't difficult, that's what he'd been wanting to do all along. But I made him stop en route so I could tell Amos where I'd gone.'

'Is that why we lived in Wales but you always talked about the Cotswolds?'

'Yes, we went abroad for a few years, Italy, Spain, Yugoslavia, all over, really. Then Wales and around Cornwall and the West Country. I came back here after Jacko and your parents were killed in that accident.'

'You left the police looking for you for weeks.' Linklater glared at Amos as well as Mary.

'I'm sorry, Chief Inspector, but I had no choice; it wasn't like it is today. You'd have returned me to my stepfather and put Jacko in jail. I couldn't let that happen.'

'But why didn't you tell me about Squires — that morning when you came to say goodbye?' He'd always thought there'd been more to her abrupt flight than she'd said — had thought Stubbs had been knocking her about again. Which was why he'd not spoken up in Stubbs's defence when the police were hounding him.

'For the same reason I never told Jacko — he thought my stepfather had hit me again. If I'd told either of you it was Squires you'd have gone after him and probably ruined your lives. As it turned out I had disappeared and was eventually presumed dead. Much better. Besides, by going for Squires you'd have given the game away, and my stepfather and the police would have found out I was alive. No, I decided to bide my time.'

'And what about Frank Squires?' asked Linklater. 'Vernon's father.'

'What about him?' Ma asked blankly.

'I think Vernon might have killed him,' Amos replied. 'Especially after what you've just told us. Otherwise why has Vernon been so desperate to stop Jack's paddock being dug up? Frank supposedly committed suicide but I've got this hunch that he and Vernon rowed.

'Picture Vernon Squires's position. He knows he hit you and you fell. He hears that sickening crack as your head hits the slab and then you lie lifeless, all the breath knocked out of your body. He panics and leaves, believing he's killed you.

'Next morning you're missing! No one can

find you. What does he think? That his Dad had buried you, I imagine — in that part of the garden where you fell, which Vernon subsequently made into a paddock. Whereas, his Dad finds the blood on the concrete and knows Vernon used his car that night. Maybe Frank knew Vernon was keen on you. Anyway, when he hears you've disappeared he accosts his son, accuses him of killing you; but he's so drunk they can't have a sensible conversation — pool their information and figure out what must have happened. Afraid his father is having an attack of conscience over hiding the body, Vernon kills Frank to keep him quiet — just like he did Brenda; justifying it to himself as doing his miserable old dad a favour.

'Which is why he reacted in such an extraordinary way when Naomi approached him in the paddock the other night. She's the exact image of you at that age — and Vernon obviously believes you died. Of course I knew you hadn't, but I wanted to understand why he was creating about Jack's intentions. For all I knew he might not have reacted at all. But when he came out with: 'My father killed Mary Walters,' because of the state he was in I believed him. It was only after he tried to kill me at Long Cast and had come in Bruce's car that I realized it was Vernon I'd seen that night, not Frank. Then everything fell into place.'

'And you made us all think that you'd picked the first available young woman to play the part — said she came from one of the other villages. It had to be Naomi, didn't it!' Jack shouted. 'But Ma just said Vernon Squires knew about Jacko — so why didn't he tell people about that, say she'd probably run away . . . or that Jacko had killed her.'

'Again, for the same sort of reason that he hasn't wanted anyone to associate him too closely with Brenda. He didn't want people to make any connection between him and Mary. That way they were much less likely to stumble on what he thought was the truth . . . and start digging up the paddock. And he was right. For forty years no one dreamt of his involvement.'

'And Squires would have been relieved when Jacko didn't come looking for him; after all he wasn't to know I hadn't told Jacko who I was going to meet.'

Jack was beaming. 'It explains why Vernon wanted to protect the whole paddock — and why he couldn't just move the body. He'd no idea where it was!' He turned on Amos. 'I still don't see why you didn't tell me? I was worried sick about how I was going to break the news to Marion.'

'I had to play for time, that's all. I eventually realized the two might be linked, Brenda's murder and Ma's disappearance — but I didn't know how'. Amos turned to Ma. 'You could have told me about Squires now. Why didn't you?' What would she say?

For a few seconds Ma considered her feet again. Looking up, she said, 'The truth?' Amos nodded, unblinking. 'Because I wanted revenge.'

Linklater and Jack grunted. Amos relaxed, relieved. He believed that. 'So what was all that about the tape?'

'I was afraid you'd ask me that. All right . . . ' She took a deep breath. 'Our people saw the lamb put in the river and then watched you arrive to haul it out.'

'What?' All three men sat forward on their seats.

'I know, I know. Bruce Squires did it. We guessed someone might've phoned you so we stole the tape — we had no idea what it was all about but thought the tape might come in useful.' She turned to Linklater. 'I know this seems odd to you, Chief Inspector, but that's because you're not a gypsy. We're so used to being accused of everything that goes wrong, if not framed for it, we thought this might be yet another incident we were going to get blamed for.' To Amos she said: 'Same reason

Jem and Aaron were persuaded to help you over the car thefts but daren't tell the police what they knew — for fear they'd be accused of being involved in it.'

Linklater nodded.

'I still don't see why you didn't tell me?' Amos said.

'Because I wanted to get Squires myself!' In that edge to her voice Amos glimpsed again the hidden strength behind that fascinating face. 'Anyway, I soon realized it was much better to let you do the unmasking, otherwise our people were likely to get into even more trouble, all for my gratification. That's when I decided to protect you instead.

'I'm sorry, Amos, yes, we used you. It all went wrong when, thinking I was being paranoid about Squires, I too became convinced of Quartermaster's guilt — and allowed Jem and Aaron to relinquish their vigil after he was arrested.'

No longer comfortable so close to long buried emotions, Amos struggled to his feet.

'Can't stay here gossiping all day, Ma. Thanks for breakfast.' He'd always wondered what had happened — now he knew. 'Just needed to show them you're alive and well and living on our doorstep.'

★ ★ ★

343

One night towards the end of the summer, when the air was warm and smelled of dew-damped straw, the gypsies lit their fire and brought out their antique lanterns. While Napoleon rooted around the huge compost heap with his cousins, the young people danced and Amos and Ma sat quietly in the shadows.

'When you announced Brenda Smith's legacy to the village, giving Naomi a house, and arranging things so Jem could take over the garage after Mrs Squires went away . . . I thought we should have a party to thank you.'

Amos squeezed her hand. 'Oh, I nearly forgot.' He reached into his pocket. 'I found this. Thought you might like it back.'

He handed her the silver bracelet engraved with her name, the one he'd first given her forty-four years earlier. Turning it over, she read the inscription inside and smiled.

We do hope that you have enjoyed reading this large print book.

Did you know that all of our titles are available for purchase?

We publish a wide range of high quality large print books including:
Romances, Mysteries, Classics
General Fiction
Non Fiction and Westerns

Special interest titles available in large print are:
The Little Oxford Dictionary
Music Book
Song Book
Hymn Book
Service Book

Also available from us courtesy of Oxford University Press:
Young Readers' Dictionary
(large print edition)
Young Readers' Thesaurus
(large print edition)

For further information or a free brochure, please contact us at:
Ulverscroft Large Print Books Ltd.,
The Green, Bradgate Road, Anstey,
Leicester, LE7 7FU, England.
Tel: (00 44) 0116 236 4325
Fax: (00 44) 0116 234 0205

THE BODY IN THE MARSH

Katherine Hall Page

Faith Fairchild's husband, the Reverend Thomas Fairchild, learns that nursery school teacher Lora Deane has received threatening phone calls. And she's not the only resident of Aleford, Massachusetts, who is being terrorized. Some local environmentalists, protesting about the proposed housing development that will destroy Beecher's Bog, have become targets of a vicious campaign of intimidation — reason enough for Faith to launch into some clandestine sleuthing. But when a body turns up in the charred ruins of a suspicious house fire, Faith is suddenly investigating a murder — and in serious danger of getting bogged down in a very lethal mess indeed!

A DEAD MAN IN TANGIER

Michael Pearce

Pig-sticking is a dangerous sport . . . for the pigs and the huntsman. While pursuing that recreation Monsieur Bossu gets stuck himself. A police matter? Perhaps, but in the Tangier of 1912 who are they answerable to? The new international committee to which Monsieur Bossu was Clerk? It is decided that Seymour of Scotland Yard will investigate. He can be safely disowned if things go wrong in a country caught between the ancient and the modern, where traditions are harsh. Soon Seymour realizes that getting to the truth of Monsieur Bossu's demise will bring him in danger of getting stuck too . . .

THE FINAL CURTAIN

Ken Holdsworth

With shoulder-length blond hair and cornflower-blue eyes, Ronnie Simmons is quite irresistible to his fellow actors — of both sexes — and in the jaundiced opinion of his boyhood friend, TV soap actor Nick Carter, he loses his heart with regularity. So it is surprising when Ronnie's sister, Susan, begs him to talk her brother out of his latest relationship. Being between jobs, Nick sets out for the rural backwater where Ronnie is appearing with an Arts Council sponsored touring company — but behind the idyllic pastoral facade lies a disturbing mystery, and Nick is soon involved in violence and murder . . .